THE WHISPERING

THE WHISPERING

Sarah Rayne

This first world edition published 2014
in Great Britain and the USA by
SEVERN HOUSE PUBLISHERS LTD of
19 Cedar Road, Sutton, Surrey, England, SM2 5DA.
Trade paperback edition first published
in Great Britain and the USA 2014 by
SEVERN HOUSE PUBLISHERS LTD.

British Library Cataloguing in Publication Data

Rayne, Sarah author.
  The whispering. – (A Nell West and Michael Flint haunted
  house story; 4)
  1. West, Nell (Fictitious character)–Fiction. 2. Flint,
  Michael (Fictitious character)–Fiction. 3. Haunted
  houses–England–Fens, The–Fiction. 4. Choirs (Music)–
  Fiction. 5. Horror tales.
  I. Title II. Series
  823.9'2-dc23

ISBN-13: 978-0-7278-8363-6 (cased)
ISBN-13: 978-1-84751-505-6 (trade paper)

All Severn House titles are printed on acid-free paper.

Severn House Publishers support the Forest Stewardship Council™ [FSC™],
the leading international forest certification organisation. All our titles that
are printed on FSC certified paper carry the FSC logo.

MIX
Paper from
responsible sources
FSC
www.fsc.org   FSC® C013056

Typeset by Palimpsest Book Production Ltd.,
Falkirk, Stirlingshire, Scotland.
Printed and bound in Great Britain by
TJ International, Padstow, Cornwall.

ONE

Memo from: Director of Music, Oriel College, Oxford
To: Dr Michael Flint, English Literature/
Language Faculty

October 201—

Michael,

A note to wish you well on your journey into the deepest Fens. Fosse House is apparently in rather a remote spot, but I'm sure you'll be all right, once you actually get there. It's a pity Luisa Gilmore didn't feel able to put you up at the house for a couple of nights, but I expect you'll fare well and forage sufficiently at the local pub. I've never met Miss Gilmore, but she's always been very helpful in our exchange of letters. She's a bit of a recluse, I suspect, and possibly a touch eccentric, but at seventy-odd years of age anyone is allowed a bit of eccentricity, I should hope. She's never married, and she's lived in the house all her life. But what's more to the point is that one of her ancestors was part of the ill-fated Palestrina Choir – actually inside the Liège convent when it was destroyed – so there could be a wealth of primary source material in the house.

The OUP are keen on our idea for a book focusing on the musical influences on the work of the Great War poets. They're also what they term 'pleasantly surprised' at the level of sales for our joint book on the influence of music on the Romantic Poets last year, and they even mentioned receiving an email from a TV company about making a documentary based on it. I dare say it won't come to anything, and I expect it's all a flea bite compared to your Wilberforce books (incidentally my small niece is an avid reader of them), but I do feel we've made a modest contribution to the field, and this new *oeuvre* should add to that.

I'm looking forward to the results of your sojourn at Fosse

House, but do try to stay clear of any peculiar happenings while you're there. You seem to attract such odd occurrences. We heard snippets of rather intriguing gossip about your exploits in Derbyshire last year, and if Owen Bracegirdle in the History Faculty can be believed, there were some extra-ordinary shenanigans in Ireland a couple of years before that. (Dr Bracegirdle is given to exaggeration, however, not to say outright flippancy).

Kind regards,

J.B.

Email from: *Owen Bracegirdle, History Faculty, Oriel College, Oxford*
To: *Michael Flint, English Literature/Language Faculty*

Michael –

I know you'll have had a note from J.B. about his new book, and I expect you're smiling with pleased anticipation at the prospect of getting to grips with all that romantic, tragic poetry forged by the Great War.

J.B. asked me if I thought you could cope with the extra workload, to which I said certainly you could, you were equal to anything. You might look like Keats or Shelley in the latter stages of a romantic consumption, and your poor deluded female students might yearn, and even occasionally write a sonnet to you on their own account (listen, I know for a *fact* that one of them did that), but actually you're as tough as old boots.

Anyway, the old boy seemed more worried about how you'd cope with Luisa Gilmore. He seems to find her rather daunting, and anyone who makes J.B. jittery has to be formidable.

J.B. has invited me to contribute to the book. I think it's on the strength of my treatise *The Great War: Causes and Conflicts*, which is required reading for all sixth form history students, and if it isn't, it ought to be. I've accepted with becoming modesty, but I have to say I'll enjoy having a hand in the mix. I'll also enjoy any fiscal rewards that might be forthcoming. There's an ancient curse, isn't there, (Ovid?) that says: 'May your debts torment you.' Well, they do. The spectre of bailiffs camping out in the august halls of Oriel College is looming, although I shouldn't think it would be the first time College has seen tipstaffs.

Owen

Michael Flint, reading these two missives, thought it was impossible to know where truth ended and dramatic license took over with Owen Bracegirdle. But it would be good to have Owen's input for the book.

As for the Director of Music, it had to be said that he had honed the art of dropping subtle hints to perfection. Reading between the lines it sounded as if the reclusive Luisa Gilmore could be anything from a modern-day Miss Havisham draped in fossilizing wedding finery, to Madeline Usher falling into deathlike trances and being entombed alive by mistake, or even a contemporary version of Morticia Addams, vampiric as to nature and floury as to complexion.

But Michael was keen on the project, which would focus on the musical influences of the poets from the Great War, and flattered to be approached for help.

'Although,' he said to Nell over supper in his rooms that evening, 'the prospect of driving into the fens in October isn't very appealing. Particularly if Madeline Usher's hosting the party.'

'Yes, but you'll like burrowing among old papers and journals and whatnot,' said Nell, who was inclined to regard Ushers and Addamses as frivolous distractions. 'And you'll like working on the book. Plus, if there's been a serious TV approach about that first one, you need to bash out another as soon as possible.'

Michael pointed out that books of this kind did not lend themselves to being bashed out overnight, that Michaelmas term was apt to be crowded, and also that he was committed to produce a new Wilberforce the Cat adventure for Christmas. As if on cue, the real Wilberforce padded into the room and sat down on a sheaf of proofs cataloguing his latest exploits, which Michael had been trying to read for his editor.

'Yes, but you're used to meeting deadlines,' said Nell, shooing Wilberforce off the proofs. 'And it'll be good to switch roles for once. I'm usually the one who goes yomping off into the wide blue yonder to buy stuff for the shop while you stay smugly at home in the ivory tower.' She grinned at him, and Michael wondered if he would ever stop finding deep pleasure in seeing her curled into the deep armchair like this, her hair lit to polished bronze by the light of the desk lamp. 'And here's another thing,' said Nell. 'While you're delving into the history of the ill-fated Palestrina Choir in the Liège monastery—'

'I still don't know what the ill fate was—'

'No, but while you're looking, you could see if there are any treasures Morticia Addams might be considering selling. Anything that might have found its way to England from Liège,' said Nell. Seeing his look, she said, with affectionate exasperation, 'Michael, darling, Liège is in Belgium. And Belgium means beautiful handmade lace and Flemish tapestries and Delft pottery – all of which would look very nice indeed in the shop. To say nothing of any canvases that might bear the signature of Anthony van Dyck, or Pieter Bruegel or—'

'Well, all right,' said Michael. 'But I'm only there for a couple of days, and I doubt I'd know Delft from Pyrex.'

'And,' said Nell, smiling, 'you'll be so immersed in the Great War and all that heartbreaking poetry of those young men who fought, that you probably won't notice a Bruegel if it falls on your head.' She paused, then with a kind of reluctant anxiety said, 'Come back safely, won't you?'

'I will. Behave while I'm away, won't you?'

'To make sure I do, how about if we misbehave tonight?' said Nell, with the sudden slant-eyed grin that transformed her from a purposeful seller of antiques to a very sexy imp. 'Just very privately and discreetly, but fairly spectacularly?'

'Have I got time to feed Wilberforce first?'

'Five minutes.'

'Oh, God, where's the tin-opener.'

The drive to the Fens and Fosse House took place two days later and was against a gathering storm that brewed itself up from the east and cast flurries of leaves and small branches against the car's windows. Michael eyed the skies with misgiving and tried not to think that invisible, mischievous celestial stagehands were setting the scene for a suitably Gothic backdrop so that Morticia Addams or Madeline Usher could make a grand entrance.

He had set off buoyantly, optimistic that he would find his way to the Fens easily because he had finally succumbed to buying a satnav, which Nell's small daughter Beth said meant he would never get lost again. The satnav had seemed a good idea, and Michael had managed to attach it to the dashboard, and had diligently followed the polite directions. Unfortunately, when he was about forty miles clear of Oxford it worked loose, and by the time Aylesbury was reached, it detached itself altogether and fell on the floor with a dismal crunch. Michael spent the next twenty miles listening to the now-drunken slur of the electronic voice which appeared to have lost all knowledge of the present whereabouts and might as well be saying, 'Here be dragons,' like the old maps on unexplored areas.

After that, he disconnected it, disinterred the road maps from the glove compartment and then, with the idea of getting into the mood of the era he would be researching, switched on a Palestrina tape which the Director of Music had lent him. The voices of the *Nunc Dimittis* filled the car with eerie beauty, summoning up images of dim, quiet churches, grave-visaged statues, and massive and ancient books with ornate gilt clasps and illuminated pages.

There had not been much time before leaving to find out much about the Palestrina Choir, other than that it had been formed in an ancient monastery in Belgium in 1900 to commemorate the start of the new century, and was named for the sixteenth-century composer of sacred music. One of the reference books had said that the Choir was still remembered, in Liège, as tragic, and until quite recently older inhabitants could be found who would relate how the Choir had sung the accompaniment to its own death throes. This was intriguing, although it could mean any number of things. It could also be a figment of someone's gothic imagination.

Michael drove through the rather bleak landscape. There were deep, straight drainage canals, and occasionally massive sluice gates – grim reminders of the constant menace of flooding in these parts. At intervals were expanses of mud flats or salt marshes. Strong winds whipped across their surfaces, making thick, oozing ripples. Tiny villages were scattered around, providing a reminder that humans had settled here from a very early era – the Romans and the Iceni, wasn't it? Michael started to enjoy the feeling of entering an England whose roots went so far back. There was a bleak beauty to the landscape, and seeing a distant church spire against the thickening skies he remembered as well that this was a part of England that was soaked in sacred lore and memory; this was the 'Holy Land of the English', with its proliferation of cathedrals and churches, and its tradition of monasteries and reclusive saints and hermits. Hermits and recluses. It brought his thoughts back to Luisa Gilmore who had apparently passed her entire life in this place.

He had hoped to check in at the pub, where he had a room booked for two nights, but an unplanned diversion a few miles outside a place with the delightful name of Poringland meant he had added forty-five minutes to his journey. This was nothing to do with the satnav's innards being crunched up, it was simply that Michael had missed a turning, which anyone could do. Clearly, it would be as well to drive directly to Fosse House, so that he could at least introduce himself to his hostess before going in search of the pub.

The roads were wide and there was hardly any other traffic, and he found Fosse House without much difficulty. The sun was setting with a Turneresque rowdiness of oriflammes across the horizon, but the storm was still grumbling menacingly over the North Sea and the wind was dashing itself against the car's sides. Michael began to wish he was back in Oxford.

But here, at last, was the gateway to the house – tall, once-white posts with a somewhat insecure wrought-iron gate. Beyond them was a fairly long drive, fringed with thick shrubbery and elderly trees. Driving cautiously and slowly, Michael could not see the house, but he could see lights shining beyond the trees – erratic glimmerings, like the mischievous beckoning of will o' the wisp marsh people . . . Or was it the corpse candles of a ghostly funeral, because if ever there was a gothic setting . . .?

He could not see the house, though. Was it shrouded in mystical mist, and only permitted to make itself visible once every hundred years? Did it rise up out of the Norfolk marshes on the occasion of some macabre anniversary, to lure unwary travellers?

It was neither of these things, of course. It was invisible from the first few yards of the drive simply because the trees obscured it. Michael rounded a slight curve in the drive and there it was, coming gradually into view through the trees as they dipped and moved in the storm-wind, as if tantalizingly and deliberately revealing a piece at a time. Fosse House, making a slow, dramatic entrance through the mists. The home of the enigmatic recluse Luisa Gilmore, whose ancestor had been part of a sacred choir that had sung to its own death throes.

It was not, of course, Roderick and Madeline Usher's mansion of gloom, but Michael thought it was not far off. It was four-square as to construction and greystone as to fabric, and there were sprawling patches of discoloration on the walls as if some inner disease had seeped through. The windows were tall and narrow, each one surmounted with curved thick stone lintels like frowning eyebrows. It was the most unwelcoming house Michael had ever seen, and he was guiltily relieved to think he would not be staying in this faded grandeur overnight. Dim lights showed at a couple of the windows, although they were so dim that it was remarkable they had been visible from the drive.

As he went towards the main front door something moved on the rim of his vision. He half-turned and caught sight of a figure walking around the side of the house. Probably someone had heard his arrival and was coming to meet him. Michael waited, but the setting sun was directly in his eyes, and he thought after all there was no one there. Or perhaps it had been a bird flying across the light. He was about to walk on towards the house when the movement came again, and this time there was no doubt. Someone was coming through the shrubbery, and whoever it was moved quickly and lightly. The figure of what looked like a young man wearing a long overcoat. As if suddenly becoming aware of Michael's presence, the boy stopped and looked directly at him. Michael received a brief impression of fair hair and pale features. At the same time a breath of wind stirred through the trees, and words reached him, fragmented as if broken up by the distance, but perfectly clear.

'*Mustn't let them find me . . . You do understand that, don't you . . .? For my sanity's sake, I mustn't be caught . . .*'

The words made little sense, and the figure was already backing

away. But a ray of the setting sun touched the face, and Michael
saw that, as he had thought, it was a young man, barely more
than twenty or so. He had deep-set eyes and a small scar on one
side of his face. Or was it a leaf that had blown there and clung
to the boy's cheekbone?

The whisper came again. '*You do understand . . .? It's important that you do . . . I must get into the house, before they catch
me . . .*'

It seemed inconceivable that this totally strange young man
could be addressing these words to Michael, but there was no
one else about. Uneasily aware that this might be some local
ruffian, fleeing from the police – he said, 'It's all right. I understand they mustn't find you.'

The boy did not look like anyone's idea of a ruffian. He put
up a hand in what might be a gesture of acknowledgement, then
turned and went back around the house's side. Michael waited,
but nothing else happened, and whoever the boy had been, and
whatever his reasons for getting into the house were, it was
nothing to do with Michael. He would mention it to Miss Gilmore,
though, and there would probably be some perfectly innocent
explanation. But by now he would have given a great deal to be
able to get back into his car and drive as far away as possible
from this house. It was not just that it was bleak and remote, or
that elusive young men whispered sinisterly in its gardens; it was
that he was finding it unpleasantly easy to visualize dark echoing
rooms beyond those walls – rooms that might hide decaying
memories or cobwebbed humans, or in which forgotten tragedies
might still linger and sigh. Nell would look at him quizzically
if he said that to her, and tell him the place was nothing more
than a slightly run-down old house, and what did he expect in a
house standing in the most waterlogged part of the country?

The thought of Nell's sharp bright logic brought a semblance
of reassuring reality back, and Michael stepped up to the massive
old front door, and reached for the heavy door knocker. It fell
against the thick oak and echoed sonorously inside the house.
Michael waited and was just beginning to wonder if Fosse House
was empty after all when there was the sound of footsteps from
inside. They were slow, rather uneven footsteps, and he remembered that Luisa Gilmore was in her seventies.

The door opened, and a thin lady stood in the doorway. A dusty light illuminated a large hall behind her.

With only a faint question in his tone, Michael said, 'Miss Gilmore? I'm Michael Flint.'

'Dr Flint. Come inside,' said Luisa Gilmore, and, as if conforming to all the opening lines of sinister ladies dwelling in remote mansions, added, 'I've been expecting you.'

She stood back, and Michael stepped over the threshold.

TWO

The inside of Fosse House was much as he had expected. It was vaguely shabby and run down, and there was a faint dimness everywhere – not so much from lack of care as gradual decay from the damp that must seep through the walls and stones and lay a quenching bloom on mirrors and bright surfaces.

But if the house was run down, its owner was not. Luisa Gilmore was certainly in her seventies and she leaned slightly on a walking stick, but as she led Michael across the big panelled hall, although she limped slightly, her movements were sharp and coordinated. She did not appear to subscribe to modern ideas about preserving youth or keeping up with modern fashion; she wore a dark-blue dress of the style Michael thought was referred to as classic, and there was a shawl around her shoulders – although that might be against Fosse House's coolness. Her hair, which was silver, was brushed in a general style that, like the dress, might have belonged to any era.

She ushered him into a room which she referred to as the small sitting-room but which was still twice as big as Michael's own sitting room in Oxford. It was not very well lit, but when she sat down in a wing armchair, gesturing him to a seat facing her, the light from a low lamp fell across her face and he thought that she must have been very good-looking in her younger days. But he also thought her pallor was more than the pallor of age – that it might be the pallor of illness. Or was it Morticia Addams after all? *Don't be absurd.*

He expressed to Luisa the gratitude of himself and the Director of Music for being allowed access to Fosse House's annals.

'I hope you'll find useful material,' said Luisa. 'Would you like a cup of tea or coffee before you drive along to the village? Or perhaps a glass of sherry?'

It was clear she did not want him to start work that evening and even clearer that she would prefer him to go as soon as politeness allowed, so Michael thought sherry would be the easiest and the quickest option. It came in fragile, thin-stemmed glasses, and it was so rich and strong that it would probably lay him flat before he had driven fifty yards. Setting it down after three sips, he explained how he hoped to approach the task ahead.

'I'll let you have a note of everything I make use of, of course, but while I'm here I don't need to intrude on you or your day at all. If you're happy to leave me with the various papers on the Palestrina Choir I'll just quietly get on with it.'

'You will have lunch here, of course.'

'Well, thank you. There's no need for you to go to any trouble. Just a sandwich will do.'

'It won't be any trouble. I have cleaning and cooking help on several mornings. Someone will be coming in tomorrow morning, and lunch can be prepared for you.' So might a duchess have referred to unknown underlings who would do whatever they were bidden.

'Most of the papers are in the library,' she said, getting to her feet. 'I'll show you before you go – I thought it would probably be the best place for you to work. Let me go ahead, then I can switch on lights for you. This is rather a dark house.'

'I liked the lights you put at the front windows when I arrived,' said Michael. 'It was very welcoming to see that.'

She gave him rather a sharp look, but only led him across the hall without speaking. Michael noticed that the slightly limping gait was more strongly marked than he had previously realized. He also saw that she glanced uneasily around as they went, and he wondered if she was not alone in the house after all. Was there someone here she did not want him to know about or to meet? He was about to tell her about seeing the boy earlier, but as soon as she opened the door to the library he forgot about Gothic heroines and young men with leaf-blown scars. The atmosphere and the scents of old leather and vellum, the crowded shelves and stacks of what looked like manuscripts and unbound books, beckoned invitingly and insistently. Come in and unravel the past, said the books and the stored-away papers. Find the pathways into the long-ago, for it's not very far away, not that particular part of the past you're looking for. On a more practical note, there were several deep, soft chairs drawn up to the old fireplace, as well as a large library-table under the window.

Michael smiled at the room and knew if the research took longer than the planned two days it would be no hardship.

Luisa drew the curtains against the night. 'The storm is returning,' she said. 'If you listen, you can hear it coming in from the fens. I sometimes think it almost sounds like whispering voices.' Without giving him time to think how best to answer this, she said, 'So you will be as well to set off now, Dr Flint. With a storm brewing, the road from here to the village centre is an unpleasant one in the dark.'

Michael was about to say he would leave right away, when he caught sight of a thick folder placed on the table, together with a deep cardboard box, both clearly marked 'Palestrina Choir: 1900–1914'.

It was impossible to ignore them. He sat on the edge of the table and opened the folder, which contained thick wodges of handwritten notes on various sizes of paper, clearly from several different decades. The box held a mass of miscellaneous material, including envelopes of what looked like press cuttings, old theatre or concert programmes, and a number of music scores in a cracked plastic sleeve. These last were largely incomprehensible to Michael, but J.B. would seize on them eagerly. In addition were several pages of typed notes, which looked as if they had been taken from reference books, and which, at first glance, gave a brief outline of the Choir's creation.

He was distantly aware of his hostess saying something about the contents of the room having been sketchily catalogued some years ago – something about someone writing a thesis which had never been completed – but he scarcely heard, because a sheet of paper, half folded inside an old envelope, had partly slid out from the clipped papers. It was a letter, handwritten but in writing so erratic that Michael received the impression that urgency or despair had driven the pen. The stamp on the envelope was foreign, and did not convey anything particular to him, but the letter was on thin, age-spotted paper, and the date at the top was November 1917.

He could not, out of courtesy to his hostess, sit down and read the entire thing there and then, but he had caught sight of the first few sentences and the words had instantly looped a snare around his imagination. The direction at the top was simply to 'my dearest family'.

They're allowing me to write this farewell letter to you, and I
should be displaying bravery and dignity in it, so that you all
remember me in that way. Only I can't do so, for I am facing
a deeply dishonourable death – and an agonizing death – and
I'm filled with such terror that I'm afraid for my sanity . . .

For my sanity's sake I mustn't be caught, the young man in the
shadowy garden had said. There could be no connection with
this letter, though. This was one of the heart-rending farewell
missives that soldiers wrote before going into battle – the letter
that was sent to their families in the event of their death. The
reference the writer made about facing a dishonourable death was
slightly odd, though. Had he been an army deserter, facing a firing
squad? But in that situation would he have been allowed to write
to his family?

It took all of Michael's resolve to put the folder back on the
table, but he did so, and then realized that a phone was ringing
somewhere nearby, and that his hostess had gone out of the room
to answer it. He remained where he was, looking longingly at
the folder. Who were you? he thought, and he was just thinking
he might have time to read more when Luisa returned.

'It seems there is a problem on the road to the village,' she
said, and Michael heard the note of strain in her voice. 'A short
while ago the storm brought down a tree, and it's lying across
the road just outside the house.' A brief shrug. 'It happens here
at times. But it means the road is impassable and likely to be so
until tomorrow when they can clear the tree. I'm sorry, Dr Flint,
but it will be impossible for you to reach the village tonight.'

'Can I drive round it?' asked Michael, after a moment. 'Or
go in the other direction? There's surely a pub or something
where I can get a room.'

'I'm afraid not. The tree is almost immediately outside the
gates. Even if you could drive in the other direction, that's more or
less a straight run until you come to the coast road. There're a
few odd houses, but no pubs or inns.' With an obvious effort,
she said, 'So of course you will stay here.'

She did not manage to completely conceal her reluctance, but
Michael thought it was because she had suddenly been faced
with the practicalities of an unexpected guest. He said, 'All right.

Thank you. But you don't have to go to any trouble. I can make up a temporary bed for myself somewhere.' Banishing recollections of his many culinary disasters, he said, 'I can even sort out a meal this evening.'

'That won't be necessary. The girl who comes in the mornings prepared a casserole today. It only needs heating and there will be more than enough for two.' With a return to her previous imperious air, she said, 'We will dine at seven.'

It will be all right, thought Michael, standing in the large bedroom on the first floor. This is simply an old house, a bit creaky and whispery, a bit gloomy. But it's in the depths of the Fens, for goodness' sake, so it's entitled to be gloomy and whispery. As for the boy I saw earlier, he was most likely a local, caught where he shouldn't have been. He remembered he still had not mentioned it to Luisa, and thought he had better do so over dinner.

And, looked at in a positive light, staying here might mean he could get to know Luisa a bit better – they would be eating together this evening, and she might open up about her family, which could be interesting and also useful.

On closer investigation, the house was not as bad as its exterior suggested. It was a bit dingy, and there was an overlying dimness in most of the rooms which might be due to the damp, or simply to some thrifty person having put low-watt light bulbs in all the fittings. Most of the rooms looked as if they were closed up, and Michael thought Luisa probably only used two or three of them. It was rather sad; a house like this ought to be filled with people. He wanted to believe that Luisa had a large family who frequently came to stay, but when he remembered how definite she had been about not being able to offer a couple of nights' hospitality, he doubted it.

His bedroom opened off an L-shaped, partly galleried landing and had dark, old-fashioned furniture and a deep bed. There was a slightly battered radiator which, when Michael tried the dial, clanked into a reasonable degree of heat, and sheets and blankets were to be found in a linen cupboard. By the time he set out his washing things in an outdated but adequate bathroom, he was able to inform his reflection that it would be quite safe to stay here for one night. He did not examine his use of the word 'safe'.

It was not quite six o'clock, and the folder with the sad, desperate letter was calling to him with a siren's lure. If nothing else, he could at least read the whole thing before tracking down the dining room for dinner with Madeline Usher. Presumably, Fosse House was not so far into Gothic or baronial tradition that somebody bashed a bronze gong for dinner, and Michael supposed his hostess would find him when the promised casserole was ready.

Flurries of wind blew spitefully through the ill-fitting windows, and when Michael went past what seemed to be a chimney wall he could hear the gale moaning inside it. Luisa was right, it did sound like whispering voices. Perhaps that was all he had heard earlier in the garden.

The walls of the main landing were partly panelled, and a series of framed photographs and prints hung on them. Some of these looked as if they were of Fosse House, and Michael paused to study them more closely.

The shots were nearly all rather smudgy groups, the faces indeterminate, and without names or dates they were not very informative. The sketches were fairly bland landscapes, probably local scenes, but one sketch was not a landscape, and it drew his attention at once. It hung at the far end of the landing, partly in shadow, and it was not very big, perhaps twelve inches by sixteen. But even from its shadowy corner, it was vivid and imbued with life. It showed a spartan-looking dormitory with wooden-framed bunk beds and deal tables. Young men, wearing some sort of uniform, sprawled on the beds or lounged over the tables, some apparently playing cards or even what could be chess with home-made pieces.

Michael found the sketch disturbing. At first he thought it was because the room was obviously a prison, with the men having the air of animals herded together. But as he went on looking, he began to realize his sense of unease was not engendered solely by the bars at the narrow windows or the glimpses of an enclosed yard beyond them. It was because the young men were being watched – and apparently without their knowledge. Three or four other men were standing outside the narrow windows, peering furtively in. Even depicted in pencil, their faces were unmistakably sly and gloating. They wore uniforms with an insignia lightly drawn on the arms and shoulders, and spiked helmets. Michael knew next to nothing about military history or uniforms, but he thought it was a safe guess that these were the distinctive headgear of the Imperial Prussian Army. Then was this a German prisoner-of-war camp? If so, it was a curious thing to find in an English country house. Or did it tie up with that letter dated 1917?

He stepped closer to the sketch, trying to make out more details, and it was then that he saw the figure seated on the edge of one of the card schools. The young man was dressed carelessly and casually like the others, but the artist had taken more trouble with the details. The deep-set eyes under the slightly untidy hair were distinctive, and on one cheekbone was sketched a small mark – a mark that might have been a leaf that had blown there and become stuck.

It was an exact replica of the young man Michael had seen earlier. The young man who had feared for his sanity and had begged not to be caught. But it could not possibly be the same person. In any case he had only seen the boy for a few moments and he might not be remembering him clearly. But he knew he was, and with the intention of finding something to dispel his wild imaginings he took the sketch down and carried it to a nearby wall light to examine it more closely. In one corner was a squiggle of unreadable initials – presumably the artist's – and beneath it the words '*Holzminden,* November 1917'. Michael thought Holzminden was a place rather than a name, and he foraged for the notebook without which he seldom moved to note the details. It could all be checked later. The sketch itself might even be something Nell would find interesting and want to investigate, although pictures were not really her province.

The sketch did not seem to yield any more clues, and Michael replaced it. The likeness would be due to nothing more than a strong family resemblance, and it had nothing to do with his research into the Palestrina Choir, and the music and poetry of the Great War.

He walked slowly along the landing, studying the rest of the display. The photographs included several sepia faces in romanticized surrounds, but there were later ones as well, mostly from the 1940s. It looked as if Fosse House had been used as a small hospital of some kind in WWII; there were photos of the house with nurses and young men in wheelchairs on the lawns. Near the end, half in shadow, was a shot of a long room which Michael thought was at the house's front. It seemed almost to echo the Holzminden sketch; again there were young men in uniform, some clearly badly wounded, others happily waving crutches or plastered arms at whoever had been behind the camera. As in the sketch, some were playing cards. Others were reading newspapers and looked as if they had put their papers down to pose for the photograph. A typed label proclaimed it as having been taken in Fosse House in November 1943.

There were no prying faces in this, but standing in the doorway watching the others was a man who conveyed the air of being apart from the rest. He was not quite in the light and there was a blurred look, as if he might have moved at the moment the shutter was pressed. Michael felt a tremor of unease. It could not be, of course, and yet—

He held the photo closer to the light, and the unease deepened, because he seemed to be looking at the man from the Holzminden sketch. Or was he? Yes, there again were the deep-set eyes, the distinctive cheekbones, and the blown-leaf birthmark or scar. It was undoubtedly the same man. Except that it could not be. He could not be in the sketch and the photograph, not twenty-five years apart and looking exactly the same. Nor could he have been in the dark gardens of this house earlier tonight.

Whatever the explanation, it was an odd thing to come across. Michael could not escape a curious feeling that this young man, whoever he was, had somehow been picked up out of 1917 and dropped into a slot in 1943. And then dropped into the gardens today, as well? It was patently absurd. He studied the blurred edges of the boy's figure in the later one. Could some kind of double exposure be the explanation? Had someone tried to photograph the 1917 sketch and superimpose it on the 1943 one – perhaps wanting to depict the links between the two wars or create a montage? But the boy was seated at a table in 1917 and standing in a doorway in 1943, and it did not look as if the photograph had been taken with anything more than a box Brownie. He went down the stairs, still trying to think of an explanation.

The hall was wreathed in shadows, and only the faintest light came through the narrow windows on each side of the door. Michael glanced round, wondering if he should switch on a light

– always supposing he could find a light switch – then saw a figure walk across the right-hand window immediately outside. He stood still, expecting to hear a knock at the door, hoping this might be news to say the tree had been cleared already and wondering if he should answer the knock when it came.

But the knock did not come. Instead the door rattled and creaked heavily, as if someone was leaning against it. Someone's trying to get in, thought Michael. Is it the boy I saw earlier? Should I open the door or call Miss Gilmore? Moving quietly, he went up to the window and tried to see out. But it was too dark and rain streaked the window. He waited, but the door was motionless, and there was only the keening wind and the rhythmic tapping of the rain against the windows. Perhaps it had only been the storm he had heard, and the reflection of tree branches blown against the windows. He repressed a shiver and headed for the book room.

As soon as he opened the folder containing the letter, he felt its sadness all over again. The faint concern about an intruder and the puzzle of the sketch and photo receded, and he smoothed the letter out carefully, then turned it over to read the writer's name. The signature stood out clearly. Stephen Gilmore.

Stephen. Did that name fit those features? Michael thought it did. Saints and martyrs and an English King. He turned the letter back and as he did so a scrap of fabric that had been in the envelope slid out. There was a small star and an insignia. Stephen's regiment or unit and his rank, presumably. Had this been sent to his family after Stephen had suffered whatever shameful death had been waiting for him?

Nell, delving into the histories and provenances of the antique items she bought and sold, had sometimes said that to turn up old documents was like having a hand reach out from the past and feeling long-ago fingers curl around yours. It was a friendly sensation, she said. But as Michael began to read Stephen Gilmore's letter, he was aware only of apprehension. There's something terrible at the end of all this, he thought. It might not be contained in the letter, but I think it's contained in this house. No, I'm being absurd.

Forcing himself to be objective, he began to read, but he was strongly aware of the fear and desperation that had driven Stephen's words.

The horrors I experienced at Passchendaele – those squalid, screaming deaths in the mud, and the constant rain of shells from the Bosch – will be nothing compared to what is ahead now. I could wish I had died at Passchendaele among good comrades, knowing I died for what was right and just . . . That would have been an honourable death – you would all have been proud of me and there would have been memorials – church services. My female cousins would have thought of me as romantic and tragic. The boys would have talked of me as a hero.

This was hardly a conventional farewell letter. Michael glanced at his watch. Half past six. He had time to finish it before dinner with his hostess. He resumed reading, and, as if in eerie echo of his thoughts, the next lines also referred to time.

There's no clock in here, but I can feel the minutes ticking away . . . I'm filled with such despair, I'm afraid for my own sanity . . . I was mad once before, so I've been told, and I believe I may easily become mad again . . . Pray for me, please, for I can see no way of escape. And, oh God, if I could see Fosse House again – if I could see the clear pure light when it falls across the fens, and if I could walk up the tree-lined carriageway and see the lamps burning in the windows as dusk falls . . . Light the lamps for me, though – do so every evening at dusk – for perhaps I may still somehow find my way home.

I promise you – all of you at home – that I am innocent of this charge. Even if I must die at the hands of Niemeyer's butchers, I will find a way to convince you all of my innocence. I must find a way. If it takes twenty-five years – if it takes a century, I must – I *will* – prove my innocence.

Did they light the lamps for you, Stephen? thought Michael, torn with pity. Does someone still do so? Because I saw lights when I came along the drive earlier, and they were faint, strange lights, as if they were the glimmer of lamps from some lost, long-ago world . . .

Stephen had also written that if it took twenty-five years, or if it took a century, he would prove his innocence. And only fractionally over twenty-five years later, in November 1943, his image had been blurrily captured on a photograph. A century after he had written those words, Michael had seen him walking through the gardens of Fosse House.

It was just after seven o'clock. His hostess would certainly expect punctuality from her guest, however unwelcome and unexpected a guest he might be.

As Michael went in search of the dining-room, he spared a thought for Oxford, and hoped that all was well there.

Memo from: *Dr Owen Bracegirdle, History Faculty,*
               Oriel College, Oxford
To: *Director of Music, Oriel College, Oxford*

Here are the promised preliminary notes about the Great War. You'll see that I found some interesting snippets on several of the War Poets – Robert Graves in particular. Apparently he was at school with one of the Gilmore family, which I think is the gang Michael Flint is currently chasing in Norfolk, so we might find a very useful tie-up there.

I do apologize for sending handwritten pages and I hope everything is readable, but you'll appreciate that the current electricity problem means I can't print them out in the usual way or, indeed, even type them. I should mention, at this point, that the power failure really isn't Dr Flint's fault. It was impossible for anyone to predict that Wilberforce the cat would become unaccountably entangled in the electrical wiring in the meter cupboard, resulting in a massive short-circuit which plunged most of College into Cimmerian darkness. Nor had anyone the least notion that the wiring was so interconnected and interdependent as to make a single, isolated short so disastrous.

Remarkably, Wilberforce himself escaped unscathed. I can't help feeling that a lesser animal would have been frizzled to a crisp, but according to eyewitnesses he walked away with nothing worse than singed whiskers and a trodden-on tail – the latter due to a second-year who was coming out of the buttery at the time. (I don't know the details of why the second-year was in the buttery in the first place, and I'm not enquiring, and he isn't one of my students, anyway.)

We're promised that light will be restored soon, but the workings of electricity companies are as intricate as a Tudor Court, so no one has any huge expectation of it. I hear the kitchens have announced a moratorium on the planned lamb and ratatouille, and there's a mass exodus arranged for the evening, either to the Turf or the Rose and Crown.

If your own part of College has been affected, and if you haven't any engagement for this evening, you're most welcome to join my group at the Turf. I'm dining early though, because I want to call on Nell West afterwards – you'll remember that her shop adjoins that excellent antiquarian bookseller in Quire Court. She phoned earlier to say there are two or three useful-looking books on WWI presently in their stock, all by fairly reputable authors, and that one appears to include some letters from a POW officer who had some contact with Siegfried Sassoon. I haven't any of the titles on my own shelves, and Nell has arranged to borrow the books for the evening so I can see if they're worth buying. I should say I'm ever mindful of College budgets and of the Bursar's blood pressure, and the books are actually from the second-hand rather than the antiquarian section (a nice distinction, I always think), so they aren't likely to cost very much.

The fiscal arrangements you propose for my own involvement in all this are very acceptable. It's a terrible world when academics have to consider the sordid subject of coinage, but so it is. I'm sorry if you've heard a rumour that I'm on my beam ends, but I can assure you that any such rumour stems merely from finding myself unaccountably without funds at the Rose and Crown one night, after I had ordered a round of drinks and a platter of sandwiches. Matters were settled honourably the very next day, and the report of my impending bankruptcy was an exaggeration.

Regards,

O.B.

THREE

The casserole was very good and so was the wine served with it. Michael wondered if Luisa dined like this every night, alone and in semi-state, sipping a distinguished claret, the table laid with damask napkins and silver. It was difficult to imagine her eating off a tray in front of the television. He had not, in fact, seen a television at Fosse House yet.

Over the meal, Luisa made conventional enquiries about Michael's room, then went on to ask about the proposed book.

Michael said, 'I think the Director of Music is very keen to include a section about the Palestrina Choir. I've only read a little about it myself. My involvement is mostly to do with the poets of the Great War – of how music influenced their outlook and their work.' He hesitated, then said, 'It sounded as if the Choir had a troubled life.'

She had been picking at her food in a rather desultory fashion, and she now abandoned it altogether. 'In its early years it achieved considerable success, but its eventual demise was tragic, Dr Flint.'

'You had an ancestor who was part of it – have I got that right?'

'Yes. Leonora. Her father was an English Gilmore several generations back. A several-times great uncle of mine, I think. He had married a Belgian girl and they lived in Liège.'

'The home of the Choir?'

'Yes, it was within the convent of Sacré-Coeur. Leonora entered the convent's school in 1907 when she was nine.' She glanced at Michael as if to assure herself he was genuinely interested, then went on. 'By that time the Choir was well established. Wealthy people were wanting to place their daughters in the school because of the music tradition—'

'And Leonora was in the midst of it,' said Michael thoughtfully.

'Yes. Her childhood had not been very happy, Dr Flint. Her parents had given her no sense of self-pride, and she grew up believing herself unworthy of the – the warmer emotions of life.'

'How sad,' said Michael, after a moment.

'Life is often sad. But she enjoyed Sacré-Coeur – she loved the music and the companionship of the other girls. The music touched something in her she had barely known she possessed.'

A part of Michael's mind was registering that Luisa was almost speaking as if she had first-hand knowledge of Leonora's emotions, but he merely said, 'She sounds an unusual girl.'

'Oh, she was.' There was definite eagerness in her voice now. 'She was only sixteen when the Great War broke out, but she—' She broke off, as if something had interrupted her, and turned her head towards the curtained windows as if she was listening to something. Or is she listening *for* something, thought Michael, slightly startled.

'Is something wrong, Miss Gilmore?'

'Did you hear that?' Her face had paled and the bones stood out sharply. 'Dr Flint, did you hear it?'

'Only the storm,' said Michael. 'I did think I heard someone outside earlier, but—'

'What did you hear? Dr Flint, *what did you hear?*'

'Just vague noises,' said Michael, concerned by the note of urgency in her voice, but unwilling to worry her by saying he thought someone had tried the front door. 'It's a wild night, isn't it, and—'

He stopped, because now there were unquestionably sounds outside, and they were not from the storm. Someone was walking along the garden path immediately outside the dining-room window. He looked across at Luisa, saw that her eyes had dilated with fear. Aware of a beat of apprehension he got up from the table and went towards the window.

At once Luisa said, 'Don't open the curtains.'

'I'm only going to see if anyone is out there.'

'There's no need,' she said in a strained voice, then sat up a little straighter, as if making a physical attempt to draw about her the remnants of composure. 'You mustn't open the door—'

'Miss Gilmore, I'm sure I heard someone. And when I arrived here earlier I thought there was someone in the gardens. Let me take a quick look outside—'

'No,' she said sharply. 'No, please don't. It's quite all right. This house is a good two hundred years old. I'm afraid it's a bit creaky.' Her colour was returning, and her voice sounded normal again. 'Houses can be a bit like people. Creaky and sometimes erratic.' A sudden, surprisingly sweet smile showed briefly.

'I've often thought that,' said Michael. He was just trying to decide whether he ought to investigate the footsteps anyway, or whether he should try to nudge her back on to the subject of Leonora and the Choir, when she said, 'Have you had enough to eat? There's cheese and fruit left out in the kitchen if you want. And coffee can be filtered very quickly.'

It was a polite dismissal. Intruders, imaginary or real, had been relegated to their place. So Michael said, 'I've had more than enough, thank you, and it was very good. But a cup of coffee would be welcome. I'll take it into the library if that's all right. I can put in another hour's work, perhaps more. Can I fetch the coffee? Bring yours in here?'

'That would be kind of you. The filter machine only needs switching on. There will be milk in the fridge. I take mine black, with no sugar.'

Michael nodded and found his way to the kitchen.

He took his hostess's cup to her, but before pouring his own he went up to his bedroom to phone Nell. He had suddenly found that he wanted to hear her voice very much. If anyone could dispel Fosse House's eeriness, it would be Nell. With that in mind, he told her about hearing the whispering on his arrival.

'Michael, my love, you're so suggestible, you'd hear ghosts in a supermarket car park,' said Nell. 'I'll bet you drove up to that dark old house – it is a dark old house, I suppose? Yes, I thought it would be – and you saw it as the setting for cobweb-draped Victorian skeletons, or the background to somebody's graveyard elegy, not to mention doomed Gothic heroines.'

'I wish,' said Michael, already feeling better, 'that you weren't able to walk in and out of my mind quite so easily.'

'It's always a nice journey though,' she said, and Michael heard the smile in her voice. 'What did the whispers say?'

'They were quite macabre,' said Michael, hesitating.

'If a dark old house has a whispering voice, it's bound to be a macabre one. Seriously, what did the whispers say?'

'About trying to hold on to sanity – that seemed to be the main burden of the song. And about not being caught, for sanity's sake.'

'Those are quite sibilant words,' said Nell thoughtfully. 'I'll bet what you heard was simply the storm wind blowing down the guttering.'

'I expect you're right,' said Michael. 'Thanks, my love. You've put me back in touch with reality. You always do put my feet back on the ground.'

'Well, you send my head into the clouds quite often, so that balances out.'

'I'll tell you about something I've found here that might do that properly,' he said. 'No, it isn't a Van Dyck or a Delft dinner service – it's quite an unusual framed sketch with the date 1917 on it.' He briefly considered whether to mention the unnerving fact that Stephen Gilmore appeared in a photograph of twenty-five years later, and decided that the whispering was more than enough gothic content for one phone call. Instead he described the sketch carefully, and was aware of Nell's instant interest.

'Did you say Holzminden? Michael, are you sure about that?'

'Yes, I am. What exactly is Holzminden? Or should I say, where is it? Because it sounds like a place rather than someone's name.'

'It is a place. It's a town, or it might even be a city, in Germany – Lower Saxony, I think. I'll have to look it up. But I think it was originally one of those medieval settlements that existed under the rule of a princedom or a dukedom. Turreted castles and stone arches, and Wolfenbuttels, I expect. *But* there was a prisoner-of-war camp there in the First World War—'

'And?' said Michael, hearing the suppressed excitement in Nell's voice.

'Well, it sounds as if what's in Fosse House might be a First World War prison-camp sketch. Sketches from the Second World War prison-camps sometimes come up for sale – they can be anything from heartbreaking to inspirational, and they're some-times worth as much as eight hundred or even a thousand pounds, depending on their provenance and where the sketch was made and what the paper is. The prisoners would trade cigarettes for paper and pencils, or use bits of cardboard from food packing. But Great War sketches are quite rare, and the Holzminden ones – well, they're practically Shakespeare's thirty-eighth.'

'Shakespeare probably wrote more than thirty-seven plays—'

'It's difficult to separate legend from reality about the Holzminden sketches,' said Nell, so focused on the subject that she hardly heard

Michael's remark. 'A great many authorities maintain they never existed. That they're only a myth. But if you've found one— Are you sure it's a POW camp in the sketch? Not a hospital?'

'Well, there are bars at the windows and even some German soldiers peering through them at the prisoners. Oh, and there's an engraving or a painting on one of the walls – a slightly stylized outline of a black eagle, wings spread, claws out.'

'The German Imperial emblem,' said Nell eagerly. 'Michael, if that sketch is real, it would be a tremendous discovery. I'll see what I can find out about it.'

'Don't spend too much time on it. I shouldn't think it's the genuine article, and in any case it's not likely to be for sale.'

'I'd like to turn up some details, though,' she said. 'It'll be a good project while you're away, and while Beth's in Scotland with Brad's aunts.'

'Have you heard from her? Is she enjoying herself?'

'She's having a whale of a time and the aunts are thoroughly spoiling her. When she phoned this afternoon, she said she was going to buy a kilt for you and a tartan bow for Wilberforce.'

'God help us all.' Michael had a sudden irresistible picture of Wilberforce indignantly adorned with a tartan bow. He said, 'Is everything all right there?'

'Yes, everything's fine. Listen, though, I'd better ring off, because I've arranged to borrow a couple of books from next door for Owen – Great War stuff that he thinks might be useful for J.B.'s book. He's calling round shortly to take a look at them. So I'll see if there's anything about Holzminden at the same time. Shall I email anything to you?'

'There's no Internet connection here and the signal isn't brilliant on the phone, either. I'll be back in a couple of days anyway. But if the sketch is genuine, I do wonder how it got here.'

'Never mind how it got there, if it's genuine, I wonder if Luisa Gilmore knows what she's got,' said Nell.

'And if she'd let you sell it on her behalf?'

'Of course.'

Michael replaced the phone and, before he could forget, made some notes for a new Wilberforce chapter, in which Wilberforce found himself in Scotland, becoming entangled with a set of bagpipes, which the ever-inventive mice had booby-trapped. He would email the idea to Beth when he got back to Oxford, and they would have one of the sessions they both enjoyed, working out how it could be written, and what Wilberforce's eventual fate might be.

Going downstairs he realized he was deliberately ignoring the Holzminden sketch, and he was so annoyed with himself that he deliberately stopped in front of it and inspected it again. But it did not seem to have any further information to give, and when he unhooked it to examine the back, there was only a sheet of brown paper, glued to the edges of the frame. Michael was aware of such a strong compulsion to tear the paper off to see what might lie underneath that it took a considerable effort to replace the sketch.

He collected his coffee from the kitchen and carried it into the library. There was a degree of reassuring familiarity about the room, and it was nicely warm. Once the table lamp and an old-fashioned standard lamp had been plugged in and switched on, pools of soft light lay across the piles of books, picking out gilt lettering here and there on a calf or leather spine. Michael opened the laptop and reached for the Palestrina file. He was finding it difficult not to keep remembering Luisa's moment of evident fear at supper, or her violent repudiation of the possibility that someone could be walking through the garden.

She did hear it, though, thought Michael. I know she did, because I heard it too. And I heard someone trying the door. No, I didn't. It was birds in the eaves or water chugging down the guttering, that's all.

He set Stephen Gilmore's letter to one side and began to sort through the top layer of the file. There was a remarkable diversity of stuff: letters and notes, concert programmes, a few dog-eared photographs with nothing to show who the people in them were or where the photos had been taken, old receipts and bills that might have nothing to do with the subject in hand, but that were interesting in their own way.

As he made his own notes, there were sounds that the storm was returning. Rain lashed against the windows and the old house seemed to be filling up with rustlings and whispering draughts. Several times the curtains stirred, making Michael jump and look quickly over his shoulder.

It was interesting to speculate how some of the papers he was finding had reached Fosse House. He turned up what appeared to be a letter to one of the nuns at the Liége Sacré-Coeur convent. How had this found its way from Liège to this remote corner of England? It was written in French, of course; Michael was aware that the French spoken in Belgium varied from region to region, but as far as he could make out, this seemed to be the straightforward form of the language – it was 'French' French. His knowledge of the language was patchy and also somewhat rusty, but he thought he could get the gist of it.

My dear Sister Clothilde . . . Permit me to express the appreciation of those of us fortunate enough to attend the beautiful concert by your Choir at Saint Jacques' Church last month . . . This was fairly easy to translate, but there followed what Michael thought were technical musical terms, which were beyond his ability. Then the writer went on to say something about how the music would have gladdened – or it might be delighted – Signor Palestrina's heart. *He would have much enjoyed listening to his own* Nunc Dimittis *and the* Kyrie *. . . Also, the Bach* Cantata *were beautifully sung.*

More incomprehensible details, presumably about the music, followed this, together with a spattering of names of people who had attended, but it was the closing paragraph that made Michael blink and look along the shelves for a French–English dictionary. Surely there would be one here . . .? Yes, there it was, battered and dog-eared, but perfectly serviceable. He seized it gratefully and returned to the big desk.

The letter-writer talked about *caché* and *l'écran* and *si triste*. *Caché* was hidden, of course, and *triste* was sad. But what was *écran*? He turned over the dictionary's pages. Here it was. *Écran* was screen. Which meant the closing sentence said, more or less, *So sad that the chorus must always be hidden behind screens.* Michael frowned and traced the final few sentences with the help of the dictionary. *However, there is an ancient and honourable tradition for their kind, dating back to Vivaldi, I believe. I am glad* (or was that delighted again?) *to have your assurance that your own girls continue to submit with docility to this . . .*

FOUR

Michael stared at the letter. So the girls of the Palestrina Choir, in their remote convent, had been hidden behind screens when they sang. Why? To protect their innocence from lascivious masculine eyes? Had Leonora Gilmore been among them? But the concert had been in a church, for goodness' sake, and the Choir had presumably been chaperoned as diligently as a clutch of Regency maidens. And the letter-writer referred to the girls as 'always' having to be hidden, which suggested the practice was part of the normal routine of their day. Had there been something wrong with them? Physically? Mentally? Luisa had said Leonora's childhood had been unhappy – was there a clue there? Probably he was making much out of little. Still, he would look out that reference to Vivaldi; there might be a lead there he could follow.

He emptied another of the envelopes from the box. It seemed to contain mostly old letters and a few curling newspaper cuttings, and it looked as if some Gilmore boy had attended Charterhouse, because there were a number of smudgily-printed notices about various school events, and alumni newsletters. Michael flipped through these, not seeing anything relevant. He was about to close the file when a letter clipped to one notice caught his eye. It dated from the early 1920s and was addressed to 'Dear old Boots' and signed 'Chuffy'. It referred to the two of them having been at Charterhouse in the years prior to the Great War and expressed a hope that Boots might toddle along to the next Old Carthusian bash on the grounds that it would do him, Boots, a great deal of good to get away from his books for a while. Chuffy wrote:

> All work and no play. And I know your cousin, Stephen, was at the old place a few years ahead of us. What happened to him? I heard one or two odd tales about him, but I hope he came through the War all right. We lost a lot of good chaps, didn't we? I'm sure I remember Stephen being a

chum of Robert Graves. I'm afraid some of the chaps bullied
Graves a bit – we all thought he was mad, and it was only
later I heard he feigned all that mad stuff as a defence against
the bullying. I think some of the others felt a bit rotten about
that. For all his strangeness Graves came through the War
all right though, and I know he wrote some cracking poetry,
not that I'm much of a one for poetry; I can never understand
the half of it. I think Stephen came in for some of the
bullying, as well – didn't he try to run away one term, saying
later that the only place he felt safe was his home in the
Fens? But then the beaks put him and Graves in the choir
and that seemed to calm them both down.

There followed mentions of several pieces of music which the
Charterhouse choir had sung, but about which Chuffy had only
imperfect recollection, not being much of a one for music – 'you
know me, old boy'. The music in question was largely Handel and
Vivaldi with, according to Chuffy, 'stuff by some cove called Tallis
that mixed all the different voices in together, but in a perfectly
lovely way, like eating Neapolitan ice-cream or those layered
pastries at Selfridges. Anyway, old bean, if Stephen is still around,
perhaps he'd like to come along to the next bunfight with us'.

Michael liked Chuffy's breezy bonhomie, and since Robert
Graves had been a notable War poet, he listed the composers
against Graves' name as possible influences. It was sad to read
about Graves having feigned insanity to beat off school bullying.

*'They said, years later, that it was from Robert I got the idea
of pretending to be mad . . . But they didn't understand that there
were those of us for whom madness was a reality . . .'*

The words lay like cobwebs on the air and Michael turned
sharply to look at the room. He's got in, he thought. He's found
a way in. Stephen, are you here? But there was no one in the
room, and after a moment he went to the window and pulled back
the curtain slightly, careful to stand back so he could not be seen.
Was someone out there? He could not see any movements, but the
rain was still falling and it was impossible to be sure.

The carriage clock over the fireplace chimed ten and somewhere in the house a door opened and closed. Luisa called out
that she was just locking up and would bid him goodnight.

'Goodnight,' said Michael, wondering if he should offer to help with the locking up. But she probably had her own routine, so he closed the library door. There was the sound of the bolts being drawn across the main door. He can't get in now, he thought.

It was twenty past ten and Michael thought he, too, would call it a night. Normally, he would not be thinking of going to bed for another hour at least, but it had been a long drive, and Fosse House had sprung a few surprises. It was remarkable that in all the wealth of fictional and factual or speculative literature about ghosts, no one mentioned how exhausting it was to encounter them – or, at least, to encounter something approximating to them. Even if Fosse House's spooks turned out to be nothing more than creaking roof timbers, Michael felt as if he had run a ten-mile marathon. That being so, he would go up to bed now, then make an early start in the morning.

A low light was burning on the stairs, and Michael went quietly along to his bedroom, pleased to discover the radiator had ticked its way to a fair degree of warmth.

But although the room was warm and the bed itself deep and soft, the wind was still whipping across the Fens and Michael kept thinking he could hear whispering voices inside it. By half-past eleven he was still wide awake and wondering whether to go down to the library to see if there was any relatively light reading on the shelves. But perhaps that would disturb Luisa. He refused to acknowledge that he did not want to walk through this house at such an hour, punched his pillow, and lay down again.

The clock had crawled round to midnight, and he was at last sliding into the hinterlands of sleep, when he was jerked awake by a sound that was neither the keening wind, nor even glugging plumbing. It was the sound he had heard earlier – the sound of the front door being rattled. He's trying again, thought Michael with horror. He didn't get in earlier, and so he's come back because he thinks everyone is in bed. I'll have to do something – alert Luisa – phone the police.

He pulled a sweater over his pyjamas, thrust his feet into shoes and opened his bedroom door. He was not going to engage in any single-handed heroics, but he could at least go as far as the galleried part of the landing and look down into the hall from above.

The wind was still gusting angrily at the windows, causing the worn frames to rattle like dry, dead bones. The drapes at the long windows stirred as if invisible hands clutched at them, and Michael, reaching the landing, saw with relief that the low light was still burning, so that at least this would not be the classic walk through the dark old house. He peered cautiously over the rail. The dim light sent shadows chasing across the floor of the vast hall below, and the trees immediately outside the windows moved their branches back and forth. It was absurd to think their shadows were forming into the outline of a human figure – a figure that was trying to get into the house to be safe . . .

He went down the stairs and across the hall. The thick old door was still and silent, the heavy bolts in place. Michael put his hand on the surface and felt it creak slightly. Old timbers. Old frame, probably badly-fitting after so many years. Nothing more.

Two narrow windows flanked the door, each with a padded window seat, and Michael went to the nearer one and knelt on the faded velvet, peering out. The glass was old and slightly uneven, and rain streamed down it, distorting the view of the dark gardens beyond. Even so, he did not think anyone was out there. It's all right, he thought. The house is locked and secured and it's perfectly safe.

'Safe . . . Yes, I always felt safe in this house . . .'

Stephen, thought Michael, whipping round to scan the shadowy hall. But Stephen had been dead for nearly a century.

He was about to return to his room when a new sound reached him, and something moved at the head of the stairway. Michael's heart bumped into overdrive, because a figure had walked across the landing above him and was slowly descending the stairs. A figure in whose pallid face the eyes were deeply shadowed so that they resembled dark pits, and who walked with a curious uncoordinated gait as if propelled by some invisible force outside of its control.

He stifled a gasp and instinctively pressed back into the concealment of the window alcove. But before his mind could form Stephen's name and image again, a thin light fell across the figure and he saw that it was Luisa. Michael, his pulse-rate returning to near-normal, drew a deep breath of relief, and prepared to explain about investigating suspicious noises. Then he saw that no explanation was necessary. Luisa appeared to have no awareness of his presence or even to see him. She was not using the walking stick, and the dreadful puppet-like quality to her movements was unnerving. Her eyes were open, but they were glazed and staring straight ahead. She's sleepwalking, thought Michael. That's all this is.

He had an idea that sleepwalkers should not be woken abruptly, so he remained where he was in the window recess, and waited. Luisa crossed the hall. She was dressed as she had been earlier in the evening – the plain dress with the woollen shawl held in place by a silver brooch. No ethereal, floating draperies for this one, thought Michael. Unseeing, unhearing, Luisa unhooked the chain across the door, then reached for the two bolts on the front door, and drew them back. There was a soft scrape of sound, and then the groan of the hinges as the door opened slightly. Night air, cold and rain sodden, gusted in, spattering moisture on the oak blocks of the floor. The dark shapes of the old trees lay across the oak, and for a moment Michael thought they formed into the outline of a man standing in the doorway. Then it was gone. Luisa closed the door, slid the bolts back, and replaced the security chain.

She's let him in, thought Michael. She heard him trying to get in, and she's opened the door to him. There was no one there, but Luisa thought there was, and she thinks she let him. In a minute she'll go quietly back up to bed.

But Luisa did not. She went to a small bureau in a corner of the hall and from a drawer took what Michael, narrowing his eyes in the uncertain light, saw was a key. Still moving slowly, Luisa went to a section of the panelling, and Michael saw for the first time that a small door was set into the wood: not a concealed or a secret door, simply a door that was so much part of the wood that it was almost unnoticeable. Luisa unlocked it, pushed it open and stepped through.

Michael stared at the dark oblong. He was uncertain what he should do, but perhaps he ought to make sure Luisa was all right before going back to bed.

The door in the panelling was slightly ajar; beyond it was a flight of stone steps, in semi-darkness. Of course there would be shadowy stone steps, thought Michael, wryly. What else is ever behind a low door in a wall? Do I go down those steps? Oh hell, why not? All he wanted to do was make sure there was nothing down there that might pose a threat. Like the shadowy figure of a man with a blown-leaf scar . . .?

The steps looked old – certainly as old as the house, if not older. They were slightly worn at the centre, and Michael was irresistibly reminded of the steps in Ayesha's temple, in Rider Haggard's *She*, worn by the constant use of one person only – the immortal Egyptian Queen who had walked up and down them for two thousand years.

He stepped through the doorway, expecting to be met by chill dankness, but although it was noticeably cooler, there were no scents of mould or packed-earth floors.

A thick stone wall enclosed the steps, but as he went down they opened up, giving a clear view of an underground room at the foot. And after all that it was a perfectly ordinary cellar, of the kind that most houses of a certain age had. There was a stone floor and plain, whitewashed walls. Massive timber joists and thick pillars appeared to underpin the floors above, and seeing them, Michael had a sensation of oppression from the rooms and walls directly overhead.

It was fairly dim in the cellar, but there was enough light from somewhere to see that Luisa was kneeling at what, after a moment, Michael recognized as a prie-dieu – a prayer desk, generally found in private houses for devotional use. In front of the prie-dieu was a small table with two candles in holders and a small crucifix. The candles were not lit, but a small oil lamp had been, casting sullen shadows over the room. Luisa's head was bowed and her hands were clasped in the classic prayer attitude.

None of this was especially worrying, but it was faintly puzzling. Did Luisa regularly follow this eerie ritual? Did she unlock the door every night to let some shadowy figure in, then come down here? If so, it could explain why she had been so reluctant for Michael to spend the night here. But why, with the whole of Fosse House at her disposal and no one to question her actions, would she have a makeshift chapel in this chill, inaccessible room? Was it a remnant from the house's past – perhaps with a religious connection? But it was at least four hundred years since any kind of religious oppression had held sway in

England, and Fosse House did not seem old enough to have priests' holes or secret chapels for Papist practices.

Still slightly concerned, Michael ventured down two more steps, which gave him a wider view of the cellar. As well as the prie-dieu there was a small writing desk with a chair drawn up to it; on its surface was a thick-bound book lying open, together with a second lamp, unlit.

In the far corner was a low table, half covered with a length of dark velvet. No, it was not a table, it was an immense oak chest, waist-high, iron bound, and with a domed lid. The velvet was bunched and creased, and it was possible to see that a thick chain with a padlock was wrapped around the chest. Michael had been thinking the cellar was not sinister, only rather sad, but seeing this chest and the heavy chain, he was aware of a dark unease. Why the chains? What was so valuable it had to be kept in an underground room and secured so firmly?

Luisa got up from the prie-dieu, bowed her head – again it was the classic gesture before an altar – then crossed to the desk and reached for the second lamp and the matches standing nearby. Michael was aware of a jab of apprehension as the match flared up, but Luisa's movements were smooth and assured. She adjusted the funnel of the lamp with the ease of familiarity, then sat down. Reaching for the book, she opened it, picked up a modern biro and began to write in it. Diary? Journal? Whatever it was, her whole attitude was one of utter absorption and Michael thought he could have stomped down the staircase in spiked mountaineering boots without her noticing.

But whatever all this was, and however odd it seemed, it was nothing to do with him, and Luisa appeared to be all right. Michael went quietly back up the steps and closed the door softly. Somewhere in the house a clock chimed the half hour past midnight. He was wide awake, and the prospect of lying restlessly in the old bed was not inviting. Could he put in another spell of work? Yes, he could. And if he left the library door ajar he would be able to see and hear Luisa emerge from the cellar. He still had a nagging concern about her – which was absurd, since she most likely descended to that underground room on any number of nights, and appeared to have done so without any noticeable harm. But he would like to be sure.

The library was warm and friendly. Michael switched on the desk lamp, reached for his notebook, and opened the file containing the Charterhouse letter from Chuffy. That part of the file did not, however, appear to contain any more nuggets, and after a quarter of an hour of turning over the faded, dog-eared pages, he abandoned it, and picked up another one. The contents of this looked older, but most of the documents were in French, and Michael, aware of his imperfect knowledge of the language, sighed at the thought of struggling with more translating. Perhaps Luisa would let him take everything back to Oxford where someone in Modern Languages would most likely zip through the papers with contemptuous ease.

But on the first of the pages were three words that sparked his interest. Liège. Holzminden. And Leonora.

Those three again, thought Michael. Are they linked? Leonora's certainly linked to Liège. But Holzminden seems linked to Stephen and can't be anything to do with Leonora. Or can it? I'd better remember this isn't an ancient mystery I'm uncovering, it's just a fact-finding task. And it's the Choir I'm supposed to be pursuing, with Leonora as a subtext.

Probably, the pages would only lead down a cul-de-sac, and most of the file would be on the lines of Chuffy's letter, or a collection of dull missives from some French connection of the Gilmore family, which somebody had thought worth keeping. But Michael thought if he was going to be burning midnight oil while his hostess wrote up her journal below stairs, this would be as good a place to start as any.

The clipped-together pages with the reference to Liège and Holzminden were written in a graceful hand, but Michael saw right away that it was not a form of French that would be easy to translate. It did not seem to fit into the category either of straightforward French or of the Flemish form spoken in parts of Belgium – although he was not sure if he could differentiate one from the other. I can't do it, he thought, torn between annoyance and disappointment. Then he looked at Leonora's name again, which appeared several times on the first page, and he remembered the Holzminden sketch and Stephen, and the impression that there was something here worth pursuing gripped his mind again. He would make a stab at this letter, because, after all, he had managed a fairly respectable translation of the letter to Sister Clothilde earlier. If nothing else, he might be able to pick out a few phrases and see if it was worth going on. He reached for the French–English dictionary again.

Stephen's letter had conveyed no sense of what Nell called a friendly hand from the past, but the letter in front of him felt different. Michael had the illogical impression that he might like the writer.

The opening sentence was relatively easy. It translated as, 'I write this a little for myself but also for anyone who may one day read this, my own account.'

So far so good. Michael moved slowly down the page, making frequent use of the dictionary, at times finding it difficult to get at the meaning. French was not the writer's native language, and at times he – it was certainly a 'he' – had not used or known the right word. But by the time Michael reached page two, the rhythm of the writing was starting to fall into place.

The carriage clock chimed one o'clock, but Luisa had not yet come back upstairs, and Michael thought he would stay with this odd, intriguing narrative a little longer. It was half-past one when he sat back and regarded the rough translation he had made so far. He had no idea if it could be believed or if it was some long ago attempt at a work of fiction. The places and the dates seemed genuine, although that did not prove anything, because how many novelists took a genuine historical event and hung their story on to it?

He began to read through his translation, double-checking some of the words against the dictionary. He had made several guesses and a few assumptions, and he had skipped some sections which appeared to be descriptions of irrelevant places or people, but in the main he thought he had grasped the gist of the narration.

After the initial opening sentence, the writing was vivid and a remarkable picture started to unfold.

FIVE

I must explain, from the very beginning, that I was never a small-time thief. I've always thought – and worked – in a large way.

I have never understood why people steal inferior items. It is just as difficult – and equally risky – to steal the cheap or the tasteless as it is to steal the valuable and the elegant.

So without wishing to appear conceited, I will tell you, my unknown reader, that I only ever stole the very best. Almost always I was successful in my work, and at times I was even quite rich. There were other times, of course. Times when I had to flee a house or a city – once an entire country – for fear of creditors. As well as creditors there are other unpleasant people – the English have the word *bailiffs* for them, and they are a disagreeable species who actually move into one's home and summarily remove possessions to pay one's debts. I always avoided the ignominy of actually coming face to face with them, but there were occasions when I only avoided it by resorting to such ploys as climbing out of a window, or pretending to be an uncomprehending servant of the household. Once I feigned sickness, although on that occasion I narrowly escaped being taken to an infirmary where God knows what could have happened.

So I have been poor and I have been rich, and I prefer infinitely to be rich, for I have a great fondness for the good things of life. Well-cut clothes, silk shirts, good food and wine and a comfortable – if possible, luxurious – house or apartment in which to live. I like dining in the homes of the wealthy and influential, and I also enjoy the company of ladies whose lives allow them – by which I mean give them enough leisure – to be beautiful. Here I should make it clear that although I have bought many lovely things and stolen many more, I have never bought or stolen ladies. The many enjoyable associations I have formed have been entirely of the ladies' free choice. I will admit to having a weakness for raven-haired, porcelain-skinned ladies, preferably of impeccable lineage. But I am a gentleman and I do not give names.

This weakness, however, made my association with Leonora Gilmore all the more surprising and also unexpected, since Leonora possessed none of those attractions. A strange little creature, with a face like a pixie from some painting depicting a fantastical scene. I once arranged for what I like to call the transfer of a Hans Makart painting – I think it was called *Titania's Wedding Feast* or something similar – in which one of the attendant sprites resembled Leonora so greatly, she might have sat as a model for the painting. She did not, of course; apart from the fact that Makart was painting long before Leonora was born, her own upbringing would have stopped her. I never met her parents, but I formed an opinion of repression and coldness.

I would have liked you, thought Michael, coming briefly up out of the narrative. Even though you were clearly a roaring snob and it doesn't sound as if you had a moral to your name, whoever you were, I still think I'd have liked you. What your journal is doing in an English house in the twenty-first century though, I can't imagine. But you knew Leonora – God knows how or where, but you did, and on that score alone I need to find out more about you.

He read on:

I have made something of what people would call a speciality in my work. The occasional painting, certainly, but more particularly the small and the exquisite. Silver snuffboxes, enamelled patch-boxes, jade figurines. Jewellery, of course. Icons, naturally.

One of my more cherished memories is of a visit to an exhibition of religious icons in Moscow. I had gone there in a professional capacity – which is to say I intended to liberate at least four of the choicest icons – and I had several

discerning clients (I prefer to call them clients) eagerly
awaiting them. None of the clients knew, not with any
certainty, that I stole the objects they so greedily purchased,
but most of them must have guessed. However, they all
knew that if they were to inform the—

Michael had not been able to find an exact translation for the
next word, but he thought it was a reasonably safe bet that it
was intended to convey police, or the equivalent.

—it would have meant the end of their supply of jewellery
and beautiful objects. More to the point, it would also have
meant the end of my career and a sojourn in prison.

I found it very useful that in old Russia – by which
I mean the Russia of the Mongols, the land of the Firebird
– it had never been customary to sign icons. That often
meant there was no provenance. My grandfather always
held that if a piece did not have a provenance, then all that
was needed was to create one for it, and the more exotic,
the better. My father specialized in stealing jewellery, but
my grandfather was a very good forger and he taught me
something of the craft. He was also extremely skilled at
replacing genuine artefacts with his own creations. If you've
ever been in the Hermitage Museum in St Petersburg,
(although now we have to say Petrograd), and stood in
front of a certain portrait with, let us say, Tzarist connota-
tions . . . Let's just say he fooled a great many people, my
grandfather.

But that evening at the icons exhibition, as I walked
through the warm, perfumed rooms, I overheard someone
say to a companion, 'A beautiful exhibition. Some very rare
pieces.'

The companion replied, half serious, half jocular, 'Let's
hope Iskander hasn't heard about this evening's display.'

The other man said, curiously, 'Is that his real name?'

'God knows. I've heard he has several aliases. They say
he switches names to suit whatever villainy he's currently
engaged in. But whether he's called Alexei Iskander or
something else entirely, if he knew about tonight he'd have

cleared most of the rooms inside ten minutes, and our exhibition would be over.'

I didn't clear the rooms, but I did appropriate six icons, all of them beautiful, all of them highly valuable, although the speaker was wrong about the time it took me. It was a little under eight minutes.

And so I come to the real start of my story, which begins in the disastrous year of 1914.

1914. It's almost like a milestone, that date. A dark, bloodied landmark jutting out of history's highways like a shark's tooth, warning the human race never to venture into that kind of darkness again. (I make no apologies for the extravagance or the emotion of that sentence; a man may surely succumb to emotion when describing the rising of the curtain on the most brutal, most wasteful war of all time.)

Censorship was still muzzling books and newspapers in Russia at that time, and thousands of people had no idea that Europe was a simmering cauldron, fast approaching boiling point. People in cities probably knew something of the situation, and because I was living in Moscow I suppose I knew as much as most of them – which is to say not very much at all. But I did know that the balance of power which several countries had striven to maintain was starting to crumble. That was hardly surprising considering the complexity of political and military alliances. If you pull out one strand of an intricate tapestry, the entire thing will unravel, and by the summer of 1914 several strands had been pulled with some force. I've never unravelled a tapestry (although I've acquired and sold a few most profitably), and I certainly never fully unravelled the tangled strands of Holy Alliances or Bismarck's League or any of the Austro-Hungarian pacts.

I am still not entirely sure why I felt such a compulsion to become involved in those snarled strands. I wonder now if my profession had begun to bore me – even if it was becoming too easy. Perhaps I wanted a new challenge, or perhaps I simply wanted to be able, afterwards, to say that I had been part of it all, that I had been there amidst the tumult and the chaos, not exactly helping to make history, which would have been a massive conceit (even for me), but to witness history being made. Recording history for future generations. The more I thought about that, the better I liked it.

So I set about persuading several newspaper editors to take me on to their staff as a freelance war correspondent, because war there surely would be, even the optimists agreed about that. I explained to them that I would be a highly suitable person to send to the troubled areas of Europe to write about the unrest. Not only was I able to write interesting and informative prose, I said, but I had travelled quite extensively. I had reasonable proficiency in French, I could make myself understood in German and I even had a smattering of English as well. 'Smattering' was something of an exaggeration there, but they accepted my claim, (fortunately without putting it to the test). What really clinched the matter, though, was that without actually saying so, I managed to convey that I had the entrée to a number of privileged houses. I do think I did that rather well, and if they ended up believing I dined at the Kaiser's table regularly and was on intimate terms with several members of the Imperial Royal House of Habsburg, it was entirely due to their own naivety.

So a number of agreements were made. The financial remuneration varied from paper to paper, but on one topic the editors spoke with the same voice. That was the matter of the censorship laws. Did I understand I must not write anything that might be construed as seditious or subversive?

I did.

And would I give my word as a gentleman (ha!) that I would not write or imply anything that might be regarded as propaganda or likely to incite anarchy?

I said politely that my word could be considered to be given, and could be regarded as my bond.

In fact I have met many anarchistic and even revolutionary-minded people who make delightful and stimulating companions, although sometimes inclined a little to bigotry and fanaticism, and curiously averse to regular washing, as if they consider their ideals too high-minded to be bothered about soap and water. For myself, I had then, and have now, no particular animosity towards the Romanovs.

I did have considerable animosity towards the miserliness of some of the newspapers employing me, though. The travelling costs turned out to be paltry, barely enough for even the most basic of train journeys. Indeed, at one point I began to wonder if this entire scheme might as well be forgotten, but the compulsion to see what was happening in the world, to know about it at first-hand – to *record* it for others to read – still had me by the throat as viciously as a wolf in a winter forest.

I should make it clear that my contempt for the meagre travelling expenses was not born from mere hedonism; I am perfectly prepared to sacrifice comfort if the cause is sufficient. What I am not prepared to do is travel in third-class railway carriages, where the only seating is wooden benches, where the washing facilities are non-existent, and where the only food is the greasy bread and fat bacon brought by other wayfarers for their private sustenance. It would have been undignified to ask for more money though, so before leaving I made a few judicious sorties into a number of rich homes. The careful selling of the items I removed provided funds for more acceptable travelling conditions, and I left Moscow in a first-class compartment, ate my meals in a well-appointed dining-car, and slept in the best hotels until I reached my destination.

My destination. That exercised me a good deal. Simply, I could not decide where I should go. The kaleidoscope of power-balance and of friendship and enmity between countries had been shifting with bewildering rapidity throughout that summer – so much so that I changed my mind half a dozen times.

But it was becoming clear that Germany wanted France. And to get France, the German armies had to take the neutral countries that lay between. Above all, they had to take Belgium – small, peaceable Belgium with its gentle defences but its key position. That meant my articles

could only be written from one place. The place I
strongly suspected was about to become the epicentre of
the fight.

And so it was to Belgium that I went.

Michael had translated with reasonable ease to this point, but
from a cursory glance at the next couple of pages it looked as
if 'Alexei Iskander' had merely been making background notes
about the opening moves of the war. The page was spattered with
the names of Prussia and Austria, together with mention of the
German Chancellor Bismarck and also the German Army Chief
of Staff, along with a few references to the Habsburg Archdukes
and Duchesses. It seemed safe to assume that most of these
references were detrimental.

He was just thinking he would try to translate at least another
couple of paragraphs in the hope of getting to Iskander's arrival
in Belgium and his meeting with Leonora, when he was pulled
out of Iskander's insouciant world by the realization that footsteps
were coming up the steps from the underground room.

He went cautiously to the door and peered out. Luisa was
emerging from the underground room, her eyes still with the
same unfocused look, and her movements still disconcertingly
puppet-like. She closed the door in the panelling, locked it, and
returned the key to the drawer in the small bureau. Michael
watched her ascend the stairs and waited until he heard her walk
across the landing and open and close her bedroom door. It was
just on two a.m. He closed Iskander's journal, switched off the
laptop, and went determinedly up to his own room, undressed
and got into bed.

Surprisingly, he slept extremely well. He had expected the images
conjured up by Iskander, as well as the trip to the underground
room, to keep him awake, but the old bed was comfortable, and
he did not wake until the soft bleeping of his travel alarm at half-
past seven. It was a good feeling to realize the night had passed
and he would not need to spend another one inside Fosse House.

Seen by day, the house was no longer the brooding mansion
of fiction, and the storm had blown itself out. Thin sunshine
slanted in through the old windows and painted a pale gold haze

across wood and glass and silk. The silk was frayed, the wood dull and the glass grubby, but seen like this the house had a dim charm of its own, and Michael could sympathize with Stephen Gilmore's longing to come home and to see the lamps glowing in the windows as he walked along the drive.

Last night, when Luisa had murmured about breakfast, Michael had at once said he would forage for himself, then make an early start in the library. Accordingly, he went along to the kitchen, where he made toast and ate a bowl of cereal. After this, he took himself and a second cup of coffee along to the library.

When he opened the curtains a faint mist lay over the gardens. The library windows looked across to an old walled garden, with a wrought-iron gate. Michael wondered if he could go out there to take a look later on. There was something intriguing about walled gardens – they were the kind of green and darkling places where secrets might linger, and where the enquirer was warned not to trespass, not to speak or even whisper, in case, in the words of the de la Mare poem, 'perchance upon its darkening air, the unseen ghosts of children fare'. Seen at this hour, Fosse House's walled garden looked as if ghosts of any age might congregate there.

Somewhere in the house a clock chimed eight o'clock, and, as if answering, from beyond the house came a deeper chime of some distant church tower. A bird flew out of a tree and twitteringly dive-bombed the lawn for its own breakfast, and the spell of the old garden splintered. The chimes died away, and Michael forgot about ghosts and sat down at the big leather-topped table, to step into the past.

SIX

Nell was having a good morning.

Before opening the shop at ten, she had arranged for a longer loan of the books borrowed for Owen Bracegirdle which Owen, the previous evening, had thought might be very helpful, and would almost certainly buy. The bookseller in Quire Court, learning who the potential customer was, expressed himself as perfectly happy to grant an extension. He observed that since Dr Bracegirdle, whom he knew slightly, was accustomed to the jealously-guarded treasures of the Bodleian and on page-flipping terms with assorted incunabula, it was unlikely in the extreme that he would tear the dust jackets or spill gin on the pages. Appealed to for help, he thought he did have one or two volumes about WWI POW camps and vanished artefacts from that war, and proceeded to scurry along his shelves like an energetic grasshopper.

'Did you say Holzminden? Where exactly is it?'

'Lower Saxony.' Nell, feeling it incumbent on her to help with the search, followed him along the shelves, navigating around the piles of books on the floor which the bookseller had not got around to cataloguing. 'I looked it up. It's one of those places dating back to the eighth or ninth century. Princes of the Wolfenbuttel line dodging in and out of its ownership, and various monastic settlements, and a royal charter in eleven-or-twelve hundred.'

'I haven't heard of the place,' said the bookseller, 'but I'm sure I've got— Ha! Here it is.' He extracted a large tome from the end of a shelf, blew dust off its leaves, and presented it beamingly. 'There are several chapters in this about internment camps in that war. He's something of an authority, the author. There might be a reference to Holzminden. Oh, and this one as well.' He darted at another section of shelf and seized an even heavier book. 'You're more than welcome to borrow both of them for the afternoon.'

'Thank you, Godfrey. I won't tear the dust jackets or spill gin on them, either,' said Nell.

She carried the books back to her own shop. Beth was in Scotland for the entire week and Quire Court was never particularly busy on Wednesday afternoons, so after she had finished applying Danish oil to a beautiful but neglected Regency escritoire destined for a customer in Hertfordshire, she had a snack lunch then curled up in the little office behind the shop.

The more promising of the books was called *Fragments of Great War Treasures* and had several index references to Holzminden and to the sketches themselves. It was slightly annoying, however, to discover that the author wrote about the sketches with an air of faint contempt, as if feeling a pitying amusement for anyone sufficiently credulous to actually think they might exist. He or she wrote:

> They are almost certainly apocryphal. Indeed, it would not be making too strong a statement to place them with such ephemeral objects as the Holy Grail, the Lost City of Atlantis and/or Avalon, and the missing jade zodiac heads of China.
>
> In my opinion, the fabulous Holzminden sketches fall squarely into these categories – and I use the word 'fabulous' in the sense of fabled or mythical. They even have a sinister legend attached to them, one that might have come out of an M.R. James ghost story or even, (God help us), a Sixties horror film. No real credence can be given to the legend, of course, but I am including it as a curio.

Nell, who liked and admired M.R. James's stories and found some horror films quite entertaining, turned to the title page to see who the author of these rather sneering put-downs might be, and was unreasonably annoyed to discover that it was a certain B.D. Bodkin, whose works she had sometimes consulted, and with whom she had in fact exchanged correspondence last year while trying to provenance some Victorian watercolours. But she wanted to know more about these sketches, so she read on. He wrote, didactically:

> Reports vary as to how many sketches there are. But most sources agree that there were probably two. The belief is

that the sketches were done while the artist was under
sentence of death, and that he had been driven mad by his
approaching execution. One source, (uncorroborated),
suggests that the taint of madness clings to the sketches.
That macabre legend has clung to the sketches down the
years and has no doubt added to their notoriety.

Well, B.D. Bodkin, thought Nell, I'd very much like to hear what
you'd have to say if you knew there's a framed sketch hanging
in a dark old house in the depths of East Anglia, with the legend
'Holzminden 1917' inscribed on it. I suppose you'd say it was
a fake. I suppose it might be a fake. Or perhaps a copy of an
original – yes, I'd better keep that possibility in mind.

But one of the sentences from the book had stuck in her mind.
The taint of madness clings to the sketches.

Nell certainly did not believe that statement, any more than
B.D. Bodkin did, but she was aware of a prickle of unease at
the knowledge that if one of those sketches really was inside
Fosse House, Michael was shut in with it – until tomorrow at
the very least. It did not matter, of course. And yet . . .

And yet with no knowledge of the legend, he had already talked
about hearing whisperings in the house. A whispering voice, he
had said; a voice that had murmured about needing to keep a hold
on sanity . . . I do wish he hadn't said that, thought Nell.

She was no longer as vehemently sceptical about the supernatural
as she used to be – she had had one or two strange and inexplicable
experiences over the last couple of years, and her scepticism had
taken a few dents. She had come to the rather unwilling acknowledgement that it might be possible for strong emotions or
events – particularly tragic or violent events – to leave a lingering
impression within a house. Under certain circumstances, it was
just about credible that people with a particular sensitivity might
pick up on those fragments. Michael had certainly done so at least
twice. But she refused to believe there was anything malevolent
inside Fosse House, and by way of emphasizing this, she carried
on reading what else B.D. Bodkin had to say.

He did not say anything more about the sketches, but he had
devoted a whole section to extracts from letters written by a
German officer who had been an attendant at Holzminden camp.

They had been taken from a privately-printed volume of memoirs originally published in the mid-1950s, and were signed simply 'Hugbert' and addressed to 'My dearest Freide'. The translation from German to English seemed quite good, although some of the phrasing was a little stilted.

The letters seemed to have earned their place in the book because Hugbert had had some brief contact with Siegfried Sassoon. There were several missives referring to Sassoon, whom Hugbert had seen while guarding the Hindenberg Line in Verdun, remarking that even from a distance he looked peculiar, but then everyone knew the English were a peculiar race. Nell made a note of the pages in case this might be of use in the Director's book, then turned to the later letters, which probably had been included to give a little more background to Hugbert and to Holzminden.

The first one was dated September 1917.

> My dearest Freide,
>
> All goes well here, but Holzminden camp is bleak – an old cavalry barracks they have adapted for British officers, and a grim place. But anything is better than those weeks in France.
>
> Today we were told that our Camp Kommandant, Colonel Habrecht, is to be replaced. We shall miss the Colonel, who is elderly but has a kindness for his men (you remember how concerned he was when I suffered from bunions last month?), and he views the prisoners with much humanity. So I was very sorry when there came an announcement that his second-in-command is appointed in his place. This is Hauptmann Karl Niemeyer, and the appointment is of much regret to several of us, for he is a very harsh man and already imposing a strict regime. I take a great risk in writing that, but I know, my dearest Freide, that you will not allow anyone to read it, and I do not think letters to our loved ones are being opened, and anyway I am a trusted staff member and it is known that you are I are affianced. Last evening I showed your photograph to Hauptfeldwebel Barth while we were having supper together, and he thinks you are very fine and I am very lucky. I, too, think so.
>
> Today we had two new prisoners – a young Englishman

and a Russian. The Englishman is quiet and withdrawn, but agreeable to the bed and locker he was allotted, but the Russian glared at everything and appeared to consider it all beneath him. I said to the Hauptfeldwebel that perhaps he was an aristocrat – he has that air of thinking himself better than his fellow men – but the Hauptfeldwebel said no, he had been a newspaper reporter – a war correspondent, scavenging the countries of Europe to write about what was happening, and I was gullible and too easily-impressed.

'He is a man of the people, just as we are ourselves,' said the Hauptfeldwebel, which is the kind of comment he often makes, his father having been a butcher in Braunschweig and Hauptfeldwebel Barth being sensitive about it. Not that there is anything wrong in being a butcher, and I believe his Bockwurst was the finest a man could eat.

'But he will be planning to write about us and about the camp,' said the Hauptfeldwebel, 'so we should make sure to treat him with care. We do not want people thinking we give out cruel treatment, for that would reflect badly on the German Empire. Also, it would mean I should not be considered for promotion, and nor would you.'

'And there is the Hague Convention regarding the treatment of prisoners of war,' I said.

'This is perfectly true.'

The Russian's name is Alexei Iskander, and I think the Hauptfeldwebel was right about him recording all that happens here, for within an hour of arriving at the camp Iskander was demanding writing materials.

I found a notepad and pencils, and he sat on his bunk, writing away as if his life depended on it. The Hauptfeldwebel tells me he will not be permitted to send his scribblings out, but does not rule out the possibility of Iskander finding a way to smuggle them out. At worst, he will squirrel them away and arrange for publication after Germany wins the war, so we must not baulk at reading what he writes, and if necessary destroy it.

This is important, so after supper, while the prisoners were all in the bathhouse, I searched Iskander's locker, which I disliked doing very much, for I am not a Prying Paul.

[*Editor's note: It seems likely that the translator mistook the exact wording here and that Hugbert meant Peeping Tom.*]

But everything Iskander had written was in Russian so I have no idea what it says, although I do not think it will be very complimentary. As you know, I am liking to improve my knowledge of all languages, for it is never known when that might be useful to a man. My English is a little improved since talking to some of the prisoners, but I could not make any sense of Iskander's Russian journal.

He is going to be difficult, that is already clear. He has already denounced the evening meal as disgusting pigswill and demanded better provisions. The Hauptfeldwebel said, in his sarcastic way, that perhaps Russian caviar and vodka would be acceptable in place of the sausage and cabbage dish, to which Iskander, cool as a cat, said certainly it would, but he would specify the caviar was *ikra*, which was superior to most kinds, and that with it came *kummel*, since he did not care overmuch for vodka.

I wish only to be with you again, and I am,

Ever your devoted Hugbert.

P.S. My bunions are much improved. You will be glad to know this.

The second letter had been written a couple of weeks later, and it appeared that Hugbert had got to know the English prisoner who had arrived with Iskander a little better.

He is a strange young man. There are times when he sits in complete silence, not moving, staring ahead of him, as if he can see things other people can not. This morning, he suddenly reached for my hand and said, 'I am not mad, not any more. You must not let them think I am mad now.'

Iskander, who happened to be in the room at the time, told me afterwards that he believed the Englishman had been ill after the battle of the Somme.

'Mentally ill,' he said. 'They told me he would sit in a corner of the room and stare in the same way.'

'At what?'

Iskander gave one of the shrugs I always find a little

theatrical. 'Who can say?' he said. 'He will have seen many horrors inflicted on my countrymen and his.' A pause. 'Inflicted by your countrymen.' He is never one to miss an opportunity for insolence, although somehow he manages to stop short of crossing the line and risking punishment. Before I could think how to answer him, he said, 'I have heard it called the Hundred Mile Stare— Ah, I see you know of it.'

'I know it as the Ten Mile Stare.'

'It means the same, no matter the distance. They stare towards a distant horizon so they will not have to look at the nightmares that lie in their immediate path. Ten miles, a hundred, a thousand, even. The greater the nightmares, the further away they try to look.'

I said (I could not help it), 'But you have seen nightmares yourself?'

'Oh yes,' he said, and for a moment his eyes took on an odd expression and I thought he was going to tell me more of what he had experienced before coming here. But he only said, 'Yes, I also have the nightmares and the demons – I think you have them, also,' he said, with a sudden disconcerting look.

I did not reply – there are some things that are not for sharing, Freide, and certainly not with those with whom one's country is at war.

Iskander appeared to understand this – for all his arrogance and rebellious ways, he has a certain sensitivity. He said, 'Mine are not nightmares filled with screams of agony as men choke in mud and blood in the trenches of France. Or of men who live for days with legs blown off or eyes shattered, and finally die amid the stench of their putrefying wounds in their nostrils. Those, I believe, are this young Englishman's nightmares.'

I said, 'What are your nightmares?'

'I do not have any,' he said, but something flickered behind his eyes. Then he made an impatient gesture, as if to push away these memories, and began to harangue me about the quality of the bedding on the men's bunks. When I said the sheets were standard army issue, and the prisoners fortunate to even have sheets, he said, 'God help the Prussian army.'

I was deeply affected by his description of the English boy's nightmares, though. Perhaps I shall try to talk to him a little. It is not in my requirements to do so, but I feel great pity. War is a terrible business, Freide. I have sometimes questioned—

[*Editor's note: It appears that the rest of this sentence was heavily scored out, as if Hugbert feared to set down his thoughts about the war on paper.*]

I acknowledge, though, that Iskander is right about the sheets, for I find they cause a troublesome irritation in areas which are difficult to reach with soothing ointment. You will forgive my referring to such parts of the anatomy, but we are affianced and should not have secrets.

Ever your devoted,

Hugbert.

Nell thought Hugbert sounded rather endearing. Perhaps it might be possible to track down a copy of his privately-printed letters. Would B.D. Bodkin be likely to help there?

Before she could talk herself out of this, Nell looked out last year's correspondence with B.D., and was pleased to find an email address at the head of his letter about the Victorian aqua tints. She flipped on the laptop and typed a careful email to him, politely reminding him of their correspondence last year, and explaining that she was currently engaged in some research on the Great War and had found *Fragments of Great War Treasures* interesting and informative. The letters from the Holzminden officer, Hugbert, had been particularly intriguing, and she wondered if there was any possibility of obtaining a copy of the privately printed collection. Any information about the whereabouts of a copy, or even contact names or addresses that Mr Bodkin could provide, would be very greatly appreciated.

She read it over, thought it struck the right balance between friendliness and professionalism, and sent the email before she could think better of it, after which she closed the laptop and returned to the book. It would be nice if there was more from Hugbert, but it looked as if this particular section was ending.

There was more from him, but it was only a short note:

My very dearest Freide,

It is possible I shall not be able to write regularly after sending this, for I am ordered to special duties, and I will be leaving Holzminden tomorrow in company with Hauptfeldwebel Barth. I am not permitted to tell any details yet, but it is a result of dreadful tragic events that took place here three days ago. I must not say more, but I will tell you that I always knew Iskander would cause trouble, and the poor young Englishman—

[*Editor's note: The rest of this sentence was not readable, although we are unclear as to whether this is because Hugbert thought better of what he had written and crossed it out, or whether his letters were, after all, opened before reaching his fiancée, and this part was censored. Either way, he seems to be indicating that the two prisoners – the Russian, Alexei Iskander, and the unnamed Englishman – were at the root of what he calls tragic events in Holzminden.*]

There has come a direct order from Hauptmann Niemeyer which I cannot disobey. The Hauptmann spoke to me most solemnly and earnestly, telling me what was wanted, then saluting my bravery.

I think I am singled out for this task in order that the Hauptmann can receive regular reports of our mission. It is known that I am a frequent correspondent with you, my *liebling*, and also with my parents, so I am thought able to write letters clearly and sensibly. I am to be accompanied by Hauptfeldwebel Barth, who is not very skilled with composition, although excellent when it comes to the frying of bratwurst, and we cannot all be accomplished at everything.

I should be glad if you will visit my parents as often as you can over the next few weeks. Your loving presence will help them not to worry. But of danger there is not very much, so you should not have concerns.

As always, your very devoted,
Hugbert

SEVEN

I t was six o'clock. Nell locked the shop door, put the security shutters in place, and went across to the annexe behind the shop where she and Beth lived.

She put Bodkin aside and scanned the index of the first of the books lent by the bookseller. Would Holzminden be here? Yes, there was what looked like an entire chapter describing the camp, which had been opened in 1917 for British Officers. It had been a fairly small set-up, but had achieved a modest notoriety by being the scene of a successful escape – ten men out of twenty-nine escapees made it back to Britain – and also because several moderately well-known figures had been held there.

'The escape was effected by means of the men digging beneath the camp to beyond the walls of the compound,' wrote one of the contributors, and in somewhat school-masterish fashion went on to describe the means and methods employed by the men. Nell skimmed this; the details of the actual digging and the tunnel's length, and the home-made bellows system for the air system would probably be of interest to serious students of such things, and they were certainly reminiscent of WWII legends and the films. John Mills being frightfully stiff-upper lip in Colditz, and Steve McQueen bouncing across the terrain on a motorbike amidst a hail of bullets. But they did not get her any nearer to the legendary Holzminden sketches or to the Gilmore family or even to Hugbert.

There was, however, some good primary source material. The *Daily Sketch*, it seemed, had called Holzminden 'the worst camp in Germany', castigating the commandant, Hauptmann Karl Niemeyer, as arrogant, vindictive, given to pilfering prisoners' food parcels, and unpleasantly devoted to the curative powers of solitary confinement. Niemeyer, thought Nell, pleased to find this link. Hugbert's commandant, whom he disliked, and who sent him on some kind of task.

As well as this, there was a lively account from an unnamed

Russian war correspondent who appeared to have found himself incarcerated in Holzminden shortly after it was opened. He had apparently written a series of articles about the camp, several of which had been translated for the book. In one of the articles, the journalist described the Kommandant, Hauptmann Karl Niemeyer, as a devil, fierce as ten furies, clothed in a Prussian officer's uniform, swinging the scaly horror of his folded tail as he regarded his hapless victims.

'As for the camp itself, it was a stone-built, iron-hued devil's citadel, akin to the evil ditches of Malebolge,' he had added.

Nell, intrigued by the macabre but powerful imagery of the words, plundered the quotation books on her shelves, finally tracking the sources as Dante's *Inferno* and Milton's *Paradise Lost* respectively. Could the journalist possibly be Hugbert's arrogant Iskander who had known about the demons and the Ten Mile Stare, and had then in the same breath complained about inferior sheets and poor cooking? It was probably stretching coincidence a bit.

'There must never be another war like the one that has just been fought and – mercifully – won,' the journalist had written. 'But if there should be, then the cruelties of the kind inflicted on prisoners in Holzminden must never be repeated.'

The next words seemed to jump off the page and smack into her eyes.

'The sketches made while I was in Holzminden show some of the conditions of the camp very clearly—'

The sketches made in Holzminden . . . Nell stared at the words. Did that mean this unnamed journalist had been the legendary artist of the sketches? Or did it mean he had been there when the artist created them? The article continued:

—but they cannot convey the misery and the despair. Nor can they convey the madness that entered the souls of some of the men – many of them barely twenty years old, many of whom had witnessed the worst horrors of warfare already. There is something which has come to be called the Ten Mile Stare or even the Hundred Mile Stare, and it is a terrible thing to see. It's not a wild or even a pain-filled look, more a heart-rending determination to look beyond the horrors – to focus on a faraway skyline or a landscape where the horrors have melted and there is only safe familiarity.

I met one young man at Holzminden for whom that safe familiarity was his home in England.

'When the nightmares come,' he said, 'I try to see the tree-lined carriageway of my family's home with the lamps burning in the windows at dusk. They would always light the lamps for me – for all of us. We would see them like beacons when we walked towards the house. It's one of the things I try to remember.'

How immensely sad, thought Nell, closing the book.

She would have liked to be able to tell Michael what she had just read – to see his eyes take on the familiar absorption, and see him tilt his head in the characteristic attitude of intense listening, and to know he was instantly understanding the emotions the article churned up. It was good to remember he would be back the day after tomorrow. Nell would suggest he came to supper in Quire Court; she would cook a really nice meal and while they ate he would tell her about Fosse House, and she would tell him what she had found as contribution to his research. This was a very good thought.

She had not expected to hear back from B.D. Bodkin very quickly – she had not even known if she would hear from him at all – but when she checked her emails, he had sent a reply.

Dear Nell West,

I do indeed remember our association last year, and I'm glad I was able to help with the Victorian watercolours. The rather charming 'Water Meadows' sequence, as I recall.

This was unexpectedly friendly, and Nell, encouraged, read on.

I greatly enjoyed compiling and writing *Fragments of Great War Treasures*, which took me down some unexpected byways and highways. I didn't read all of the privately printed letters you refer to, but I did have some brief contact with the family of the letter-writer – a nephew and niece, I think – to obtain permission to use the extracts.

I can therefore let you have the title and ISBN number of
the collection. I recall I borrowed the book from the Bodleian,
and there's no reason to suppose they don't still have a copy.
Kind regards and good luck with your research,
Bernard D. Bodkin

The ISBN number for the letters followed, together with the
exact title of the letters, which was: *The Letters of Hugbert
Edreich, 1916–1918*. Printing had been in 1955, by 'Freide
Edreich', in 'loving remembrance of a dear husband'. There was
also a translator's name, which Nell, who had a smattering of
school German, but had not had to call on it for many years,
was relieved to see. Altogether, this was very satisfactory, and it
was surprisingly amiable of Bernard D. to be so helpful. Nell
was prepared to forgive him for his preachy dogmatism over the
Holzminden sketches.

Owen might be inclined to spare an hour to accompany her
to the Bodleian to help track down Hugbert Edreich's letters. It
was the kind of research that would interest him, and he would
be familiar with the loan system, which would make the task
easier. But when Nell dialled his number it went to voicemail,
so she left a message, explaining what was wanted.

As she put down the phone, she wondered how Michael's
research was going.

Michael had spent the first part of his day in feeling slightly guilty
at spending so much time on the journal notes left by Alexei
Iskander, because Iskander, entertaining though he might be, was
not what Michael was here to research. Yes, but Iskander knew
Leonora, said his mind. And Leonora is the link to the Palestrina
Choir, and Liège is a link to the Great War. So it's not straying
too far off the path. Perhaps I'll allow myself an hour to translate
just a little more, then if it starts to seem like a cul-de-sac I'll
abandon it.

But he knew he would not abandon it, and after he had translated
two more pages, he knew it was not a cul-de-sac.

'It was the beginning of August when I reached Germany's
eastern border,' wrote Iskander in his careless, erratic French,
which Michael was finding increasingly easy to translate.

I had had an interesting journey – and a very useful one. There are a number of excellent hunting-grounds in the countries that lie between Russia and Belgium, and although the Kaiser's Prussian soldiers were advancing steadily towards Belgium, I thought there was time for me to make a small detour into Vienna.

It was not exactly a small detour, if I am honest, but the railway service was proving to be admirable and everyone should see Vienna at least once. I saw it for the first time that summer, and I do feel it could easily become a spiritual home for me. It's a city of culture and gracious living. The very cobblestones are soaked in music, and it's as if the city thrums with the cadences of Mozart and Strauss and Schubert, and with all the romances and tragedies and triumphs of those gifted composers. Wonderful. The Viennese, as a race, are warm and welcoming; their hospitality is delightful, their women are beautiful, and to the traveller they offer the best they have in the way of food and wine. More to the point, Vienna has many great houses and palaces which are ideal for an enterprising thief. I found a number of small and valuable objects which, given a little sleight of hand, could be abstracted and sold most profitably. There are as many receivers in Vienna as there are in any city of the world, and after one or two abortive attempts, I found several.

Michael had had to guess at Iskander's meaning in this last sentence, because the French–English dictionary did not give a translation for several of the words. But he was fairly sure Iskander was referring to fences.

I visited the concert halls of Vienna, too: *Wiener Hofoper* – the Court Opera – and the Golden Hall in the *Musikverein*, but there were simply too many people about for me to ply my trade there with any safety. So I allowed myself a holiday on those evenings, and bathed in the music, and relaxed in the company of a lady who was occupying a gilded box at a performance of *The Marriage of Figaro*, and who was amicably disposed towards the sharing of a

quiet supper after the performance. This supper, taken in
her apartment, was a very pleasurable experience. The
rooms were rococo, the lady was voluptuous, the wine
was luxurious, and when I say I relaxed in her company,
I do not mean I was relaxed for the entire time. The
English Bard has said that wine provoketh the desire but
taketh away the performance, but that was never the case
with me and certainly not on that evening, and perhaps
Shakespeare was never privileged to enjoy Chateau
Margaux anyway.

I should like it understood that I did not, on that occasion, ply my disreputable trade, although there were many
beautiful and valuable objects in the rooms. But there are
rules about these things, and I hope at heart I am still a
gentleman. I left the rooms unplundered, the lady satisfied,
and walked virtuously home through a rose and gold dawn,
with the sun rising like a glowing jewel over the
Schönbrunn Palace. (From which any readers of this
journal who know Vienna will realize that the lady's
apartment was in the wealthy quarter of the city. Of course
it was.)

It was the beginning of August – a hot and windless
August – and Vienna was buzzing with the news that
Germany had officially declared war on Russia and on
France. This, though expected, was still chilling. But even
in those early days it was becoming apparent that Germany
had overreached and underestimated, and that in particular
it had underestimated Belgium. The Kaiser, with his
customary bombast and arrogance, now tried to negotiate a
free escort through Belgium in order to invade France.
Belgium refused, as any self-respecting country would; in
fact King Albert indignantly pointed out that Belgium was
a country and not a road, at which the Kaiser flew into a
rage and promptly ordered out his armies and told them
to invade, and take, Belgium.

It was exactly as I had foretold – although I have to
acknowledge a great many other people had foretold the
same thing. But if ever a spur was needed to hasten a
traveller's footsteps, this was it. I bade farewell to the

City of Music and Dreams, and resumed my journey to Belgium.

Not wanting to attract any notice, and aware of being in a country with whom my own was now at war, I abandoned the railways and resorted to more discreet methods of travel. It was less comfortable, but it was better to be uncomfortable and alive than to travel in luxury and end up spitted on the end of a German bayonet. Sometimes I walked, but usually I was able to get rides in horses and carts. It was not unpleasant to jog along the country lanes, perhaps with a farmer bound for market, or a tinker plying his wares.

I travelled for an entire two days with a small band of gypsies, sharing their supper when they made camp and joining in their music. They are interesting people, the Romanies, with vivid history and colourful traditions and wild passion-filled music. Also, their idea of food and drink is generous and their ladies very friendly. We parted company with regret and declarations of undying friendship, although, to be fair, that last may have been due to the quantities of wine consumed.

I reached the outlying districts of Germany in the late afternoon, and if I narrowed my eyes and concentrated I could make out the ancient city of Liége in the distance. Even from a distance I could see the silver strands of the Meuse River and the faint outlines of several of the twelve forts encircling the old city.

As I approached Liége I was aware of an unrest – it was a curious sensation, almost as if something, some invisible force, knew that a massive conflict lay in waiting. Rather as someone may suffer a headache just before a thunderstorm. I had no explanation for the feeling then and I do not have one now, but walking through the wooded areas between Germany and Belgium, listening for the marching feet of the invading armies, I felt as if something had been wrenched away from its roots, as if some natural force had become distorted and something dark and heavy was trickling into the world.

Nearing Liége, seeing those grim towers built over twenty-five years earlier to repel invaders, I felt as if a vast, tightly-stretched drumskin was being tapped somewhere close by. I could not quite hear it, but I could feel it, as if I were lying on a railway line, hearing a train approach. On and on it went, in a rhythmic tattoo. I knew what it was. The marching of armies. The Kaiser's forces advancing on Liége.

Iskander's words were so vivid that when Michael leaned back from the table for a moment, he had the impression that the echoes of those armies were reverberating across the years, rippling against his own mind.

He was reaching for his pen again when he realized that the sounds were not from the past at all; they were here in the present. They were real sounds, and they were not drumbeats – they were footsteps. The slow, soft footsteps Michael had heard last night and that had frightened Luisa during supper. Tap-tap . . . Like a faint, blurred rhythm.

It's Stephen, thought Michael with a lurch of apprehension. He was here last night – he got into the house – I saw him. And now he's coming back. He's walking down that path, he's coming through those bushes now, and he'll try to get in again. Will Luisa let him in again?

'Let me in . . . Please let me in . . .'

The words lay like clotted cobwebs on the air, the sounds half shrivelled in the sunlight. It's because they've travelled across a century, thought Michael. They're clogged by dead men's dust – by the antique dust that's lain unswept. Unswept antique dust . . . is that from *Coriolanus*? God help me, I'm hearing whispering voices from a man dead for nearly a century, and I'm quoting bloody Shakespeare!

I'm not really hearing the whispers, though, he thought. I've fallen asleep for a few moments – the warmth of the sun on those windows – or maybe Luisa Gilmore laces her coffee with cannabis.

'Let me in . . .'

A cloud moved across the sun and the garden dipped into shadows, and the whispering faded. The antique dust has settled back into place, thought Michael. Either that, or I've woken up.

He turned determinedly back to the paper-strewn table and Iskander's journal.

As I walked towards the fortress towers of Liège, I could hear the marching feet of the soldiers with more clarity. I tried to convince myself they were growing fainter, but they were not, of course. They were getting louder and closer.

The forest was behind me by this time, and ahead were fields. I went across those fields like a fleeing hare – I swear I had not run so fast since the night when I had to make an unplanned retreat from the Volkov-Yusupov Palace, along with a pair of gold candlesticks, an ormolu mantel clock, and something I believed might be a hitherto-unpublished poem by Alexander Pushkin. (The poem turned out to be a forgery.)

On this particular day, however, I was not burdened with candlesticks or fake Pushkins, and I reached the edges of the German fields safely and thrust my way through a gap in the hedge. I was close to one of the fortresses now – a chimney-like structure, stark and forbidding, rearing up into the afternoon sky like a black jutting tooth. I paused, wondering if I dare try to get into the tower and hide. But wouldn't they try to take possession of those towers anyway? Then I saw that to the right of the tower – perhaps the length of a small field away – was a low, rambling greystone building, with a small bell tower and, rising above its roofs, the outline of a cross.

A convent. And convents were places of sanctuary; they had the same immunity from violence and invasion as churches.

I went across that short distance at the speed of the Hound of Heaven fleeing down the arches of the years.

EIGHT

As soon as I neared the convent's walls, I became aware of music trickling from the windows – thin sweet music, young girls' voices, blending and weaving together in the most heart-scalding perfection I had ever heard. And I may be a thief and a man of few principles, but I can appreciate beauty as well as anyone else, and I stood there for several moments, listening, feeling a balm lay its hand across my soul.

Then I remembered the soldiers and I glanced over my shoulder. But they did not seem to be very near, so I walked normally and openly to the ancient door at the convent's centre. If you're about some nefarious deed, to act furtively will only draw attention to yourself. 'Walk in as if you own the place,' my father used to say. 'And the chances are that most people will think you really do.'

All through what came later, I remembered how the gardens of Sacré-Coeur had looked and felt on that afternoon. During the worst days, I occasionally managed to believe I was still walking through those colours and scents, and that the world around me had remained serene. And although my knowledge of flowers is mostly confined to florists' establishments, when my mind revisits Sacré-Coeur even now I can see and identify the flowers: the rich purple and deep pink windflowers, and the snapdragons and poppies, and I can smell the foaming lavender.

But even on that afternoon I was aware of a sense of dislocation, because this was a country about to be invaded. War does not belong in serene old gardens, with the warm scents drugging the emotions far more surely than ever the perfumes of Arabia did. War belongs to winter, to grey, angry rainstorms and spiteful blizzards, so that the misery and the pain and the fury blends and blurs with the lashing elements.

I had intended to go up to the door at the centre of the convent and politely request food and rest for a few hours.

Once it was a monastic tradition that the weary wayfarer was offered food and a bed for the night, and there was no reason to think that had altered much over the centuries. But the music was still weaving its gossamer strands, and almost without realizing it, I followed it. I have listened on many occasions to beautiful music in spectacular settings, but I had never before listened to the Evening Prayer sung in a convent with the soft light of the dying afternoon bathing everything in rose and gold. I should like to record that I experienced a conversion as I stood there – that the music and the tranquillity of Sacré-Coeur worked a reformation on me and changed my life. They didn't, of course.

The singing was coming from a chapel at the side of the main convent: a small low building with narrow windows that had heavy strips of lead and beautiful coloured glass inset. By standing on tiptoe I was able to peer through the nearest window. There were perhaps twenty nuns inside, all kneeling in prayer, and the chapel was small, but very lovely. I could see statues and carvings and exquisite Mass vessels on the altar. And icons. Oh my God, those icons. My mind instinctively began to compile a list of people who would pay lavishly and unquestioningly for any one of them.

I raised myself up a little higher to see better. The soft sweet chant was still filling up the chapel, but of the chanters themselves there was no sign. I scanned the aisles and the arches again, but I could only see the soaring arches and columns, a low inner door at the far end, and several high, intricately carved rood screens set across one of the aisles.

Rood screens.

Rood screens are, more or less, panels of open wooden tracery. They're a kind of leftover from medieval times: a flimsy partition – largely symbolic – dividing nave from sanctuary. In Russia we have a similar structure, called an iconostasis – but instead of being beautifully carved wood an iconostasis is a small wall of religious paintings and icons. (I think I acquired my love of icons from being taken, by devout parents, to church services, and studying the icons while everyone else was murmuring the responses.)

There was no reason why Sacré-Coeur's chapel should not have rood screens, and there was even less reason for me to find them faintly sinister. But I did, for the simple reason that the singing was coming from behind the screens. The Choir was not merely separated from the small congregation, it was completely hidden. Why would a small remote convent do such a thing for a normal evening service?

Before I could begin to think about this in any detail, I became aware of other sounds beyond the haunting strains of the *Deus*. Footsteps. Marching feet, sharp and insistent, and shouted orders in German. The soldiers were here – they had crossed the border into Liège, and they were tramping through the old gardens towards the chapel.

From the sounds it was a fairly small detachment – certainly not the entire battalion – but it struck dread into my heart. Remaining where I was in the semi-concealment of a thick stone buttress, I looked back into the chapel. They had heard the sounds, that was at once clear. The singing was faltering, and although the service was continuing, several of the nuns were turning round, bewildered by the sounds.

The soldiers were crossing the gardens by now, seemingly heedless of where they trampled, making for the main door and shouting out for admittance. Within the gardens a strident voice was issuing commands to enter the building and take possession of it.

'Find rooms we can use,' called this hard, harsh voice. 'Sleeping quarters, kitchens. Make them habitable. The others will be here before nightfall.'

'They aren't opening the door,' said someone.

'Then break it down.'

There came the sound of rifle butts being hammered against wood, repeated blows. I flinched, imagining the lovely old oak being damaged under the blows.

'We can't do it,' said the same voice after a few moments. 'It's thick, solid oak – it would take a battering ram to break it open.'

'Then find a door that will open or that we can break down.'

'The chapel,' said another voice. 'I see a chapel. That won't be locked.'

'But we can't force our way into a chapel,' said a third, worried voice. 'The nuns are at prayer— I can hear them—'

'The nuns you will deal with,' snapped the officer – I could not see his uniform so I did not know his rank. 'You will deal with them as you would with any female who resists,' he said, and there was a lick of lechery in his tone. Someone responded with what was probably an obscenity, and there was a shout of laughter.

This, clearly, was a reconnoitre party, and the men intended to make Sacré-Coeur their headquarters. If the nuns allowed them to take over the convent it would be a bloodless process, but if they did not, the soldiers would sweep the entire community aside as uncaringly as if they were flies to be swatted, and if blood were spilled, they would not care. I stood there with those worn old stones at my back, with that music still wrapping its cadences round me, and I was vividly aware of two facts. The first was that the nuns would not meekly allow the soldiers to take over Sacré-Coeur so that they could possess Liège and then Belgium. It would not be in their natures. The second fact was that any resistance the nuns might attempt would be useless. They would not have the strength or the numbers, and even if they did, they would not know how to fight such an onslaught. I did not know how to fight it either, but I did know about escaping from importunate bailiffs and angry husbands, and those principles (that word is possibly not the most apposite one here) could be applied now.

I ran around the sides of the chapel until I found what I was looking for – a low arched door leading directly inside. I threw it open and sunlight from the gardens streamed into the dim old chapel, laying harlequin patterns across the floor. As I stepped into that well of gentle light, into the scents of candle smoke and incense, it was as if the layers of prayer wrapped around me, and I thought – I can't break into this. I can't fracture this tranquillity and disturb these women. Then I remembered that the soldiers would unquestionably disturb them, and I strode to the centre aisle and faced the small congregation.

There was a gasp of shock, and some of the nuns rose to their feet. One – an imposing authoritative figure, certainly the Mother Superior – came towards me, gesturing me to go back.

In the best French I could manage, I said loudly, 'Forgive me, but you are all in great danger. German soldiers are in the grounds – preparing to invade your country. But if you come with me now I may be able to get you away.'

They did not take it in. Of course they did not. They had been rapt in prayer, in the service, in the music, and they were confused, as if suddenly faced with too-bright sunlight after hours of darkness. Then several of the younger ones stood up, but Mother Superior at once rapped out a command.

'All remain in your places. Sister Jeanne, continue to play. It is the time for the *Magnificat.*'

The small bespectacled nun seated at the organ glanced at me. She started to say, 'But Sister Clothilde—'

'It is an order, Sister.'

The tradition of obedience held strong, and little Sister Jeanne bowed her head. The massive organ chords began to roll forth, and from behind the rood screens, the silver and golden voices started again, thready and uncertain at first, then with more confidence.

I went towards the rood screens, intending to push them aside, but the soldiers were already at the door, blocking out the sunlight. As they entered the chapel, the current of air sent the candle flames flickering wildly, casting grotesque shadows across the chapel, making the soldiers seem like striding giants. Their hard boots rang out on the marble floor, and they took up positions across the main aisle, the altar at their backs. One of them went to stand by the organ, and two more stood like sentries on each side of the main door. All had rifles, and all grasped them firmly. I stepped unobtrusively back into the shadows of a deep alcove – not from a craven wish to hide, but to try to work out an escape plan for the nuns.

The commanding officer – I recognized his voice – said, 'Who is your Mother Superior?'

'I am Sister Clothilde, Mother Superior of Sacré-Coeur.'

'Then, Sister, we are taking over your convent. Belgium is claimed by the Kaiser – it is his route into France – and this place is to be the headquarters of this battalion until our task is complete.' He paused, then with relish said, 'Until Belgium falls.'

He spoke in extremely bad French – even I could tell that – and some of the words were German, but the nuns understood him.

There was a silence, then several of the older nuns came to stand with the formidable Sister Clothilde, their faces white and set, although the younger ones still cowered back in fear.

Clothilde was not afraid, though. She said, sharply, 'Belgium will never fall. Leave our chapel. This is God's house, and we will not submit to the brutality of you or your Emperor.'

I dare say she could not have found anything that would have infuriated and insulted the soldiers more. I'm not actually sure if she cared, though, and she delivered the words with a precision and authority that would not have shamed Bernhardt or Duse.

The officer was certainly infuriated. He turned to his men and issued a series of orders, speaking too rapidly for me to follow. Whether the nuns followed it I don't know, but as the soldiers moved towards them, their rifles raised threateningly, they seemed to square their shoulders in readiness, and they stood their ground. I stood my ground as well, frantically looking round the chapel to find a means of creating a diversion.

The young nuns were still huddled together in a frightened bunch, but when Sister Clothilde turned to look at them, they responded as one, going to stand with her. Sister Jeanne stood up again, but Clothilde called out to her – I think this time it was something about maintaining the silver cord of prayer to the Lord – and Jeanne nodded. The music began again, and after the first few notes, the singing started once more. The soldiers were momentarily disconcerted and I was not surprised, because while the organ music seemed to be a natural part of the chapel, that cool, intricate chant, apparently coming from nowhere, had an other-world quality to it. But the officer gestured impatiently, and they went purposefully towards the small inner door, which presumably led through to the main convent.

Sister Clothilde was ahead of them. She whisked across the chapel and took up a stance in front of the door.

'Stand aside,' said the officer, angrily.

'I will not.'

'You force us to use violence against you, Sister.'

'Then do so. I shall not flinch.'

Clothilde stood her ground, and I felt deeply shamed that I was still cowering in the shadows and not rushing out there to slay the soldiers. But to do so would be useless; they would shoot me at once. Instead, I began to edge stealthily towards a massive statue on a stone plinth – Christ displaying his glowing heart, with all the love and compassion that traditional image conveys. The plinth was easily four feet high, the statue itself another three; if I could topple the statue to the ground it would create such a crashing disturbance that the nuns might be able to make a run for it.

The older ones had followed Clothilde's lead, ranging themselves with her, effectively blocking off the door. The music and the singing were continuing, but Jeanne's hands were stumbling over the chords, and sobbing broke out from behind the rood screens, splintering the music into ugly fragments. At this, Clothilde turned towards the screens and issued another of her ringing commands. This time I heard and understood better – she was ordering the sisters and the singers to hold fast to the prayer, for the prayer and the music were the sure and certain bonds through which would come God's help. God would not fail them, she cried. There was the ascending note of the fanatic in her voice, and there was certainly the gleam of the zealot in her eyes, and it was clear she meant to defy the invaders no matter the cost.

But even the most extreme of militant Christianity was

not going to fell ten or a dozen trained soldiers, all of them armed, none of them particularly sympathetic to women – at least, not these women – and the soldiers moved towards the door, their rifles held out.

The singing was still struggling to maintain its momentum, and there was something so heart-rending about those frightened, determined voices that renewed determination washed over me. A dozen more steps – perhaps a dozen and a half – and I would be within reach of the stone plinth. I would have to trust to luck that the statue was not cemented down, and I would also have to trust to luck that the nuns and whatever was behind the rood screens would respond fast enough for an escape.

I am not sure if Sister Clothilde was entirely sane at that point. From where I stood I could not hear very clearly, nor could I entirely follow what she was saying, but I think it was something about not yielding to the emissaries of Satan and standing firm in the face of Satan's armies. Mad or sane, she had a grandiloquent line in rhetoric.

The officer said, in a cold voice, 'You expect us to shoot you, Sister?'

'We will die in God's love.'

'So you have a hankering for the Martyr's Crown,' he said, very sarcastically. 'Well, we shall disappoint you over that, for we do not commit murder if we can avoid it, at least not against *religieuses*. But there are other methods of persuasion, Sister.' There was a gloating lasciviousness in his voice, and he rapped out another of the orders to the soldiers. I thought one of them hesitated, but the others moved at once, grabbing the arms of the two youngest nuns and pulling them into the main aisle.

I took several more steps nearer the statue, praying not to be noticed, hoping none of the sisters would remember I was there and give away my presence.

'Well, Sister?' said the officer. 'We have two of your choicest pigeons. Now will you stand aside and let us into the convent?'

'I will not. Sisters, stay brave. God's love and His strength are with you.'

The two young nuns were struggling and sobbing, and
I don't think they really heard her. They both wore what
looked like the garb of novices, and one of the soldiers had
pulled away the headdress of the smaller one. Beneath it
she had cropped hair, soft and silky, like a baby's. She
looked about seventeen and even tear-streaked and terrified
she was extremely pretty. The men reached for the headdress
of the other and snatched that off as well, standing around
the two girls, laughing and jeering.

'Now, Sister,' said the officer to Clothilde, 'you see what
is about to happen, I think? My men have not seen females
for a very long time. Will you allow us into your convent
to use it for our headquarters, or do I persuade you to do
so by letting my men make use of these two choice little
morsels?'

(He may have used words other than morsels, but my
German was not equal to translating obscenity.)

Whatever words he used, there was no doubt about his
meaning. Sister Clothilde turned white to the lips, and Sister
Jeanne let out a cry of fear and anguish.

But, 'We do not allow you into God's house to practice
your brutality and wage your war on innocent people,' said
Clothilde. 'We will never allow it, no matter the cost.' Her
eyes flickered to the two girls – one of them was trying to
cover her poor shorn head, and the pity of it slammed into
my throat. 'No matter the cost,' she said again.

One of the nuns added, challengingly, 'And Belgium will
never surrender. Even if you kill all of its people one by
one, it will not yield to you.'

'It will not,' said Clothilde. She looked at the two girls
and then at the avid-eyed soldiers. 'If you wish to perform
that act of savagery, take me instead,' she said. 'I do not
care, and God will understand.'

The officer laughed, and the sound echoed mockingly
around the chapel.

'We prefer younger meat,' he said. 'But if we have to,
we will take you one by one until you agree to let us into
your convent. You understand me? One by one. All of us
in turn.'

Clothilde stared at him. 'I understand you,' she said. 'But we will resist you with the small strength we have.'

'I think, Sister, that you will not resist for long,' said the officer. 'Perhaps after the third or fourth time – when your nuns are screaming with the pain and humiliation – you will be begging us to take over your convent.'

The two sentries from the door moved into the chapel then, whether to watch what was about to happen, or simply to make sure no one tried to escape, I have no idea, but it meant they now stood between me and the stone plinth with its statue. I managed to dart behind a stone column without being seen, but anger and frustration swept through me in a scalding flood.

The two novices were thrown to the ground, the soldiers standing around them, already loosening their belts. Two of the older nuns moved, as if trying to go to the girls' assistance, but the soldiers barred their way.

The faces of all the men were avid, and in the light from the flickering altar candles and the rays from the setting sun, their eyes gleamed with lust. The anger surged up again, and I tensed my muscles, ready to make a run for the stone plinth. To hell with being seen or shot; if there was any justice in the world, I would manage to send the statue crashing to the ground and pray to whatever gods were listening that the nuns would have the wit to escape in the ensuing mêlée. But before I could do so, the same two nuns ran forward again, straight at the soldiers, their hands outstretched to push the men away from the two novices. It was brave in the extreme, but it was also fool-hardy in the extreme, and of course it was fatal. As if by reflex, the two sentries lifted their rifles and fired several rapid rounds. Screams filled the chapel, and the two nuns fell, clutching gunshot wounds. Blood spattered over the quiet old stones, and across the lovely old organ, and Sister Jeanne screamed and recoiled from the bench, cowering against the wall.

'Play the prayer,' cried Clothilde. 'God is listening – God will not abandon us. The *Magnificat* . . . "The Angel of the Lord declared unto Mary, and she received the Holy

Ghost . . ." All of you, join with me – trust in God, in our
Blessed Lady—'

The terrible, the macabre and pitiful thing, is that they
tried to obey her. Jeanne made her trembling way back to
the organ bench, and fumblingly started to play, and after
a few chords, the ragged, fearful singing came in. It was to
the accompaniment of those sounds – that music – that the
soldiers held down the two young novices – both of them
too frightened to resist – and raped them. They did it there
on the prayer-drenched stones, one after the other, with the
blind, watchful statues, with the slippery tainting blood
everywhere, and the nuns they had shot lying dead on the
ground.

I am not ashamed of many things in my life, but I have
always been deeply ashamed that I did not move sufficiently
fast to stop that particular brutality. But hearing the sobs
and the cries, I ran out of the shadows, straight at the stone
plinth. I am no hero – I would like to repeat that for my
reader – but I do not think any man could have cowered in
hiding and done nothing to help those women. So I bounded
across the chapel, straight at the statue.

To some extent I had the advantage of surprise – the
soldiers had no idea I was there – and by the time they did
realize it, I had reached the plinth and was throwing my
whole weight against it. There was a panic-filled moment
when I thought the statue was not going to move, then it
shuddered and there was a harsh, hard sound of stone
scraping against stone. The soldiers spun round, levelling
their rifles. They saw me, and they fired, but by then I was
behind the statue and the plinth, and the bullets buried
themselves in the statue. Sprays of stone-dust clouded out,
and under cover of this I pushed again at the figure. The
teeth-wincing scraping came again, and then, with a kind
of stately menace, Christ's figure began to move. I pushed
it for the third time, and this time it dislodged from its base.
For a moment the emotive, legendary features reproduced
in hundreds of statues and paintings, slowly – oh God, so
slowly – toppled forward.

They say you often get more than you planned for in life

and that was certainly the case in that chapel. Not only did the statue fall, it took the plinth with it. They both went crashing down, hitting the ground with an explosion of sound, painful and deafening. Lumps of stone and fragments of shattered marble flew out in every direction, and the sound of the crash reverberated through the small chapel, causing the glass to shiver and dislodging several of the Mass vessels from the altar. Huge eruptions of dust billowed out, snuffing the candles, plunging the chapel into an eerie, grey-tinged gloaming. But worst of all, the organ pipes, jarred by the crash, thrummed with angry discordance, sending out ugly confused sounds as if the organ itself were wounded and moaning in agony.

The soldiers were running everywhere, gasping and coughing from the dust that was clogging their lungs and causing their eyes to stream, trying to regroup. They could not see me – I could barely see them, in fact, but I had been behind the dust explosion and I was probably in better shape than anyone. Sister Jeanne half fell from her organ stool, looked about her in fearful confusion, then turned to where I stood, as if in appeal.

I pointed to the rood screens. 'Get them all out at once. Get everyone into the convent then barricade yourselves in,' I said. 'If I can dodge the soldiers, I'll get out and try to send help to you.'

It was a jumble of French and heaven-knows what other languages, but she understood well enough, and nodded, turning to the screens. One had fallen and was leaning drunken and splintered against a column. The other was still in place, and it was around this second screen that I stepped.

And saw what was behind it.

NINE

I ought not to have been surprised. I certainly ought not to have recoiled in pity. But, sadly, it's an instinct most of us have – faced with the abnormal, the grotesque, with those poor specimens of humanity that nature has mistreated, we flinch and want to run away.

The scene that lay behind those screens was like something from one of the famous disturbing paintings or engravings by people such as William Hogarth or Bruegel or Goya. Scenes from asylums, from pauper hospitals. At first the canvas appears to contain normal, ordinary faces with normal, ordinary bodies. But as you go on looking, you begin to see something subtly wrong with every one of the figures. Deformities of body – perhaps even worse, deformities of mind that look out through the eyes.

Those cruel tweaks of Nature confronted me as I stepped around the screens. Twenty, perhaps twenty-five, young women, some barely fourteen years old, others probably nineteen or twenty, huddled together in a terrified cluster, their eyes wide, their faces streaked with tears and stone-dust. Every one bearing the vicious pawmark of deformity. Hunchbacked, crippled, malformed, some of the faces even bearing the unmistakable stamp of idiocy – it's pitifully obvious, that last one. As if a malicious hand smeared the raw material before it had quite set. I've heard them called the sweet and holy fools of the world, but I don't know if I subscribe to that.

But in one thing they were alike in that moment. They were all terrified, and as soon as they saw me they shrank back. God knows what terrors they must have gone through herded together here, hearing what was happening, perhaps glimpsing some of it. Many of them would not entirely have understood, but all of them would have known they were in danger.

All around us, the organ pipes were still thrumming with discordance, and through it I could hear the soldiers crashing everywhere and swearing. But the dust was already clearing, and it would only take minutes for them to recover and regroup. I had minutes to get these girls across the chapel and into the main part of the convent behind locked doors. The alternative – to get them out to the gardens and out into the countryside – was impossible.

The pitiful thing – the thing that still twists painfully at the root of my soul when I think about it – is that they began to sing again. It was as if they were offering the only defence they had, and despite the danger and the chaos, tears stung my eyes.

But mercifully Sister Jeanne was there as well, and they trusted her. She clapped her hands briskly, and I think she said, 'Into the convent, girls, and quickly, please.' They fell obediently into line, and Sister Jeanne nodded to me in a gesture that might have been a thanks or a blessing, and led them through the clouds of dust and the shuddering music from the disturbed organ pipes. I stayed where I was, seeing that despite the awkward gait of most of them they skirted the edges of the chapel nimbly enough, avoiding the soldiers, picking their way through the dust. They went through the far door, and Sister Jeanne turned and sketched the outline of the Sign of the Cross on the air. I put up a hand in acknowledgement, then they were gone, and I caught, very faintly, the sound of a key turning in a lock. I thought: they'll barricade themselves in there, and if I can get away I'll somehow get help to them.

If I could get away . . . One level of my mind – the professional burglar's level – had continued to work at its usual pace. Almost without realizing it, I had worked out that I could get through a narrow window partly hidden by the remaining rood screen. It was just about accessible from the ground, and the glass would have to be knocked out, but thankfully it was plain glass. Even in that desperate situation I would have hesitated to destroy the beautiful stained glass panels in the other windows.

The soldiers were at the far door, trying to force the lock, and the officer was saying something about finding other ways in.

Praying that Sister Clothilde and the others had had the wit to make sure all doors and windows were secured, I reached up for the stone sill, grateful for the cover afforded by the screen. But before I could lever myself up on to it, there was a movement on my right and I looked round sharply, thinking one of the soldiers had found his way here, tensing all my muscles to fight him or dodge bullets, or both.

It was not a soldier. It was one of the girls from the choir – she was cowering in the deep shadow of a buttress, and she was a thin, pale little thing with dark hair. Unlike a number of the other girls, her features were regular, although slightly pointed in the way a cat's features are or a pixie's. Her eyes were clear and intelligent, but filled with terror and bewilderment. How she had been missed by Sister Jeanne I have no idea, but here she was. On the wrong side of the locked door.

I defy anyone, in that situation, to know the best course of action. We were in a dust-swept chapel with a thrumming discordance echoing all round us, the rest of the community was barricaded behind locked doors, the Kaiser's soldiers were brandishing rifles at everything in sight, and two murdered nuns were lying in their own blood. I don't think I was ever in a more awkward or bizarre situation.

There was no time to wonder whether I could get the girl into the locked section of the convent, because clearly I could not. So, in my unreliable French, I said, 'Don't be afraid. I'm here to help. We'll climb through the window.'

I didn't really expect her to acquiesce. I didn't even expect her to understand. But she nodded and clambered out from her tiny hiding-place – I remember thinking: oh God, please don't let her be as badly deformed as some of those other poor souls. Please let her be capable of walking normally, because if she's severely crippled, we might as well surrender to the German army here and now.

As she walked to the narrow window, I saw that she limped quite badly, as if she might have one leg slightly shorter than the other, or possessed what I think is called a club foot. But somehow I got her through the window, pushing her on to the sill, and indicating to her to drop down on the grass on the other side.

'Can you manage that?' I said.

'Oh, yes,' she said at once, which was one mercy in the midst of the chaos.

I turned back to survey the chapel. And now my burglar's mind was undoubtedly in the ascendant. I thought: I've got to travel through Belgium and find help for those nuns, and I've got to do it fast. I might have to take that girl with me for a few miles.

I'm not particularly proud of what I did, but the soldiers would have looted the chapel, and to travel anywhere, it's necessary to have money – or something that can be turned into money. I went for the icons, of course. I pocketed four of them – beautiful jewel-painted things in polished frames. Then I scrambled on to the stone window sill and down on to the grass. The pixie-faced girl was waiting for me.

'What's your name?'

She hesitated, as if unsure whether to trust me that far, so I said, 'I'm Iskander. I'm a Russian newspaper reporter.'

I'm not even sure if she knew what a reporter was, but she nodded, as if absorbing these new words. Then she said, 'Leonora.'

'I wish I could say I was happy to meet you, Leonora. But it will be all right. Take hold of my hand and don't let go. We're going to run away together.'

She only hesitated briefly. She said, 'Run away? Away from here, do you mean? From Sacré-Coeur?'

'Yes. Is that all right with you?'

'Oh, yes,' she said, with a fervency I had not anticipated. 'As far as possible.'

Her hand came into mine, and together we went through the scented gardens, and into the vast waiting night of the doomed land.

The journal ended there, but Iskander's vivid word-pictures remained.

So, thought Michael, that grisly little legend about the Palestrina

Choir had been true. The Choir really had sung the accompaniment
to its own death throes. It had been a heart-rending attempt by the
girls to placate the intruders, because it had been the only thing
they had known – the only defence weapon they could offer. Like
Iskander, the pity of it bit painfully into him.

At times, translating the narrative, Michael had had to guess
at Iskander's meaning, and there had been whole paragraphs
– in one case almost an entire page – where the writing had
been too cramped – or perhaps written too hastily – to decipher
it with any certainty. But as he worked, understanding the
journal had become progressively easier, like running down a
flight of stairs – you moved so fast that your feet did not
actually touch the stairs, and yet your own momentum and
confidence propelled you safely to the bottom. Michael had been
able to skim Iskander's words so surely that he had reached an
understanding.

The chimes of a small mantel clock broke into his concentration, and he realized with vague surprise that it was two o'clock
and that he was hungry. He had told Luisa that he would happily
sort out his own lunch, and he closed his notebook and went
along to the kitchen. After he had eaten he would ask if there
had been any word about the fallen tree. In the meantime, he put
together a sandwich which he ate at the kitchen table, his mind
still filled with a kaleidoscopic blur of poetry and music and
brutality – and of that haunting image of the Palestrina Choir
humbly offering its music to the Kaiser's soldiers.

He washed up his plate and knife, and made a cup of instant
coffee, which he took back to the library. There was still no sign
of Luisa, and as he drank his coffee, he reread the letter to Sister
Clothilde which referred to the Choir being always hidden behind
screens. This was an intriguing byway for research, and Michael
began to scan the shelves to see what other sources might be on
hand. After a prolonged search during which he dispossessed
several indignant spiders of their homes, he eventually found a
battered volume on baroque choral music. It had been printed in
1910, the cover was dry and split, and the pages were badly
foxed and infused with a dry musty scent of age. But halfway
through he found a section that read:

In Vivaldi's day, many young girls were secluded from the world in conventual setting, not because they had a vocation, but so they could be trained to sing. Some embraced this training willingly, but there are many recorded instances of girls being taken from their homes by subterfuge or even force if it was thought they would be valuable additions to religious music. It was also common for wealthy families to pay religious institutions to house girls who were disfigured or mentally flawed, so that their existence need never be known.

Others came from poor backgrounds, where disfiguring diseases were rife – often due to syphilis. For those unfortunates, the convents would have been a sanctuary where they were housed and fed.

For most of their lives, these girls were hidden away. During performances and choral mass they remained behind screens – ostensibly in accordance with the Catholic tenets of preserving virginity and purity, but in reality to hide the disfigurements and, in some cases, the identities.

This practice gradually died out as medical science advanced and attitudes towards cripples and the mentally deficient became more tolerant. However, traces of the tradition lingered in remote districts – in Spain, in France, in Belgium, and also in Italy, although the suggestion of 'hidden-away choirs' inside the Vatican cannot be substantiated. There is, however, strong evidence to suggest the practice continued in Europe until as recently as the late 1850s.

Michael read this twice and found it distressing and infuriating in equal measures.

It ought not to be a particular surprise to hear that girls had been hidden away like that – not shamefully or squalidly in asylums or workhouses, but in religious houses which people would have seen as respectable and even admirable.

Had Leonora gone willingly into Sacré-Coeur? The journal gave no clue; it ended with Iskander and Leonora leaving the convent. Michael considered this. How had Iskander's journal – or what appeared to be part of his journal – reached this house?

If Iskander had been here – or if someone had acquired his belongings and brought them here – might there be other pages still to be found? This was a seductive possibility, but Michael was here to research war poets and the influence of music on their poetry, not to chase the lively outpourings of a disreputable Russian war journalist and burglar.

He worked determinedly for two hours, exploring other boxes of papers, reading ancient letters, opening aged books, some of them privately printed by forgotten residents of the house, and sorting the contents of several desk drawers. Most of these yielded nothing more illuminating than old seed catalogues or faded notices of local events, but there were two or three more letters from Chuffy, who had apparently held the Gilmore family in some affection, and had written to his old Charterhouse school friend chronicling events such as a local cricket match in which Chuffy had distinguished himself – 'I notched up fifty which I thought was a pretty good show'; the wedding of Chuffy's sister to a local squire – 'Frightfully good chap, I should think it'll do pretty well, and a cartload of cousins turned up for the wedding bash'; and details of a number of Old Carthusian get-togethers, which Chuffy, a diligent attendee, described for the edification of his old chum, listing such names as might be thought of interest to Boots.

> . . . and Robert Graves put in an appearance this time, my word, he looked so much older, but I dare say we all look older, what with the war and all, even those of us who were too young to actually serve. Graves came up to me, friendly as you like, really decent chap. We talked about your cousin Stephen, of course. Graves remembered him, in fact had heard one or two of the stories about Stephen, well, I dare say most of us heard one or two of the stories, but I always thought they were all rot, and I said so. Graves said, 'Ah, really? I'm very glad to have that assurance,' and shook my hand, and we had a drink together, well, actually, we had several. I don't mind telling you I should like to have asked him about the Somme, but I thought it better not to, because one never knows if those chaps want to talk about what they did and saw, and I know Graves was shelled. But he

and I sat together for the concert, and I noticed how moved
he was by some of the pieces the Choir sang. Some Italian
stuff, so I believe – Palestrina or some such name. I'd never
heard tell of it, but Graves seemed to know it – learned
cove he is – and said the Choir had performed it beautifully.
He said it was enough to make you want to go off and write
screeds of verse in the same rhythm and pattern.

Oh, Chuffy, thought Michael in delight, whoever you were, you're
giving me gold nuggets, and if I can find out your real name,
you shall have an acknowledgement in the Director's book. He
scribbled down the details of Chuffy's letter, then looked for a
date or an address, only to find that Chuffy had provided neither
on any of his letters, presumably thinking that Boots knew the
date and also knew where he, Chuffy, lived anyway.

What looked to be a slightly later letter referred to another
concert – the organizer of the Old Carthusians during Chuffy's
era appeared to have a considerable affinity for music – at which
there had been a specially-written piece set to the words of Rupert
Brooke's famous poem, *The Soldier.* This time Michael cursed
Chuffy for not providing dates and supposed it must have been
some kind of anniversary – perhaps it had been the ten year
anniversary of the Armistice.

Chuffy, it appeared, had not gone much for the music written
for *The Soldier* – 'awfully modern stuff, I thought it' – but had
found himself moved by the words and did not mind admitting
it. 'All that stuff about some corner of a foreign field being forever
England, and hearts at peace under an English heaven. Dashed
affecting, when you remember how many of those chaps we
knew who died over there.'

Michael assembled all of this on to the laptop, with particular
attention to Chuffy's account of the school reunions and a
reminder to himself to write to the Old Carthusian Association
in the hope that they kept records. Typing it all on to the laptop
he again regretted the lack of an Internet connection here, but
he would be able to let the Director have the notes in the next
day or so.

It was half-past four. He took his coffee cup back to the kitchen.
Rain beat against the windows and sluiced down gutters and

drains, and Michael stood looking out, thinking that Fosse House seemed to lie at the centre of an incessant downpour. He was just rinsing the cup when he realized there were other patterns inside the sound of the rain. Footsteps. Was Stephen out there again? The footsteps faded, and Michael hesitated, then thought he would open the little garden door at the far end of the kitchen and reassure himself that no one was out there.

The door was locked but the key was in the lock, and he turned it and opened the door. Rain blew into his face, and he shivered, but took a few steps out. The gardens were grey-green in the dull light, and it was like peering through a bead curtain. For a moment he thought a blurred figure darted between the thin grey layers, then it was gone, and he could see the walled garden with the wrought-iron gate. The gate was closed. There's no one there, he thought with relief, and went back inside, closing and locking the door. The rain had left faint marks across the kitchen floor. Michael looked for a cloth and not finding one hoped they would dry out by themselves.

He went back to the library, hoping for some sound that would indicate Luisa's whereabouts so that he could talk to her about the Choir, annoyed to find himself hesitant to knock on doors. But there were no sounds anywhere. Perhaps his hostess had a brief sleep in the afternoons. Madeline Usher encoffined in the ancient keep, the lid screwed down, but the beating of her heart still discernible . . .? 'For pity's sake,' said Michael angrily to himself, 'if Luisa's asleep, it's because she's nodded off over a good book!'

The library felt so chilly that he went upstairs to collect an extra sweater from his bedroom. The stairs and landing were wreathed in gloom, and he looked for a light switch, but could not see one. His room was only a few yards away, however, and he went towards it, glancing to the far corner where the Holzminden sketch hung.

The sketch was wreathed in shadows, but standing next to it was the figure of a man in an army greatcoat.

Stephen.

TEN

Stephen seemed to be staring into a distant and terrible horizon. He's looking into a nightmare, thought Michael in horrified fascination. No, that's wrong, he's trying to stare *beyond* a nightmare, because the nightmare is too dreadful to look at. But he's not real, I must remember that. He's nothing more than an image from the past.

The collar of Stephen's greatcoat was turned up as if against a cold wind, and the soft blond hair was tumbled. For the first time Michael saw that his hands were torn and bruised, the nails shredded, the fingertips bloodied. Stephen, he thought, your hands, your poor hands . . . What did that to you?

Stephen turned his head and looked directly at Michael, and a half-recognition seemed to show in his eyes.

'Don't let them find me . . .'

Michael had no idea if the words were actually spoken, or if he was hearing them with his mind, but Stephen was so young, so vulnerable, that he stopped being afraid and took a step forward, one hand held out. He thought Stephen had just made up his mind to accept his approach, but then light, uneven footsteps came up the stairs, and he turned sharply to see Luisa. She must have crossed the hall without him hearing and she was standing at the head of the stairs, one hand resting on the banister, her eyes on the shadowy figure. But when Michael looked back, Stephen had gone, and there was only a faint outline on the panelling, like a thin chalk mark.

In a dry, ragged voice, Luisa said, 'You saw him, didn't you.'

It was impossible to pretend not to understand. Choosing his words carefully, Michael said, 'I thought there was something – someone – here. But it was probably just a shadow—'

'It wasn't a shadow,' she said at once. 'It was Stephen. That means you let him in.'

'No—'

'You must have done,' she said. 'He can't come in unless

someone opens a door or a window for him. His hands are so damaged you see – he can't turn a handle or a window catch himself. It was a long time before I understood that.'

Michael stared at her, and his mind went back to how he had heard the rain tapping against the kitchen windows, and how the rhythms had formed into soft words. *'Let-me-in . . .'* He had heard that, and he had opened the kitchen door to make sure no one was out there. There had not been anyone – but a shadow had seemed to slip between the veils of rain, and there had been faint wet marks like footprints across the kitchen floor . . . I did let him in, thought Michael, with an uneasy glance towards the corner with the Holzminden sketch.

Very gently, he said, 'Miss Gilmore, supposing I did glimpse something or hear something or – or even open a door to look outside for a moment? It doesn't matter so very much, does it? Old houses often have lingering memories, and occasionally the memories can even be visual. I've encountered it before. Not everyone accepts the premise, but—'

'"All argument is against it, but all belief is for it"?' she said. 'Who was it who said that?'

'Dr Johnson.'

She smiled slightly. 'I thought you'd know.' If there had been any fear in her eyes earlier it was no longer there.

Michael said, 'I think that some people are more receptive to – to picking up traces of the past than others. Perhaps you're one of the receptive kind.'

'I wish it were that simple,' she said, then looked at him with an odd, sideways glance. 'Dr Flint, nearly a hundred years ago, towards the end of the Great War, my ancestor Stephen Gilmore was incarcerated in a German prisoner-of-war camp. A place called Holzminden.'

She did not seem to notice Michael's start of surprise, so he said, 'Were his hands damaged in Holzminden?'

'I don't know. But on some nights his hands still bleed.' A deep sadness touched her face, then she said, 'I think Holzminden damaged his mind, though. Perhaps he became a little mad because of it. I've sometimes felt—'

'Yes?'

'I've sometimes felt that his madness became stamped on this house,' she said. Her eyes narrowed, darting from side to side as if searching for something, and Michael felt a prickle of unease.

'Whatever happened to Stephen can't possibly affect you now, Miss Gilmore—'

'Dr Flint, why do you think I live here like this!' she said, angrily. 'Solitary, secluded. Shut away from the world. Why do you think I couldn't offer you the common courtesy of asking you to stay here for your research? Here, in a house with so many empty bedrooms. And why do you suppose I was so fearful when the storm forced my hand last night?'

There was an abrupt silence. Then Michael said, very softly, 'Because Stephen comes here every night.'

'Yes. *Yes.* He tries to get in, but his poor hands— And there are some nights—'

She broke off, and Michael said, very gently, 'There are some nights when you let him in?'

'Yes,' she said, staring up at him. Her hands flexed in an odd gesture, as if she was clasping another, invisible, hand. 'I don't know why I'm telling you this,' she said. 'I've never told anyone before. But you saw him. You heard him. So perhaps you understand, just a little.'

Do I tell her she seemed to have sleepwalked last night? thought Michael. That I saw her open the door? He said, carefully, 'Do you see him every night?'

'Almost every night. Since I was a young girl growing up here. When I was a little older – when I understood better – I realized that no one must ever be in this house once darkness falls, because no one must know about Stephen. If he's real – if he's still here, I have to protect him. I have to protect people who come to this house, as well.'

'From whatever – or whoever – came for Stephen?'

'Yes.'

'And if Stephen's not real?'

'Dr Flint, we both know what happens to people who see and hear things that aren't there,' she said impatiently.

Trying for a more normal note, Michael said, 'But you haven't been entirely alone all this time, surely?'

'Not entirely,' said Luisa. 'My life hasn't been completely solitary. It certainly hasn't been without purpose or interest. There are people in the village – occasional social events. And there are people I correspond with – there are a great many of those. Researchers into the Choir in particular – that began many years ago, and it's brought me a good deal of pleasure and interest. Your Director of Music is one of those researchers, of course.'

'What about your family? Friends?'

'I had no brothers or sisters,' said Luisa. 'As a child I was alone a good deal.' A shadow of some strong emotion passed over her face, but it vanished before Michael could identify it. 'In any case, I could never put into words what I heard and saw.' She paused, then in a low voice said, 'Sometimes, I think I am mad as well – that I've been infected with Stephen's madness. Can you catch insanity?'

'Of course not. And let's remember that I've seen Stephen, too.'

'Yes. Dr Flint – Michael – I think I shall always be deeply grateful to you for that.' Then, as abruptly as if a curtain had been drawn, the cool, grande dame persona returned. 'I came to tell you that I took a phone call a short time ago,' she said. 'The tree is still blocking the roads. I'm afraid it means you'll have to spend another night inside Fosse House.'

Email from: Owen Bracegirdle
To: Nell West
Hi Nell –

Thanks for your message earlier.

Of course I'll come with you to the Bodleian, and we'll caper through the catalogues and disrupt the staff in quest of your privately-printed letters. I can't imagine why you're chasing letters from a POW officer from the Great War, but you can tell me the spicy details over coffee.

Light has been restored to College after Wilberforce's foray into the bewilderment of Oriel's electricity. That means I've been able to send a more seemly report to the Director of Music on my work for his *opus*, rather than a scrawl on a couple of spare sheets of A4. I hope he takes due note of the lateness of the hour I sent it, because it doesn't hurt to let the ivory tower gang realize that lesser mortals work quite hard.

I'm sorry to report, though, that while everyone was searching for Homer's lamp for illumination, or, at worst, a few candles or a cigarette lighter, Wilberforce appears to have padded through the Gothic darkness to Oriel's kitchens. He reached them unerringly, of course – that cat could find a scullery in a stormy night without a compass – and made a quiet and efficient assault on the abandoned lamb casserole. To be fair, the casserole had already been designated as uneatable, due to being only half-cooked, and I suppose Wilberforce couldn't be expected to understand about the dangers of imperfectly-cooked lamb.

It was a pity, though, that if he had to be sick afterwards, he must needs to so on the Dean's hearthrug. It's reputed to be a Persian rug which was presented to the Dean by some visiting Eastern potentate, and the Dean is currently being placated by promises of the best specialist dry-cleaning that can be found for the rug. To help out, I have placed my soul in pawn, Faustus-like, to stop him hauling Wilberforce to the nearest vet's slaughterhouse, and it took a remarkably long time, which is why I didn't get your phone message until now. I think the Dean is suitably placated, and even if he isn't, I suspect Michael's army of cherubic eight- and nine-year-old readers would form a protest march to stay Wilberforce's execution, anyway. Your Beth would most likely carry the banner.

Let's meet at half-past nine tomorrow outside the Bodleian. I'll need to be back at College for twelve, but if we don't find your letters, we can arrange a second trip, and if necessary take in the Radcliffe.

Owen

Nell read the email, shook her head over Wilberforce's exploits, but was pleased that Owen would help with the quest for Hugbert's letters.

As she went into the kitchen to put together some supper she was glad to think Michael would be returning to Oxford tomorrow. He would probably set off fairly early and be back in good time to have supper in Quire Court. With this in mind, Nell hunted out a favourite recipe book to find something really nice to cook.

She might do rainbow trout – she had a recipe for stuffing it with smoked trout and horseradish, which was delicious. There was a bottle of Chablis in the fridge which a customer had given her for finding a beautiful set of needlepoint dining chairs, and she would buy fruit and cheese for dessert.

Michael would be all right in Fosse House, of course. But as Nell ate her supper, she kept glancing at Bodkin's book, which she had left open at the page referring to the Holzminden sketch and the taint of madness that was supposed to cling to it. She wished she had not read that. She wished, even more, that Michael had not mentioned hearing whispering voices at Fosse House.

ELEVEN

Michael had no idea how he was going to cope with a second night in Fosse House, and he had no idea how he was going to face Luisa over supper this evening, and again tomorrow morning.

Should he pretend they had never had that unreal conversation on the landing and, instead, talk cheerfully about his work? He had a wild image of determinedly describing the breezy letters from the unknown Chuffy, and of Luisa industriously searching genealogies to find out who Chuffy had been and which Gilmore he might have been writing to, both of them studiously ignoring any sounds that might herald Stephen's arrival. Or Luisa might not ignore it at all; she might make a light-hearted reference to it: 'And don't take any notice of my ancestor, Dr Flint, he usually takes a turn in the garden around this time . . .'

It was an image that defied credibility, particularly since Luisa would no doubt lead the conversation wherever she wanted it to go. It had been odd, though, to be afforded that glimpse behind the composed facade.

It was half past five, and when he went into the library it was wreathed in shadows. Michael switched on the desk lamp, grateful for the warm pool of light it cast over the leather-topped table which was still littered with notes and old letters.

He had thought work would be impossible, but when he opened the box file containing Chuffy's letters, he found he was able to step back into Fosse House's past easily, and even make some half-intelligent notes about Robert Graves and to draft a letter to the Old Carthusian Society about the setting of Rupert Brooke's *The Soldier* to music. A recording from so long ago was too much to hope for, but there was a faint chance they might have kept the setting or the score. Even a programme of the event would be a find.

Rifling a second box, he found what appeared to be the basis for an essay – perhaps even a thesis on the Palestrina Choir's history – which seemed to have been originally drafted in the early 1930s. It looked as if it might be useful, although it was slightly disconcerting to think someone else had trodden the path Michael himself was now treading. Had the unknown writer found and made use of Iskander's journal? He experienced a pang of the unreasonable, possessive jealousy known to many academics and writers. Iskander's mine! he thought, then was aware of the absurdity.

The gardens were shrouded in darkness, and Michael drew the curtains, returned to the big table, and continued working. The thesis, which was intelligently and interestingly written, began by describing how in 1899 a community of nuns in Liège had conceived the idea of marking the new century by forming a Choir within their school, and how they had named it for Giovanni Palestrina, the sixteenth-century Italian composer of sacred music.

'It was to be an integral part of the Convent's life,' wrote the unknown essayist. 'The sisters of Sacré-Coeur had the praise-worthy aim of entering the twentieth century on a strong wave of prayer and goodness, and they saw their long-held tradition of music as a way to do this. This may perhaps be described as idealistic, but it is a good precept in any age.'

Having struck this optimistic note, he – or it might be a she – then turned to the effect the Great War had had on the Choir and its environs.

'Accounts of 1914 – that troubled, tragic year for Belgium – are fragmentary and not all of them can be relied on. It was an emotional time for the Belgians, but it seems certain that the Convent of Sacré-Coeur, the home of the Palestrina Choir, was badly damaged and some of the nuns were killed in the initial invasion.'

It did not sound as if the writer had read Iskander's journal, after all. That could mean he or she had found other source material. Michael read on, hoping this would be the case.

'I was fortunate in finding a letter sent to a Sister Clothilde, the Mother Superior of the Sacré-Coeur Convent,' the writer explained. 'It was apparently written a short time after the initial invasion of Liège. By then France had been crushed by the Kaiser's armies and Belgium was occupied, which makes it remarkable that the letter reached its destination.'

Here he conscientiously added a footnote: 'This letter, along with other interesting and informative papers, is in a small museum in Liège itself (one of the city's many museums), and is part of the annals of the city's tribulations which have been preserved. The text of the letter may have lost a little in my translation, but I hope I have captured the spirit.' The letter followed:

My very dear Sister in Christ,

Permit me to send you my love and prayers in your time of sorrow and loss – but also to express my heartfelt gratitude to *le bon Dieu* for your safe deliverance. We, in the Paris House, were shocked and saddened to learn of the violent deaths of two of your novices at the hands of the Kaiser's armies, and have offered up Masses for them. Father Albert has tentatively suggested we should also offer prayers that the soldiers responsible will feel proper contrition for their actions, but most of us feel this is taking charity a little too far, although we are praying that God will help the Kaiser see the error of his ways. This, however, seems unlikely at the present, for he is a bellicose man, although I dare say many of his weaknesses can be ascribed to his withered arm.

We were horrified, also, to hear of your enforced siege – that you were actually forced to barricade yourselves in the crypt – but we are heartened to know of your courage and resourcefulness. It is certainly a pity you were unable to move the stone sarcophagus containing the Founder's body to use as a barricade (remembering our redoubtable Founder, she would have repelled all enemies purely with one of her glacial stares), but the blanket chests and oak coffers with Mass vessels seem to have served the purpose well enough and kept the enemy from the gates. It is a pity the young girls of the Choir were forced to listen to the curses and blasphemies of the soldiers as they tried to break through, but no doubt their innocence will protect them from the worst of the profanity, and presumably it would have been in the German language anyway.

God is good in that He had guided you to stock your

larders so well – also that you were able to make that frantic journey through the convent to snatch up all the food you could carry from the larders before taking refuge underground. You have my sympathies in the privations you endured during those days. Living off oaten cakes and lentils for so long is not something one would wish to do, even in Lent. But your sojourn in that particular Wilderness will have strengthened you all spiritually (even if it wrought havoc digestively). As to the sanitary arrangements you made, I shall preserve a mannerly reticence, and only say that Sister Jeanne seems to have created a most ingenious solution. I am sure your gardens will eventually profit.

We were all very interested in the unknown young man who managed to thwart the soldiers and give you opportunity to flee the chapel. I hope that when this terrible time ends – as it must do some day – you will be able to have the statue of the Sacred Heart repaired. The stonemasons' art is a noble one, although it is a pity that the nose and left foot of the Figure were ground into splinters. But I dare say they can be remodelled, and Jesus is still Jesus, even *sans* nose and several toes.

I regard that unknown young man in the guise of a messenger – a latter-day St George, overthrowing the enemy and preserving the innocence of the maidens. I would be inclined to ascribe the arrival of the small detachment from the Belgian Army at Sacré-Coeur as entirely due to that young man's endeavours as well. Clearly, he was resourceful as well as brave.

We read recently that the Prussian commander, Colonel von Bülow, was shocked and surprised by the degree of Belgian resistance, and that the siege at Liège took over a week – time he had not taken into account. This, I feel, illustrates that pride goeth before destruction, and an haughty spirit before a fall, although I suppose I must do penance for entertaining such an uncharitable thought. At least the delay allowed the British forces to lend their fighting strength to the conflict. We wept for the fall of Antwerp, though, and for the poor people forced to flee their homes.

I shall do my best to trace for you the poor young thing,

Leonora Gilmore, who was swept along by your unknown
saviour in the chapel and seems to have vanished with him.
May God grant that she was not destined to meet a worse
fate in the stranger's company, that he continued his mission
as protector of the innocent and had sufficient conscience
and honour to deliver her into safe hands.

However, I fear that with your country and mine in such
turmoil it will be very difficult for me to find out what
happened to Leonora. She sounds an unusual and intelligent
girl – it is rare for one of your Chorists to display interest
in world affairs, but I think you were right to permit her to
read newspaper accounts of what was happening in the
world.

It is too easy, in our enclosed lives, to also enclose our
minds and be unaware of the events beyond our walls. I
was slightly shocked, though, at the story of how Sister
Jeanne found copies of those two books in Leonora's locker,
and actually caught her reading one of them under the bed
sheets by candlelight after the Great Silence. It is understandable that with an English father Leonora would be
interested in the books of English writers, but I believe Mr
Somerset Maugham's private life is extremely dubious, and
that of M'sieur D.H. Lawrence is little better.

However, if I can obtain news of Leonora I will assuredly
write to you at once.

In the meantime, I hold you and your Sisters in my
prayers.

Your loving sister in Christ,
Sr Dominique
Order of the Sacred Heart

Michael sat back, his mind filled with the images Sister
Dominique's lively letter had summoned.

It was good to hear that the sisters of Sacré-Coeur had with-
stood the invasion – that they had hidden out in the crypt, eating
lentils and waiting for deliverance – which had either come
because Iskander had sent it, or because the Belgian armies had
been resisting the Germans and had come to the convent. He
reread the paragraph in which the trustful Dominique had

expressed concern over Leonora's innocence, and thought she
probably need not have worried, because deflowering virginal
seventeen-year-olds was unlikely to have been in Iskander's code.
Rogue and burglar he might have been, but Michael thought he
had possessed the principles of a gentleman.

There were no further notes after the letter, but there was,
rather unexpectedly, a further letter from the ubiquitous Chuffy,
giving details of a niece's christening at which he had stood
godfather – 'The little sprog yelled her head off, and the
godmother got potted on gin afterwards and had to be decanted
into a taxi' – and went on to express a hope of seeing Boots
at Christmas, because somebody called Bingo was giving a
party at the Club which it would be a crying shame for Boots
to miss.

Michael could not see why this should have been filed with
the Palestrina Choir history, and was just deciding it had been
shuffled together with the notes by mistake, when he turned to
page two of Chuffy's letter, in which Chuffy observed that if
Boots could not come up to Town for Bingo's festive bash, he,
Chuffy, would have to come along to what he called Boots's
draughty barracks and rout him out. Chuffy wrote:

> I always felt inheriting that old place out of the blue affected
> you. Extraordinary how a thing like that can change a chap,
> although it's a change I wouldn't mind having in my life,
> not that it's very likely, because nobody in my family has
> a brass farthing, and I'd hate to see the guv'nor hand in his
> dinner pail anyway.
>
> It's nothing to do with me, but I don't think it's good
> for you to be forever worrying about the house and whether
> it's secure after dark, or frowsting over that stuff you're
> writing. I do understand you want to find out the truth about
> Stephen, well, I dare say a good many of us would like to
> know the truth about Stephen, but all work and no play, old
> man . . . Poor old Stephen is certainly dead, in fact he's
> officially dead – I remember you coming up to Town for
> some Court thingummy that pronounced him dead. Seven
> years without anyone hearing from him or something, wasn't
> it? I recall I thought the length of time sounded frightfully

Biblical – all those plagues and famines and whatnot. But I do know that the wigged gentlemen in Lincolns Inn pronounced Stephen dead and handed you the ownership of Fosse House.

Next time you come up to Town I'll introduce you to one or two corking girls – it'd do you a power of good to paint the town red, or at least give it a few pink splodges.

Michael laid down the letter thoughtfully. It sounded as if it was the unknown 'Boots' who had been writing the history of the Palestrina Choir. He examined this deduction from several aspects and thought it stood up to scrutiny.

Stephen Gilmore had been pronounced as dead by the courts. Assuming the courts had dated his disappearance from the end of the Great War, that seemed to place Boots's inheritance of Fosse House as 1925 at the absolute earliest.

The clock, which had been ticking quietly away to itself, suddenly chimed the half hour, making Michael jump. Six thirty. Assuming dinner would again be at seven, he had just time to see if there was any more information to be gleaned about Boots and his quest.

He had not really expected to find anything, particularly since he had no idea of Boots's real name, but near the bottom of the box was a brittle, faded newspaper cutting with a smudgy photograph of a wedding group. There was no date but Michael thought the clothes looked right for around 1930.

The cutting seemed to be from a local paper, and it informed its readers of a wedding that had been celebrated in the Church of St Augustine.

The groom was Mr Booth Gilmore, and readers will remember that Mr Gilmore inherited Fosse House some five years ago after a presumption of death was declared on his second cousin, Mr Stephen Gilmore. Mr Booth Gilmore has since lived quietly at the house, pursuing various academic interests.

The bride was Miss Margaret Chiffley, the cousin of an old school-friend of Mr Gilmore – see p.4 for full details of Miss Chiffley's gown and the gowns of the bridesmaids.

A wedding breakfast was held after the ceremony at Fosse House.

This newspaper offers its congratulations to Mr Gilmore and his new wife.

So, thought Michael, 'Boots' was Booth Gilmore, and Chuffy finally succeeded in dragging his old school-friend from his ivory tower for long enough to meet and marry a suitable lady – whom Chuffy, obliging as ever, had even provided, from his own family. Chuffy was the sobriquet for Chiffley, of course. He smiled because it was a typical fashioning of a schoolboy nickname for that era. It was an unusual surname as well; it might even be possible to trace Chuffy or his descendants.

It was a shame that the faces in the newspaper photograph were too blurred to make out any details, and even more of a shame that the paper had not listed the names of everyone. He would have liked to identify Chuffy in particular. But everyone seemed to be smiling, and Michael found himself hoping Booth and his lady had been happy.

It seemed that on one level, at least, they had. Just beneath the wedding notice was a smaller clipping that announced the birth of a daughter in 1936: 'To Booth and Margaret Gilmore (née Chiffley), a daughter, Luisa Margaret. Thanks to all concerned.'

Michael was not really surprised. The dates had already been looking about right for Booth to be Luisa's father.

Luisa had referred to her parents being away, saying she had been on her own a good deal. Presumably Booth – perhaps with his wife – had travelled outside England in his search for the truth about his mysterious cousin, Stephen, leaving his small daughter in the care of a nursemaid or nanny. He certainly seemed to have visited Liège. Did that mean he had found a link between Stephen and the Palestrina Choir, or had it simply been Leonora who had interested him because of the family connection?

Michael was just deciding he would have to postpone further searches until after dinner, when he heard Luisa tapping her way across the hall, and then the sound of a door being unlocked. Did that mean she was going down to the underground room? To pray? To write in the leather-bound book again? But again the question formed as to why she should go down there to do either of those things. Because she's mad, said his mind in instant response. She might only be mad nor' nor' west, like Hamlet, but if the compass has swung round to the nor'nor' west point tonight . . .

He was just managing to convince himself that he could ignore the sounds and that Luisa would emerge in time for dinner, perfectly normal and lucid, when there was a muffled cry and a series of slithering bumps. She's fallen, thought Michael, horrified – she's tripped on those wretched stone steps and fallen down them.

He ran out to the hall and across to the door set in the panelling. It was closed, but of course Luisa would have closed it after her. For a moment Michael thought she had locked it as well, and that he would have to break it down, but when he tried the small catch, the door swung smoothly inwards. He took a deep breath and stepped through.

TWELVE

The curve of the steps hid the underground room from view, and a faint, flickering light came from below, as if the oil lamp or the candles had been lit. From the top of the steps Michael could not see Luisa, and he hesitated, still concerned, but not wanting to intrude. He had better make sure she was all right, though.

Had it only been twenty-four hours since he had stolen down these steps? In the flickering light his shadow fell blackly and eerily on the stone walls, and Michael glanced at it uneasily. Were there two shapes on the wall, as if two separate people were tiptoeing stealthily down the steps, the second one just behind him . . .? He whipped round and for a fleeting moment had the impression of someone pressing back in the dark corners.

'Stephen?' said Michael, very softly, and it seemed as if the darkness picked up the word and spun it into soft echoes.

Stephen, Stephen, STEPHEN. . . .

Then, incredibly, like dead breath struggling to form sounds, a faint response seemed to form within the echoes.

'Here I am . . . You let me in, remember . . .? I can never get in by myself – I can never open a door or a window . . . But I was the shadow you saw inside the rain, and I was the one who printed the footmarks on the floor . . .'

Michael pushed the whispers away and went down the remaining steps. There was the altar-like table he remembered and the candles. They were unlit, but the oil lamp was glowing in its corner. There was the small desk with the book and pen. Then he saw that the chair by the desk had overturned, and that Luisa was lying near it in an untidy huddle on the ground. Michael went over to kneel by her. She was not moving and her eyes were closed. Was she dead? In films and books people always seemed to know straightaway if a person was dead, even without medical knowledge. But then he saw with relief that Luisa was breathing, although she was certainly unconscious.

There was a bluish tinge to her lips – did that mean heart? Michael was not very used to dealing with illness, but there were certain basic things you did when someone collapsed. The first was to summon help, the second was to keep the person warm. He sped back up to the stairs, snatched up the phone in the hall, which was quicker than rummaging for his mobile, and dialled 999. It was a massive relief to hear a calm, clearly knowledgeable voice taking the details, and saying paramedics would be there as quickly as possible, and please to wait with the patient.

'There's a tree down in the road,' said Michael. 'Will the ambulance be able to get round it?'

The reassuring voice said he need not worry; the paramedics would come on motorbikes, and if hospitalization was needed, there were various services that could be called on. 'We're used to remote houses in this part of the world,' she said, and Michael thanked her, explained that the lady who had collapsed was in an underground room, and that he would remain down there with her until help arrived.

'Don't move her. Put a blanket over her, and see if you can call her out of unconsciousness. Try to get her to stay awake.'

'I'll try.'

'And don't leave her on her own.'

'No, of course not. Tell the medics I'll unbolt the front door so they can get in. They'll get to the underground room from the hall. There's a door in the panelling – I'll prop it open.'

'They'll call out anyway, and they'll go over the house if you don't hear them,' she said. 'Shall I stay on the line with you until they come?'

'I'm not on a cordless phone,' said Michael, who was conscious of inadequacy and would have been grateful for the friendly efficiency.

'Well, ring us back if you need to.'

'Thank you very much,' he said, and this time ran upstairs to get blankets from the nearest bed, which happened to be his own.

He had been willing Luisa to have regained consciousness when he got back; to be sitting up, the terrifying bluish tinge gone, saying she had stumbled and fallen, briefly knocking herself out. But she was lying exactly as Michael had found her. He spread the blankets over her and sat down on the floor, reaching for her hand.

Call her out of unconsciousness, the emergency service had said, and the inevitable comparison rose up – that of the cataleptic Madeline Usher, about to be entombed alive, but her mind awake and silently pleading for someone to call her out of her dreadful paralysis.

To dispel this grisly image, Michael said, 'Miss Gilmore? Luisa? Can you hear me? Try to stay awake – you've fallen, but you're all right, and the ambulance is on the way.'

Did a faint flicker of awareness cross her face? Michael could not be sure, but he thought there was a belief that hearing could remain when other senses were dormant, so he said, 'I'll stay with you, but if you can open your eyes—' Still nothing. 'Or if you can hear me, squeeze my hand.' Was there the faintest tremor of movement from the thin fingers?

He leaned back slightly, looking around the room. The stone floor and walls gave it the feel of a dungeon, but the presence of the prie-dieu and the altar-table with the crucifix, together with the desk, made it more the retreat of some religious scholar. He was just wondering if he could reach one of the candles and manage to light it, when he felt Luisa's fingers curl round his. He looked back at her at once. Her eyes were open and she was looking at him.

'You're quite all right,' said Michael very clearly. 'But I've phoned for an ambulance, and it's on the way. Are you in any pain anywhere?'

Her free hand came up to tap the left side of her chest significantly.

'Heart?' said Michael. 'Angina?' There was a faint nod, and remembering that one or two of the older dons at Oriel had angina, he said, 'Do you have a spray? Tell me where it is and I'll get it.'

'No use.' The words came on a ragged breath of sound.

'But—'

Her hand clutched his, and Michael took it in both of his hands, trying to infuse it with warmth.

Luisa said, 'Stephen—' Her eyes looked beyond Michael to

the corners of the room and distended with fear. Involuntarily, Michael looked over his shoulder, but nothing stirred.

'There's no one here,' he said. 'Stephen isn't here. You're quite safe.' Her eyelids fluttered, and Michael said urgently, 'Luisa, stay awake. You must stay awake. The ambulance won't be long.' Oh God, let that be true, he thought, and as if on cue, he heard sounds above – a door being opened, loud footsteps, and a man's voice calling that he was the paramedic and asking where they were.

'Down here,' called Michael, releasing Luisa's hand and going halfway up the stairs.

'Good God, what on earth is this place?' said the paramedic, coming down the stairs, his green emergency bag banging against the wall. But he was already kneeling down, his hands moving with professional assurance over Luisa, then opening the bag to take out stethoscope and pieces of equipment that Michael thought were heart monitors.

'Miss Gilmore – can you hear me? Are you in any pain?'

'She indicated her heart,' said Michael. 'When I said was it angina, she said yes.'

'Does she have a spray?'

'I asked her that, but she said it was no use and I couldn't get her to say where it was. I don't even know where her bedroom is and I didn't want to leave her to search for it – And you were on the way—' Damn, he thought, I'm sounding indecisive and altogether useless.

But the paramedic merely said, 'You made the right decision. Miss Gilmore, I'm going to make a few quick checks.' There was a brief interval of beeping machines and some sort of computer result. 'Ah,' he said. 'It looks like an MI, I'm afraid. Myocardial infarct – heart attack in plain terms. Impossible to know if she had the attack then fell, or if the fall brought it on. But we'll worry about any other injuries when we get her into hospital.' He produced a syringe and rolled back Luisa's sleeve. 'This is what they call a clot-buster,' he said. 'We have to be careful about giving this to anyone who's had one previously, but I think it's all right – I'd remember if we'd been called out to her in the last year, and I'm fairly sure we haven't.'

'One of the advantages of a small community,' said Michael.

'It is. I'll give her nitroglycerine as well, then we'll get her to the cardiac unit.'

'How?' said Michael, in dismay as the man opened his bag again and took out a phial and a fresh syringe. 'The fallen tree—'

'They'll airlift her,' said the man, administering the injection. He reached for his phone and tapped out a number. 'We often have to do it out here.' He spoke into the phone, then nodded, apparently satisfied. 'Ten to fifteen minutes before they reach us,' he said. 'It's a good service, and the helicopter can land in the field just beyond the main walls I should think. In the meantime, if you'll help me to carry her up the stairs, we can be ready in the hall.'

A thin spiteful rain was beating against the windows when they got Luisa into the hall, and when Michael opened the main front door the helicopter was already approaching, its propeller sounding like massive leathery wings beating on the night sky. The lights sliced through the dusk like pale, glaring eyes, and the scene began to take on a surreal quality.

The air ambulance men brought a stretcher, and between them they put Luisa on to it and fastened straps around her. Michael had located her bedroom by this time and had put washing things, together with hairbrush and comb, in a sponge bag. The bedside cabinet had two or three medicine bottles and a small spray of pink liquid. He tipped these in as well so the hospital would know what pills she was taking, then wrapped everything in a dressing gown.

Luisa was still semi-conscious, but Michael leaned over, explaining what was happening, hoping she could hear and understand. He thought she roused sufficiently to look towards the panelled door, and he said, very quietly so the paramedic would not hear, 'I'll lock that up for you. Don't worry.'

'Key—' One hand went to the pocket of her woollen jacket.

'I'll look after the key until you come back,' he said. 'Is that right? Is that what you want me to do?'

When she nodded, he took the key from her pocket, and she gave a grateful half-smile, then in a suddenly urgent voice, said again, 'Stephen—'

'Stephen won't hurt me,' he said, taking her hands. 'It's all right. I know about him, remember? I can deal with Stephen. You can trust me.'

'I know I can,' she said. 'I've written it all down. It's in my book.'

'The book in the underground room?'

'Yes.' She seemed grateful for his comprehension and unquestioning of how he knew what she referred to. 'Michael, you need to know – to understand . . . I want you to be the one who knows the truth.' Her hands closed tightly around his, and a spasm of pain crossed her face.

Speaking carefully, hoping she could still hear and understand him, Michael said, 'If it seems necessary, I can look at what you wrote in your book? Your journal? Is that what you mean?'

'Yes,' she said. 'You can read it— I trust you . . . I didn't think there would ever be anyone, not till you came here—'

'You *can* trust me,' he said as she broke off again. 'I promise I'll do whatever's necessary.' This seemed to satisfy her. She gave the half-nod again and sank back against the blankets.

When she had been carefully stowed on to the helicopter, Michael turned to the paramedic who was preparing to set off on his motorbike.

'Is there any news of whether the road's cleared yet? I was hoping I could go with her to hospital, but—'

'I should think it'll be tomorrow before they get the tree off the road,' he said. 'The storm brought a couple more down, but they're on the main roads, so they have priority. You'll be all right here, won't you?' He glanced at the house. 'Odd old place, isn't it?'

You don't know the half, thought Michael, but he said, 'It is, rather. But it has an interesting history. Thanks so much for all you've done this evening.'

'All in a day's work,' said the paramedic, smiling. 'I'll give you the number of the hospital where they'll take her.' He handed over a small card. 'You could phone in a couple of hours to find out what's happening. They'll be wanting next of kin details and so on.'

'I don't know who her next of kin is,' said Michael. 'But I'll phone anyway.'

'You'd better have the number of the local police station as well, while I'm about it. They'd know the situation about the tree.' He scribbled a number on the back of the card.

Michael waited until the helicopter had taken off and watched it wheel itself around and head off. The motorbike growled its way down the drive and turned on to the main road. He stood in the doorway for a moment, then took a deep breath and went back into the house, locking and bolting the main door. Then, in accordance with his promise to Luisa, he locked the panelled door and put the key in his pocket again. But, crossing the hall, he was conscious of Fosse House's silence – haunted and watchful – pressing in on him.

'*You let me in,*' Stephen had said.

Michael frowned and went systematically through the ground floor rooms, switching on lights. He located a radio and a television in a small sitting room on the side of the house and switched the radio on. With lights and music one could surely drive back any amount of ghosts. Feeling slightly better, he searched the kitchen for an evening meal, hoping Luisa would recover sufficiently for him to apologize for raiding her fridge. He had a sudden wild image of himself taking her out to lunch as a thank you. The prospect of sitting opposite Morticia Addams in a local pub restaurant and hearing a waitress reel off the day's specials pleased him immensely. Dammit, thought Michael, taking eggs and cheese from the fridge, I'll do it. Get better quickly, Luisa, because we've got a date.

He managed a reasonable plate of scrambled eggs with grated cheese, which he carried into the TV room, where he watched the evening news. This had the effect of making him feel slightly more in touch with normality, even though normality took the form of soaring inflation, wars in various countries, and battling politicians.

But after he had washed up, even with lights switched on, and Classic FM playing a lively Mozart concertante, Fosse House seemed to be filling up with soft rustlings and whisperings.

'*I'm still in the house . . .*'

I don't care if you're swinging from the light fittings, said Michael to Stephen's image, and went into the library and phoned the hospital to find out how Luisa was.

'We can't really give out information other than to family—Oh, you're the gentleman who called the paramedics, yes, I see.

Well, I'm afraid she's still rather poorly. Can you give me any details about next of kin?'

'I'm afraid not. I don't even know if there is any family,' said Michael. 'I think you'd better use this number as a contact for the moment.' He gave Fosse House's number, then his own mobile.

'We'll let you know if there's any change in her condition, but if you do trace any family for her, give us a call.'

It was still only a little after nine o'clock, and the evening stretched rather emptily ahead. Michael phoned Nell, explaining what had happened.

'Poor Luisa,' said Nell. 'I hope she makes it – I rather liked the sound of her.'

'A bit eccentric in certain areas,' said Michael, who somehow did not want to say – even to Nell – that Luisa had seemed more than eccentric earlier in the day.

'Will you be able to track down her family?'

'I don't know. I've got the run of the library, but I don't think I can start looking through her private papers.' Except the journal, said his mind. She wanted me to read that. 'I'm hoping it won't be necessary to rifle through her things,' he said to Nell.

'She sounds like a survivor,' said Nell. 'And you might find an address book somewhere un-private – by a phone, for instance But listen, just to put you back on track, I've been finding out a few things about Holzminden – about the prisoner-of-war camp, I mean. Godfrey at the bookshop in Quire Court – you've met him, haven't you? – produced a couple of very useful tomes. One has excerpts from letters written in 1917 by an attendant who was a guard there. Even allowing for the German to English translation, they paint quite a vivid picture of the place. I'm trying to track down the rest of the letters – apparently they were privately printed.'

Michael smiled at the enthusiasm in her voice, asked after Beth, and was pleased to hear Beth was having a good time with Aunt Emily in Aberdeen.

'I'm going to the Bodleian tomorrow to look for the letters,' said Nell. 'I've asked Owen to hold my hand and guide me through the hallowed portals. Also the Radcliffe, if necessary. I'd rather have your hand to hold, but I'd like to find the letters as soon as possible, so Owen's a good substitute. And—'

'And you've long suspected you'd never be in any danger by holding Owen's hand anyway.'

'Well, as a matter of fact I did suspect that,' said Nell. 'Ah, yes, I see. Dear Owen. But you'll be back soon, won't you?'

'I'm setting off for Oxford tomorrow.'

'Will you be able to? What if they haven't cleared the tree by then?'

'If I have to pass earth's central line— If I have to cross the foaming flood, frozen by distance, I will be with you in Quire Court when night falls on the world.'

'You do get carried away,' she said, laughing.

'The poets always say these romantic things better than I ever could.'

'Don't denigrate yourself. You're the last of the real romantics as far as I'm concerned. Ring again if you want to. I wouldn't mind if it was three in the morning when you rang.'

The house felt immeasurably safer and saner after talking to Nell, but by ten o'clock Michael gave up the struggle to work. He took the key of the underground room from his pocket and looked at it for a long time.

The prospect of going down to that room again was daunting, but Michael knew he would have to do it. *I want you to be the one who knows the truth* . . . He could dash across the room, snatch up the book, and be back up here within five minutes – ten at the most.

Before he could change his mind he went into the kitchen to find an electric torch and matches. As an afterthought, he collected his mobile phone from his room and, thus suitably armed, unlocked the door in the panelling. It opened easily, and as it swung inwards, a faint drift of still-warm oil or paraffin came up, with, beneath it, something old and sad. Michael took a deep breath, switched on the torch, and went warily down the stone steps.

The room looked exactly as he had left it. He righted the fallen chair, then shone the torch around. It was not so bad, after all. It was not somewhere he would choose to work, but Luisa had lived here all her life, and perhaps she had not minded the lingering ghosts.

He picked up the thick, leather-bound book and jammed it

into his pocket. If nothing else, it might contain names or phone numbers that would be useful to the hospital. Before he went back upstairs, he shone the torch on the oak chest in its corner. In the sharp torchlight, the scratches around the lock were more noticeable. From one angle they almost seemed to form the pattern of a snarling angry face – the kind of twisted, scowling, incredibly *old* face depicted as guardians of ancient tombs or long-buried malevolent secrets. Whatever it is, it's nothing to do with me, thought Michael, but his feet had already taken him across the stones and he was bending down to pull the velvet aside almost before he realized it. There were several deep scratches on the edges of the domed lid as well. Madeline Usher, entombed alive, after all? Struggling to rend her coffin open, clawing at the lid . . .? 'Oh, for pity's sake,' said Michael impatiently out loud, 'someone lost the key, and the lid had to be levered off, that's all.' But the memory of Stephen Gilmore's hands, raw and torn, flickered in his mind.

A good many of us would like to know the truth about Stephen, Chuffy had written. And Stephen had been pronounced dead after seven years. That means they never found a body, thought Michael, still staring at the chest.

It was nonsense, of course. The chest, if he bothered to force it open, would turn out to contain nothing more sinister than old photos or old newspaper cuttings. But why would Luisa keep them down here, inside an oak chest, bound with a thick chain and padlock? Why would anyone?

The padlock looked fairly secure, but Michael grasped it to make sure. As he did so, something seemed to wrench at the shadows, as if tearing them aside, preparatory to stepping through them. Michael recoiled, his heart punching against his ribs. Hands, dreadful wounded hands, the nails splintered, the flesh raw, reached out from the darkness behind the chest, and he gasped and fell back on the stone floor, dropping the torch. It rolled into a corner, shattering the bulb, and darkness, thick and stifling, closed down.

Michael got to his feet, frantically trying to get his bearings. Was Stephen still here? He groped blindly for the walls, willing the stairs to be within reach. He was just starting to make out vague shapes in the darkness and realizing that he had been going towards the desk instead of the stairs, when cold, dead fingers reached out and tried to curl round his hand.

Michael's nerve snapped, and he jerked back and scrambled across the room. By now he could make out the shape of the steps, and he was able to find his way up to the hall. He slammed the panelled door and leaned back against it, regaining his breath. Then he locked it, although his hands were shaking so badly he had to make two attempts, and at one level of his mind he was aware of the absurdity of trying to lock up a ghost. But he did it anyway, then he retreated to the library and slammed that door as well.

What now? The prospect of remaining in the house all night filled him with dismay. Mightn't it be better to leave at once and hope he could get to the village – or any village – with a pub and a spare room? He reached for the phone on the desk, found the card the helpful paramedic had provided, and dialled the local police number.

'I'm very sorry, sir,' said the voice at the other end, 'but we haven't shifted that tree at Fosse House yet. We've been too busy clearing the main road – it's been a wild old storm. We should get it done first light tomorrow, though. If I were you, I'd stay put.'

'How far along the road is the tree? From Fosse House, I mean?'

'Smack across the road about ten yards from the gate,' said the voice, lugubriously. 'Blocking the road altogether.'

'And how far is the village from the house? If I tried walking?'

'Oh, you can't do that,' said the man at once. 'It's a good ten miles, and in this weather— Well, you'd be drenched to the skin inside of ten minutes, and likely suffer pneumonia. You stay put is my advice, sir. The men'll be out there in the morning. But call us back if there are any problems. We'd get out to you if so. Motorbikes, you know. They can get round the tree all right.' Michael briefly considered asking if he could be provided with a pillion ride to the village, but decided against it. He thanked the man and rang off, wondering if he could risk trying to reach the village on foot. But it would mean walking along the dark lonely drive, and then along the equally dark, lonely road beyond it. All ten miles of it.

Leaving Fosse House did not seem to be an option, so Michael stopped thinking about it and instead contemplated the best way to pass the night. Should he seal himself in the library with crucifixes and garlic wreaths and all the panoply of the ghost-repellants of fiction, and wait for dawn which traditionally sent spirits fleeing? He had told Luisa that Stephen would not harm him, and he still believed that. But then he remembered again those dreadful hands reaching out of the shadows, and he no longer felt as sure.

It was at this point in his thoughts that the phone rang, and Michael, his nerves still on edge, jumped all over again. He reached for it, hoping it might be the police station calling back to say the road was unexpectedly clear after all.

But it was not. It was the hospital to which Luisa Gilmore had been taken. The ward sister he had spoken to earlier said she was extremely sorry to be giving him this bad news, but Miss Gilmore had died half an hour ago.

'I'm afraid the damage to her heart was too severe. She had a second heart attack shortly after she got here. We tried all the usual methods to revive her, but we weren't able to.'

Michael had not expected to feel such an acute sense of loss. After a moment he said, 'That's so sad. I'm very sorry indeed. I didn't know her very well, but—'

'An unusual lady,' said the sister.

'Yes.'

'We have to focus on practicalities, I'm afraid,' she said. 'We really do need to find next of kin or someone who has authority to – well, to act for her. To make arrangements.'

'I'll see if I can find an address book,' said Michael. 'Failing that, there must be someone local who will know.'

'If you could ring us back as soon as possible,' she said.

'Yes, of course.'

At first Michael thought he would phone Nell, and then he saw it was approaching midnight, and she would probably be in bed. And despite what she had said, it was a bit late to phone, especially with sad news. He would try to find the information the hospital needed instead. It might even focus his mind and drive back the spooks to make a search for an address book.

An address book . . . Or a diary?

Somewhat reluctantly, he took from his pocket the journal he had picked up in the underground room. Luisa wanted me to read this, he thought. She wanted me to understand, and she said she trusted me. And on a practical level, it might contain addresses or phone numbers of family.

But it still felt like the worst kind of intrusion, and it was some time before he could bring himself to open it. The pages were all handwritten, and as far as he could see the writing was all in the same hand. There did not appear to be any dates, and there certainly did not seem to be any names and addresses. He flattened it out on the desk, directly under the comforting light cast by the lamp.

He had intended to do no more than glance at the first few pages, after which he was going to steel himself to go up to Luisa's bedroom and look for a conventional address book. But the opening sentences of the diary acted like a magnet.

'Today was a good day, because Leonora did not come . . .'

It seemed to be a journal, pure and simple, and it did not look if it was likely to contain what Michael was looking for. Unless you counted Leonora.

He turned a couple more of the pages.

'Today I prayed for over an hour to keep Leonora at bay, but she came to me anyway . . . I wonder how much longer I can fight this . . . She feared the madness, and I fear it too . . .'

Michael paused. Despite Luisa's words, could he really read this? Wasn't it too private?

But she had said she wanted him to know.

THIRTEEN

Today was a good day because Leonora did not come. So this is the day I shall begin a diary, partly because it is 1950, the start of a new decade, but mostly because I feel so much stronger and happier when Leonora is not here.

I shall record everything important that happens, and it will be a place where Leonora cannot come – it will be my world, safe, private, and I will be able to shut her out completely . . . Please, God, let me be able to do that.

I don't know yet what important things I will be writing. I know about diaries, though. My father has printed copies of diaries written by famous people – Samuel Pepys and John Aubrey – men who lived hundreds of years ago, but whose diaries are still read today. So perhaps someone in the future will read this and wonder about me, and think how interesting it is to know about life in the 1940s and 1950s. My diaries might even be displayed in museums, so that scholarly people like father will consult them. Or I might have children some day, and they will read them, although I can't imagine where a husband to provide the children will come from, because I hardly ever go anywhere, except to church on Sundays, and we seldom have visitors in case it disturbs Father's Great Work. Also, Mother says visitors mean a lot of work and she has quite enough to do as it is; a house of this size does not run itself, we should all remember that – I could do more to help, and it would not hurt father to tidy his desk occasionally, either.

Because of Father's Work I must never be noisy or go rampaging about the house. I never do. I don't think I would know how to rampage, even if there were other children to rampage with, which there never have been.

Michael turned the page. Apart from that mention of 1950, Luisa had not dated any of the entries, but she appeared to have started

a fresh page for each new one, and it did not look as if she had
written in it every day. There were large gaps on some of the
pages, and the ink varied in colour and in quality. The writing
varied as well, and so strongly that it almost looked as if another
person had made some of the entries. This was such a worrying
thought, however, that Michael refused to give it attention.

Leonora was here today. I know she is trying to get into
these pages, but I shall not let her, I shall *not* . . . I am
stronger than she is, and as long as I remember that
Leonora is a separate person, she cannot hurt me. It's
important to keep hold of that thought. I have started
saying it to myself each night, after I've said my prayers.
I say, *I am not Leonora, I am not*, over and over again.
I think it is what father calls a Coué exercise of the mind.
He tried to teach me about Émile Coué who believed in
the power of the mind, but Mother said the concept was
beyond someone of my age and Father was wasting his
time – no fourteen-year-old could be expected to recite
mind-exercises.

I would recite the Devil's scriptures every night if I
thought it would keep Leonora away. No, I don't mean that,
of course I don't.

Leonora is trying her tricks to get into this diary, but I have
learned how to cheat her. I know the times of the day when
she tries to force her way into my head and lay her thoughts
and memories over mine, smothering them so I can't get at
them. Early evening is the time she likes best – twilight – or
sometimes the hour just before dawn.

To make sure she does not get into these pages I am
closing them very firmly after each entry and placing a
paperweight on the cover.

This morning my governess asked if I had twisted my ankle,
because she had noticed I seemed slightly lame. I do not
remember twisting it, but we have strapped it up with a
crêpe bandage. It is a nuisance, but I expect it will heal
very soon.

Today, Mother and Father are making preparations for their visit to France and Belgium. It is all part of Father's Great Work, and something they do two or three times a year. I hope that when I'm older I might be allowed to accompany them on their journeys. The prospect is a bit alarming though, because I have hardly been beyond this corner of Norfolk. I don't count the three years when Fosse House was requisitioned for a convalescent home for soldiers wounded in World War II, and Mother and Father decamped to a house in Scotland to live with Mother's cousins. I was only four at the time; we were there for four years and the memories are all bad ones. The younger Scottish cousins bullied me and made apple pie beds and tied my plaits to the bedposts while I was asleep, and there were uncles with loud bluff voices and aunts who sniffed disapprovingly at Mother. I hated them all and I hated living there, so I don't think about it, not ever. I don't even look at the photographs and sketches of Fosse House in those years – the soldiers and the nurses who lived here then – because I can't bear knowing the house had a life of its own while I was away. I think my father hated being away from the house as much as I did; he had locked up his beloved library and left reams of instructions about what could be touched in the house and what could not, and how windows on the ground floor must never be opened after dusk on account of the poisonous night air from the marshes. He took as much of his work as he could to the Scottish house, but it was not the same. He did not like doing the things Mother's family liked doing, which was shooting game and tramping about the hills, and making disparaging remarks about people who read books and foraged into the past.

Mother hated being in Scotland because she did not like her family and because she believed the soldiers would damage Fosse House while we were away. She said it made no difference that they were recovering from battle wounds, you could not trust soldiers, everyone knew that, and it was no use people saying they were mostly officers because officers were often the worst.

While my parents are away my governess lives at Fosse House, and we have lessons, which mostly I like. We study great English writers and poets – later we might read some of the French writers; my governess says my French is coming along very well, and we could try Victor Hugo or possibly the poetry of Louise Colet, although Mme Colet's private life is to be much deplored. I thought, but did not say, that at least the lady had a private life, which is more than I have.

Sometimes we listen to music. We have a gramophone in the drawing room, and I am allowed to buy records with my small allowance and Christmas or birthday money. Father sometimes listens to the records with me – those are the rare occasions when we do something together. Mother often tells us she likes music, but usually she listens to two movements of a symphony, then says she cannot sit here all afternoon doing nothing.

It was Father who told me about Leonora. She was his aunt or great-aunt or third cousin – he is not sure of the exact relationship – and she had been part of a famous choir in Belgium.

'Her name was Leonora,' he said, and with the pronouncing of the name, a curious thing happened to me. I thought: Leonora. *Leonora*. It was as if a connection had been made, as if a door had been opened, and something that had been waiting in Fosse House's darknesses for a very long time was peering out . . . Leonora, who had sung in a choir, and been afraid of something, so dreadfully afraid . . .

On Sundays we go to church and while my parents are away my governess and I take nature walks. This week, though, my foot is still troublesome so we don't walk very far.

It is quite difficult to write my diary while my governess is living in the house.

I have received a postcard from Mother and Father from Belgium. They are staying in a place called Liège. The name touches a chord deep within my mind, and reading the postcard and looking at the picture on the front, I have the feeling that Leonora is watching me.

The postcard shows an old stone building with a small bell tower surmounted by a cross, so it is either a church or perhaps a convent. I stared at it for a very long time, and I have it before me now, propped up on a corner of my dressing table where I am writing this. It's as if I recognize the place – no, it's Leonora who is doing that. How long will I have to fight her before she leaves me alone, I wonder . . .? Sometimes I hate my father for telling me about her.

The message on the postcard says Mother and Father are having a pleasant time and the weather is good. They hope I am well and ensuring the house is locked up at night.

I have found Liège in my atlas and in the encyclopedia, and it's one of those old towns soaked in the romantic history of so many European places: the small states and dukedoms with princes and margraves and little turreted castles. Reading about it, tracing its boundaries, I keep thinking: yes, I know that – and that. But how do I know? *How?*

If I ask Mother how a particular journey has been, she might say the food had not agreed with her, oily foreign rubbish and she is glad to be home, or remark how tiring it had been walking round museums and libraries and she believes she will not accompany my father next time he goes away. She always says this, but she always does accompany him. I think she does not trust him to find his way home by himself.

Father, asked about a journey, might say he had found a most useful museum in some small town, or been given access to a private library which had yielded some helpful information. But as to the people they meet and the places they see, neither of them ever seems much interested.

Today I think I may actually have seen Leonora – at least, someone I take to be Leonora. She is small and fragile-looking, and she has large dark eyes that she fixes on me as if she wants to suck out my thoughts and my memories. She is very pale and she has dark hair – too dark to be called brown, but not dark enough to be black.

It was shortly before supper and she was near the walled garden. I saw her from my bedroom window, which overlooks it. She was standing beneath a tree, looking up at me.

Later, I asked my governess if she had seen anyone wandering around, but she had not.

Am I going mad? What does Leonora want?

Does she want to take over my mind . . .?

The writing trailed off, the ink leaving splodges and what might be tear stains. Michael turned to the next page and saw, with relief, that the writing returned to its original graceful slant.

Mother and Father returned last night. Mother went straight to bed after the journey so I did not see her until lunch today. She was tired and snappish, picking at her food, and finding fault with everything that had been done in the house during her absence.

Father was wrapped in his thoughts, but he went all round the house as usual, making sure nothing had been disturbed or disrupted. This afternoon he showed me a small framed sketch he had found in a museum in a place called Holzminden. He said it was a piece of history from the Great War – a war in which a cousin of his had served and been killed – so he had asked the museum's curator if he could buy the sketch. The curator had been more than happy to sell it – he had said he believed it was one of a series of sketches. He had not known what had happened to the others – probably, they had long since been destroyed. Herr Gilmore should remember that that war – the Great War, as some called it – had been over for more than thirty years, and the recent one was more than six years since. And they were all good friends now, England and Germany and Russia and Italy, *waren sie nicht*?

Father appeared to think the curator was viewing matters through rose-tinted spectacles, but the sale had been agreed very amicably, and the sketch carefully wrapped up by the curator's assistant. Father said he was going to hang it on the main staircase of Fosse House as a little memorial to his dead cousin, and what did I think?

What I thought was that the prospect of having to see such a sketch every time I went up or down the stairs was horrifying; I did not think I had ever seen anything so disturbing in my entire life. The sketch was of a long, bleak room, with narrow beds and wooden lockers, and men in uniform sitting or lying around. The windows were small and somehow mean, and they all had thick bars across them, as if this might be a prison. So from that aspect alone it is a sad picture, somehow filled with despair, even though several of the young men look cheerful. One is sitting apart from them, and there is such hopelessness and fear in the tilt of his head that I wanted to cry for him. But the really bad part – the part I stared at in father's library with such repulsion – is that clustered at one of the barred windows are several more men, all wearing a different kind of uniform, all staring into the room with a dreadful eagerness. There is almost hunger in their eyes as they look at the men in the room. They terrified me the minute I saw them, and I know if I look at the sketch again they will still terrify me.

'What do you think?' said my father again, and I mumbled something about it being very interesting, and asked exactly what it was.

'It's an old prisoner-of-war camp,' he said. 'You see where someone has written *Holzminden* in that corner, and the date? November 1917. There was a camp at Holzminden for captured officers at the end of the Great War – mostly British officers, they were. I believe my cousin Stephen was there – he was captured early in 1917 and held prisoner. So I thought he might be one of the young men in the sketch. That's why I bought it from the museum.' He sort of brooded over it, almost lovingly – if lovingly is a word that can ever be applied to my father.

I said, 'You know a lot about him.' Father did not often talk about his research or his family, so I was careful how I asked because I wanted to hear more and I was afraid of sending him back into his shell.

'Oh yes, I do. He was older than me – I always thought of him as a heroic figure because he went off to the war.

That war wasn't like the one we've just been through, Luisa. It was crueller than you can imagine, and the young men who fought – they had no idea what they were going into. They went off laughing and singing – some of them lied about their ages to get into the army. Brass bands played at the railway stations as their trains went out, and people waved flags and hung out bunting, and cheered and sang patriotic songs. But all the time they were going into a darkness – into mud and blood and terror. So many of them died.'

'Including your cousin?'

'People have laughed at me or belittled me for trying to find out what happened to him,' he said, still staring at the sketch. 'None of them understood. I've always needed to know what happened, ever since I came to this house, because—' His eyes flickered to the window, and he got up to try the latch, as if to make sure it was secure. But even when he sat down again, he lowered his voice as if he feared someone might be standing outside, listening. 'But even after all these years, I still don't know,' he said, and there was such sadness in his voice that I wanted to put my arms round him. I did not though. He would have hated it, and we would both have been embarrassed.

Instead I tried to think of something to say that would make him go on talking, but before I could do so, he said, 'I do know Stephen was sentenced to death in Holzminden, though. I found the execution order in Liège in the museum. That's why I went to Holzminden from Liège. But I couldn't find out if the sentence was actually carried out. I needed to know, you see. You do see that, Luisa?'

'Oh, yes,' I said, not seeing at all. 'Did it say why he was sentenced to death?'

'No. That's one of the things I couldn't find out, and I must find out, Luisa, I must—'

He was staring down at the sketch, passing the palm of his hand over and over its surface, as if he was trying to draw from it the living essence. His eyes had a look I had never seen before – it made me uncomfortable. It was as if the real person – my father, Booth Gilmore – had been squashed into a dark forgotten corner, and something else was looking out from behind his eyes.

Is that how I look when Leonora tries to push me into my own dark corner so she can take over my mind?

Now I am sitting in my bedroom, staring out over the walled garden, and I am thinking that a young man – perhaps one of the very young men in the grisly sketch – perhaps a young man who looked like the early photographs we have in the drawing room of my father – had been imprisoned and sentenced to death. Would they have hanged Stephen, like they hang murderers here? Or shot him because they believed him to be a traitor or a spy? Perhaps he had been a spy. Spies are rather romantic.

I have made up little stories about Father's cousin Stephen, about him spying and being heroic and romantic. It stops me wondering what happened to him, and how he died. It stops me, as well, from remembering the look in Father's eyes as he studied the sketch.

The more I think about Stephen, the more clearly I can see him. I can see him crouching in a small stone room, and I think he is waiting for his execution, because he is dreadfully afraid.

Is this more of the madness? Is it something to do with Leonora? Did she know Stephen? Was she with him when he died? But I am not Leonora, I must cling to that undoubted fact. I am *not Leonora* . . .

But if I were . . . If I were, I could open my mind without being fearful. I would be able to see the images and the memories properly, instead of these maddening glimpses, as if a flickering candle is being held up to fragments of a dim old manuscript . . .

Dare I open my mind? Just once? What would I see and feel? I would like to feel and understand Leonora's emotions – the sheer exuberance and delight and gratitude she would have felt on that extraordinary day when she walked out of the convent with the dark-haired, dark-eyed young man . . .

FOURTEEN

The nuns must have thought it scandalous that Leonora, no more than seventeen, should flee with a complete stranger. But the Kaiser's armies were overrunning the town of Liège, they were actually inside the convent buildings, and Leonora had seen a means of escape – just as, years earlier, she had seen the Convent of Sacré-Coeur itself as an escape from her own chill, unloving home . . .

My parents often abandon me to go in search of my father's obsessive quest. Leonora's abandoned her on the steps of Sacré-Coeur, so we have something in common, she and I. Is that what has forged this curious link between us?

I think her parents' world was a tidy, orderly place, with no place for a daughter who was flawed – who had been born with a deformity of one leg so that she walked awkwardly. Unwanted is probably too strong a word, but Leonora was certainly not the daughter those two people had hoped for.

Sacré-Coeur, so respectable and respected, provided them with an answer to the problem of their imperfect, unmarriageable child. For the first few years, friends and business connections could be told how dearest Leonora was in a convent school, and very happy there. Later they would have adjusted this to how Leonora had been granted a place in the Choir School, and how wonderful that was. The concerts for Church dignitaries – the bishop – a recital in a cathedral with the archbishop present . . . 'We are so proud of her . . .'

They were so proud of their daughter that they did not trouble to attend any of those concerts, so that they might hear for themselves the pure, clear beauty of the Palestrina Choir, or meet the other girls with whom Leonora shared her life and her studies and her music. There were nights when she wept into her pillow over that.

It must have been beautiful, the music of that Choir. I have found references to it in books in Father's study: accounts of its soft, sweet music, even one or two letters which Father must have found, in his quest for his cousin Stephen, and brought back to Fosse House.

I don't know how the nuns of Sacré-Coeur explained away to Leonora's parents the fact that she ran away with a completely unknown man in the middle of an invasion and a siege. I don't think Leonora ever knew that. I don't think she cared, though.

The invasion of the convent is one of the things I can see quite clearly. I can almost smell the fear, and I hear the shots, and my eyes sting from the clouds of plaster dust when the statue of the Sacred Heart was overturned . . .

The entire convent had been at Vespers, wrapped in the music, enrapt in the intricate beauty of the singing. Leonora had been concentrating on the glowing tapestry threads of the *Deus*, careful to come in on the correct bars because Sister Jeanne had arranged a new setting, and once or twice looking forward to supper after the service.

The soldiers' entrance shredded the music into ugly, jagged fragments. Leonora and the other girls in the Choir, not realizing or seeing what was happening, had tried to continue singing, and Sister Jeanne had determinedly begun the *Magnificat*. But the sounds beyond the rood screens were too horrific, and their voices trembled into discord. They exchanged terrified glances, instinctively moving closer to one another for comfort, most of them not understanding what was happening, or why the two nuns were crying out while the men cheered.

When the Sacred Heart statue crashed to the ground, sending great reverberations of sound through the chapel, two of the rood screens fell with it, and the girls pressed back against the stone columns, plaster dust, dry and thick, billowing suffocatingly into their faces. They could see into the chapel now, and even through the clouds of dust and flying debris, they could see the soldiers tramping through the ruins, rifles in their hands, murder in their eyes. They could see two novices lying on the ground, their robes torn away, their hands over their eyes as if in shame, and they could see two of the other nuns lying prone and still, deep, dark wounds in their heads, and blood pooling around them.

Next it will be us . . . The fear crackled through them like a fire.

It was Leonora who seized on the only weapon they knew – an appeasement – an offering to the men. Raggedly, she began to chant the cadences of the *Magnificat* again, picking up the splintered threads of the music, desperately trying to weave them into the familiar patterns, praying to God – to anyone who might be listening – that the others would join in. And that the soldiers would fall back in the face of God's own music.

But although several of the girls joined in, the soldiers did not fall back. It was only when the dark-eyed man bounded through the rubble and barked out commands in bad French to Sister Jeanne to get the girls to safety that the soldiers seemed momentarily disconcerted. There was a confused interval – people scrambling across the fallen masonry, sounds of sobs and fearful cries – angry shouts from the soldiers, and running footsteps. It was only when the dust began to settle that Leonora heard the clanging of the inner door and the turning of the key in its lock, and she realized she was still in the chapel. And that the nuns and the other girls were on the other side of the locked door.

That was when the unknown man reached out his hand and said, in his difficult, heavily-accented French, 'Don't be afraid. I'm here to help. We'll climb through the window.'

She's writing as if she really could see it, thought Michael, coming out of the journal for a moment. How does she know so much? Did she find information about Leonora in this house – some information her father tracked down – and become fixated on it? Is she subconsciously drawing on that, or simply not mentioning it? There was Iskander's journal as well. Luisa could have read that when she was younger. Translating from the French would not have been very difficult for her – she had mentioned learning

French with her governess. Either or both of these explanations would fit.

He had intended to simply glance through the opening pages of the journal to find names or phone numbers for the hospital, and to do no more than skim a few more pages, in deference to Luisa's words. But at some barely-acknowledged level of his mind he had already made the decision to remain in this room and read the whole thing. If nothing else, it might distract him from listening for soft footsteps, or wondering what might lie inside the oak chest. It was a peculiar way of spending the night alone in a haunted house, but it was the precept of whatever gets you through. Wasn't it John Lennon who had said that? Michael was so pleased at remembering this snippet of comparatively modern philosophy that he wrote it down in order to prove to Nell that he did not live half inside the world of the metaphysical and romantic poets.

He glanced around the room, but all seemed quiet, and if Stephen walked the halls of his old home he did so unobtrusively. Michael adjusted the desk lamp and returned to Luisa's diary.

He was an adventurer, of course, that man with whom Leonora ran away. A rogue and a vagabond – a gentleman of fortune . . . Do I say 'gentleman'? But, in a strange way, I think he was a gentleman. He was the one who sought out people in Liège after that brutal attack on the convent. He routed out the townspeople, the young, strong sons who could fight, and he rallied them, ignoring the danger from the other troops of German soldiers already roaming the streets. He was the one who saved the nuns – that must never be forgotten.

So, a thief and a gambler, but always a gentleman.

He was a gentleman when he broke into the wealthy houses on that flight from Liège and took whatever could be taken and sold to fund their journey. He was deft and stealthy and he could enter a house like a shadow and vanish into the night afterwards without the occupants knowing.

'Only take what will not cause hardship or loss,' he said to Leonora. 'These people will not miss that – they will not suffer from the loss of that, or that – oh, or that,

we cannot possibly leave that behind for it is beautiful and
valuable . . .'

Somehow, throughout everything, he managed to send
articles to the newspapers which employed him, travelling
from place to place, as the original invasion developed into
full-blown war. Money was sent to him by incomprehensible
means – banks were sometimes involved. Leonora did not
always entirely understand how this was done; there was
something called wiring of funds, and sometimes there were
bank drafts to be collected from pre-arranged places.

When this money did not arrive as expected, or the
collection place could not be reached, the pieces of jewellery, the silver snuff boxes, the small beautiful ikons, could
be sold to provide sufficient money for travel and food. The
travel was nearly always the best available, and the food
was the finest.

'I do not settle for the inferior when I can have the best,'
he said, with his unfailing air of believing the world was
arranged for his specific enjoyment.

Even that night in the bedroom of a roadside tavern on
the Dutch/German borders, with midnight chimes sounding
romantically, with the owl-light draining the colour from
the trees, and the scent of roses from the gardens . . . Even
then, he was a gentleman . . .

'Leonora, my sweet, innocent girl, we must stop this . . .
I mustn't do this, I must not . . . We may be forced to share
a room because the others were all booked, but I can
quite well sleep in the chair – on the floor . . . I can be
honourable, and I will be. Oh, but if you look at me like
that I don't think I can be honourable for much longer . . .'

French was not his first language and the words were
fragmented, but the emotions, the sheer driving urgency of
passion, were whole and sweet and undeniable.

And here, at that part of Leonora's memories, I am faced
with a blank, brick wall, for whatever those two did that
night – and, I suppose, on subsequent nights – I have not
the knowledge or the experience of the knowledge to interpret it. I cannot enter into their emotions, either physically
or mentally. I know Iskander's emotions got the better of

him, and I know Leonora matched his passion. But that is all I know. Leonora retreats from me at that point. Her wild, dangerous, uncharted flight across war-ravaged Europe with her lover vanishes, and I am left with only my own memories where once I had hers.

I've liked setting down all that about Leonora and Iskander. It makes it all less shadowy – it makes them more real. But they were real, they lived.

Do my parents ever guess that Leonora is inside my mind? How far does it go, this overshadowing? Does she sit at my place in the dining room, and do my parents ever have the impression that it is no longer their daughter but another person who is there?

But I shall not let her take over completely, I shall not . . .

I cannot write more now. Fosse House's darknesses are closing around me . . .

There came another of the breaks, and Michael got up to pour a drink from the decanter on the desk.

Luisa's diary lay on the desk, the lamp casting a pool of soft light over its pages. The room was warm and the house was silent and unthreatening. Michael was even starting to feel a bit sleepy. But he would prefer not to actually fall asleep, and Luisa's diary might help to keep him awake. He had no idea what he would do if he heard footsteps beyond this room, or if the door from the hall was slowly pushed open.

He reached for the diary again, seeing that the next entry was in slightly different ink, and that it appeared to have been made some considerable time after the previous one.

I see I ended my last entry with a reference to Fosse House's darknesses. They were here before I was born, of course, so I grew up with them. I accepted them without thinking about them, as I accepted the other things that made up my life – the draughty rooms of the house, the exercises I was set by my governess, the sewing tasks allotted by Mother, Father's fussiness about keeping doors locked and windows secured after nightfall. The vast wastelands of silence when my mother and father went away.

They returned from Liège and Holzminden two weeks ago, because, so they said, they did not want to miss my fifteenth birthday. We had a small lunch party for the occasion; some of the ladies from church attended, along with the vicar and his family and the curate. The ladies argued about the flower rota at St Augustine's; the vicar and my father discussed Horace throughout all three courses to the exclusion of the rest of the guests, the vicar's wife and two daughters enjoyed their usual Poor-Luisa-no-friends-no-life session, and the curate upset most of a bottle of Father's wine over the tablecloth. Mother says the tablecloth is ruined, even though she soaked it in cold water and salt, damask never washes well, and it is enough to send a person straight into the arms of Rome.

But it was a small, welcome event, even with a little laughter when the vicar emerged from Horace for long enough to make a mild joke, and to wish me many happy returns of the day. Life resumed its ordinary pace after that.

FIFTEEN

It is November – when I look back I think it has always been November in this house, as if it might be trapped inside some kind of grey, hopeless Autumn of its own. And it's evening. The house should be silent at this hour – as much as it ever is silent – but it is not. It is filled with the whisperings and soft footfalls that I have heard ever since I can remember. Mother often complains about them. Bad plumbing, she says. Ill-fitting windows, or the wind blowing through chinks in the roof. An army of carpenters and builders would never cure the problems, and how a person is expected to sleep at nights in such a ramshackle, ill-kept house is beyond her comprehension.

This afternoon, with a dull light creeping across the fens, I was in the little sitting-room, finishing some sewing. Presently, Mother would come in, as she always did at that time of the evening, and say please to tidy away my work and help lay the table for supper. She would wonder whether Father would join us in the dining room, or whether he would want a tray in the library, and grumble yet again about him being eccentric, and say that eccentricity was all very well in its place, but it made a great deal of extra work in a house. Then she would say she should have married her cousin Charles.

I was pretending that just this once she would say something different. 'A young man has called for you, Luisa,' she might say. Or, 'I have invited neighbours for supper tonight, so put on a nice frock and brush your hair.' Deep down I knew it would never happen, but I liked to imagine it.

But when the door opened it was not Mother, it was Father, and he was carrying the sketch he brought from Liège together with a sheaf of papers covered in his handwriting.

'I'm glad you're in here, Luisa,' he said. 'I need your help with a little project.'

This was instantly interesting because Father never asked anyone for help, or, if he did, it was never me.

'It's about my cousin,' he said.

'Stephen? The one in the war camp? In the sketch?'

He was pleased I had remembered. 'Yes,' he said. 'I don't know if he really is in the sketch, but I'd like to think he is.' He sat down, and I saw that he was holding the sketch in the way he had when he first showed it to me – smoothing his hands over and over the glass. Once he lifted it and pressed it against his chest, and once – this was quite disturbing – he raised it and laid his cheek against it.

Then he set it down and said, 'I've had some papers sent to me by the curator of the museum in Liège – the place where I found the sketch. There are a couple of letters written by a German officer. My German isn't as good as it might be, but I did study it briefly, you know, and I think I've got the sense of what the man wrote. And there are several articles written by a Russian journalist – I can't read Russian, but some are written in French and those I can read. I expect I can find a Russian translator for the others. They both knew Stephen – the German, and the Russian journalist. It's a real find, Luisa.'

'What do they say?'

'That Stephen came home. He escaped from the prisoner of war camp at Holzminden and somehow he got back to England. He came here to this house.' He sat back, for once glowing with achievement, waiting for me to say something.

'How did he escape?'

'I don't know, and it doesn't matter,' he said impatiently, and got up and went to the window to try the latch, as if reassuring himself it was fastened. He often did this, but until now I had never seen it as anything other than what Mother called his finickiness.

'Luisa, do you ever hear strange sounds in this house? Footsteps. Soft whisperings and tappings, as if someone is—'

'Trying to get in?' I had never put it into words before – I had never even allowed the thought to form, but now that I said it I knew it was what I had thought for some time.

'Yes,' said my father eagerly. He leaned forward and there was a look in his eyes I had seen occasionally before – a look that always made me feel a bit sick and vaguely frightened. 'And someone really is trying to get in,' he said, in a soft voice. 'Someone comes to those windows almost every night and tries to get in. Asks to be let in . . .'

I stared at him, remembering the soft entreaties I had heard over the years. *'Let me in . . .'* How often had I heard those whispers, and how often had I drawn the curtains tightly, walked to another room, immersed myself in a book with my hands pressed over my ears so I should not hear. I had thought it was part of Leonora – that it was another of her tricks to get into my mind – but since father brought the sketch back, I had begun to think the *let-me-in* whisper was a man's voice. Was that because Stephen really was in the sketch, and bringing it into the house had somehow strengthened his presence here? But this was so horrible an idea that I pushed it away.

Father was watching me. 'You've heard him, haven't you?' he said, and before I could answer he continued. 'But I can see you have. I've heard him as well. Asking to be let in. I've never let him in, though – I've never dared.' His face was white and shrunken, as if the flesh had shrivelled away from the bones, but his eyes blazed with life. 'But now we must do it. Tonight, Luisa, we must let him in.'

'Oh no—'

'I must. I'll never have any peace until I do. Until I find out the truth. The people who come to live here after me – you, Luisa, perhaps your children if you have any – they won't have any peace, either. Stephen won't let them.'

I said, 'But – he isn't real. He died all those years ago. We mightn't know how he died or where or exactly when, but it's so long ago. He's just a – an old memory. Houses have old memories, and that's what Stephen is. That's all he is.' As I said it, I was thinking: please, oh please, say that I'm right.

But he didn't. He said, 'It's sharp of you to say he's a memory. So he is. But you see, Luisa, some memories can be dangerous.'

'How? What could he do?'

'It's not what he could do,' said my father. 'I think he was a gentle soul. Damaged by the war, but essentially gentle. It's what people want to do to him. You remember I told you about him being sentenced to death?'

'Yes.'

'Listen to this from the German letters,' he said, eagerly, and took several sheets of paper from the large envelope. They were covered with his neat, scholarly writing.

'It was written by an officer called Hugbert Edreich,' said Father. 'He seems to have been part of a small secret group of German soldiers who came to England for the express purpose of finding Stephen.'

'And executing him?'

'Oh yes,' said Father, eagerly. 'Yes, they came to do that.'

It's a curious thing about my father – also, to some extent, my mother – that they never seem to realize that some of things they say or do might be hurtful. Leonora's parents had been the same – I knew that. Unable to feel or imagine feelings in others. It simply did not occur to my father that I might find it upsetting to hear that a young man had been hunted down in this very house, so that he could be killed.

'The letter is addressed to Hauptmann Karl Niemeyer,' he said. 'He was the commanding officer of the prisoner of war camp at Holzminden – I've been able to confirm that. I don't know how Edreich got the letter out – or even if Niemeyer ever actually received it. Letters sent to England from the soldiers in France were censored, so that no information could be given away about placements or plans. But I don't think outward letters were quite as strictly censored. It wasn't like the last war, you know. In the Great War, people knew, in a general way, about spies, but there was no thought of the enemy actually coming into the country. There wasn't the same kind of suspicion. I don't know, either, how it ended up in Liège, except that they've gathered a great deal of memorabilia from that war. I'll read what Hugbert Edreich wrote.'

(Later, I found the letter in Father's desk, and I copied it into this diary. I don't know if it will ever be of any use, but it's another small part of Stephen.)

The strangeness in my father's eyes seemed stronger, and I glanced uneasily towards the door, wondering if I should call Mother. But he was already reading aloud, and here, on the next page, is what the letter says.

> *To Hauptmann Niemeyer*
> *Sir,*
> *I write to you at the request of Hauptfeldwebel Barth, to respectfully inform you that our task progresses well. I send this report from a small village very near to the place to which we must travel (which I do not name in case this letter is read by others). We are staying at a small tavern (the Hauptfeldwebel wishes me to assure you that we are mindful of the funds given to us and are not being excessive in our spending).*
>
> *We have been able to talk to local people, although we are careful to preserve our disguises. We are certain that Stephen Gilmore has made his way back to his family house, and is there now.*
>
> *I have suggested that the correct procedure would be to bring Gilmore back to Germany, but Hauptfeldwebel Barth fears he might cheat us again, as he and the Russian journalist, Alexei Iskander, did at Holzminden. Therefore, he intends that the sentence of execution will be carried out here. I am unsure whether this is possible – such a sentence carried out in a country other than the one where it was originally passed could be seen as transgressing the law.*
>
> *However, be assured that I shall obey whatever commands I am given.*
>
> *I send my respectful duty to you,*
> *Hugbert Edreich*

There was a long silence. Then I said, 'They came here, didn't they? They came to kill Stephen.'

'Yes, I believe they did. The death sentence had been passed in Holzminden – I don't know why or what Stephen's crime had been, but I don't think four German soldiers would have risked coming to the country at that time just to recapture an escaped prisoner of war. They came to this house to get him. I think they got into the grounds. I think

Stephen saw them or heard them, and he tried to get back
into the house to escape being captured and being—'

'Executed?'

'Yes. I think he was in the walled garden when they
came, Luisa.'

In the walled garden . . . Then Stephen was the shadow
that occasionally darted across the gardens at twilight . . .
He was inside the smudged twilight images when the trees
seemed to take on the shapes of men . . . And the echoes
trickling through my mind at dusk were his echoes as he
fled from his pursuers. *'Let me in . . .'*

'Did he get back into the house?' I said, and I could hear
how my voice was strained and desperate. 'Did he escape
them?'

'I don't know. What I do know is that there's no record
anywhere of his death. He simply vanished. So, seven
years after that war ended, I had him pronounced as officially dead by the courts. I hated doing that, you know,
but it was necessary if I was to inherit this house. It had
been empty all those years. It was falling into terrible
disrepair.' He glanced towards the window. Someone had
left the wrought-iron gate to the walled garden open,
latched back against the wall. Mother would probably send
me out to close it after supper. She would not go herself,
because she disliked the walled garden, saying it was a
gloomy old place.

Father said, 'If they did execute him, they would have
done so in secrecy. That German, Hugbert Edreich, wrote
in his letter that he wonders if the sentence would have
been legal in this country.'

'It might have been seen as murder?' I said tentatively.

'Yes. I think that's what he meant. He sounds a decent
sort of man, doesn't he?'

'Would they have shot Stephen?'

'I don't know. Shooting was one of the more usual forms
of execution, though. But we could save him, Luisa.' He
came closer to me. 'Think about it. Stephen tried to run
back to this house – he called out as he ran – he called out
to be let in. We've both heard him.'

'There was someone in the house, then? Someone who could have let him in?'

'I don't know that, either. But it's Stephen we hear, Luisa. He's constantly trying to get inside the house—' He broke off, breathing a little too fast, the dreadful mad look glaring from his eyes. I pretended it was only the light from the nearby lamp making him look like that, but I knew it wasn't. 'We could save him,' he said again.

'But he isn't real. How can you save someone from something that happened such a long time ago? Because—' I struggled with a complicated concept, then said, 'Whatever happened all those years ago has happened. You can't change it.'

'Are you sure about that?' he said softly. 'Perhaps you're too young to understand. I forget how young you are. You wouldn't grasp how Time operates. How it can travel forwards as well as backwards. It bleeds, you see, Luisa. If it's damaged, Time bleeds. And sometimes it bleeds forward.'

I don't know if I've written that down correctly, because I don't know if I've remembered it correctly – I certainly don't know if I've understood it.

'How could we save him?' I asked.

My father said, 'Tonight, when he whispers at the window, we're going to let him in.'

That was the point at which I knew he was mad.

Now I'm sitting in the library, with the curtains open to the night garden. I'm listening for the footsteps I have heard so often in this house and for the whispering that can lie on the air like torn fragments of old silk.

I'm not sure where Father is, and I don't know what he intends to do. He was silent throughout supper, but that isn't unusual, and it drew no comment from Mother. My own silence did, though, and Mother subjected me to a series of questions about my health. Some were boring, some were ridiculous, and several were embarrassing. I said I was quite all right, thank you, only perhaps a little tired.

To this, Mother at once said she was tired as well, in fact she believed she had one of her headaches coming

on, not that she expected anyone to understand or sympathize. She would take one of her sleeping tablets and hope
she was granted a reasonable night's sleep for once.

I mumbled something and said I would read in the library
before going up to bed. I had the newest Agatha Christie
mystery. Father's eyes flickered, and the shared knowledge
of what we were going to do passed between us.

The Christie book is in front of me as I write this, and
I see I have reached the part where M'sieu Hercule Poirot
is about to reveal the killer's name. I wish I could continue
reading, and I wish I could be interested in nothing more
than finding out who committed the three (was it three?)
murders earlier in the story.

But all I can think of is that *he* will soon be here. Stephen.
He's dead, of course. He can't come into this house. But
what if he does? Will I see him? Will he see me? Is he the
romantic war hero I thought him, a dashing spy, dying for
his King and country? Or is he a villain, under sentence of
death for some squalid crime, perpetually dodging those
soldiers? And who is it that he calls to in this house? Could
it be Leonora? Was she here, and is she part of Stephen's
story in some way? That thought brings a horrid, illogical
jab of jealousy.

'I've left the iron gate open to make it easier,' Father
said to me before we sat down to supper. He said it quietly,
but he said it eagerly, like a child wanting to give pleasure,
and I hated him for not understanding how much he was
frightening me, and how incredibly stupid he was to
believe in his mad idea.

A moment ago the little clock over the mantel chimed,
breaking softly into the silence, and I jumped. And it's as
if the chiming released a trigger, because something is
starting to happen. A moment ago I heard the faint screech
of the iron gate. The hinges always screech like that if
someone pushes them right back against the stone wall.
If I turn my head a little I can see into the night garden
– I can see the outlines of the trees, grey and black in this
light – and I can see the wrought-iron gate and the walled
garden beyond it. Is Stephen there?

If I stand close to the window I can hear soft rustlings and murmurings. And now there's the soft light crunch of footsteps on the gravel path that circles most of the house. Stephen. He's coming nearer, and I can see him now. A young man, wearing a long, dark overcoat. It's called a greatcoat, I think. It's what soldiers wore in that war – the Great War – Stephen's war. I see him in the way you see a piece of film projected on to a screen. Not quite transparent, but nearly so.

'*Let me in . . . You must let me in . . .*'

The words are faint and broken because the wind is snatching at them. I've wiped the mist from the glass so I can see better, and I've set the lamp on the desk so the light shines across the gardens.

He's coming towards the window . . . I cannot write any more . . .

It's almost midnight, and I'm in my bedroom. I know I won't be able to sleep until I've recorded something of what happened earlier.

As Stephen approached the house, I could hear him sobbing quietly. With the sounds came a feeling of what I can only describe as impending doom. Written down, that looks impossibly dramatic, but it's what I felt.

'*Let me in . . . For the love of God, let me in . . . Niemeyer's butchers are already in the grounds . . .*'

There was a space of time – it might have been two minutes or two hours for all I know – when I didn't think I had the courage to do what Father wanted. But those pleading words, that harsh, desperate sobbing was too much for me. If I walked out of the room now, Stephen would come to this house every night like this, begging to be let in.

'*Niemeyer's butchers are in the grounds . . .*'

I leaned forward and opened the window.

At first I thought nothing was going to happen. There was a faint spattering of rain on my hands, and then, with heart-snatching suddenness, it was as if the massing darknesses and the furtive whisperings whirled their tangled skeins up and spun them into a tattered sphere that swooped straight at me. It was like being smacked across the eyes, and as I gasped and stepped back, a cold wind blew into my face. The sobbing was nearer, and there was such fear and such despair in that sobbing, as if someone was drowning in the dark, all alone . . .

And then he was there, framed in the window, barely two feet away from me. He was young and pale, there was a tiny scar on one cheekbone, and he was looking into the warm, lamplit room with such longing that it tore into my heart.

I said, in a voice I hardly recognized as my own, 'Come into the house. You'll be safe here.'

A hand came out, and even through my fear I saw the fingertips were raw and bleeding, the nails torn almost to the quick in places. The pity of it scalded through me, but I put out my own hand and he took it eagerly, his poor torn fingers closing around mine. They were cold, so dreadfully cold, and he clutched at my hand as if I was the only thing in existence that could save him . . . There are moments in life that stamp themselves for ever on some inner level of the mind – moments that will never really fade. For me, that moment has always been when Stephen Gilmore took my hand.

And then two things happened practically simultaneously. The door of the library opened, and my father stood there. The shadowy outline in the window and the feel of those torn, cold fingers holding mine both vanished.

He hadn't been real, of course, I knew that, but it was as if something had been wrenched out of my body. A sense of aching desolation and loss swept over me, and I turned furiously to my father. 'Why did you come in?' I said, with an angry sob. 'He was here.' I pointed, stupidly, fruitlessly, to the window. 'You came in and he went away,' I said, and sat down abruptly in a chair, because I felt as if something had sucked all the bones out of my body.

'No. Luisa, look there.' My father pointed to the floor, and I saw faint damp footprints leading across the sitting-room floor and out to the hall. In a voice from which all the breath seemed to have been taken, he said, 'He didn't go away. He's here in the house.'

SIXTEEN

S o they let him in, thought Michael, leaning his head back against the chair for a moment. They both believed they had let Stephen in, and Booth Gilmore believed he could save him from the German soldiers – Niemeyer's butchers.

In broad daylight, with people around and normality everywhere, he would probably have found this no more than rather sad – an indication of the introspection of a solitary young girl and a man with an obsession. Marooned in Fosse House with its whispering darknesses and darting shadows – with his own encounter with Stephen Gilmore still vividly in his mind – he found it chilling.

He turned to the next page of the journal. The entries seemed to be from around the same period, but they were mostly about ordinary, everyday things. Lessons with the governess, church, one or two mild local social events.

On one page, though, Luisa had written, 'It is now more important than ever to fight Leonora. If she finally takes over my mind, I will have none of my own memories, only hers. There will be no memories left of Stephen – of the feel of his hand taking mine. I will not let her overpower me, I will *not*.'

Michael thought that whether or not Luisa's fear of Leonora was due to some incipient madness, it was still deeply disturbing. For a wild moment he wondered whether Leonora had eventually succeeded – whether he had sat down to dinner and shared those curious conversations with Luisa or with Leonora.

The library room was warm, and Fosse House was silent and unthreatening. Michael was even starting to feel slightly drowsy. Through the drowsiness he heard the faint chimes of a church clock, and rowsed sufficiently to count them. Midnight. The dead vast and middle of the night, if you believed the Bard. The hour when drowsy darkness rolled over hushed cities.

It was ridiculous to remember all the myths and legends about midnight, but he was absurdly relieved to realize he had crossed its symbolic Rubicon, always supposing he had been worried about that, which of course he had not. But the chimes had woken him up, and perhaps it would be as well to stay awake if he could. There were only six hours until it would start to get light, anyway. He would divide those hours into sections. First he would finish reading Luisa's journal, and then he would make a search of this room to see if he could find any more of Iskander's insouciant chronicles. He might even risk a quick sortie to the kitchen for the radio; all the stations broadcast twenty-four hours a day, and a little night music might cheer up the spooks. Or there might be a phone-in programme on somewhere. He had an immediate image of himself phoning in and explaining he was forced to spend the night in what appeared to be a haunted house so he would be grateful for any helpful ideas on how best to pass the time. It would probably bring half the weirdos in the country out of the woodwork, but it might make for an entertaining hour or so.

This reminded him he had a chapter of the current Wilberforce book still to write, and that Wilberforce might usefully be entangled in a broadcasting situation. This was such a promising idea that he reached for his notebook to write it down before he forgot it, and spent an absorbed half hour sketching out Wilberforce's foray into a local studio to act as a disc jockey, during which he dropped most of the discs, sat on the rest, and the army of inventive and gleeful mice who were always on the watch invaded the studio to plug Wilberforce into the shipping forecast instead.

Michael made a note to ask Nell's Beth what pop groups were currently in favour with the eight- and nine-year-olds who would read the book, and then, this satisfactorily dealt with, got up to stretch his legs by examining the contents of the bookshelves. In the main the titles were dry looking scholarly works, but the lower shelves held a rather ragged collection of paperbacks – Luisa's Agatha Christies, and also what looked like some of her old school-books. He pulled one or two out and flipped through the pages, interested to see the teaching methods from the 1940s.

He was just thinking he would tackle the rest of Luisa's journal when the church clock chimed one. As the single sonorous note died away, Michael became aware of other sounds from outside, and they were exactly the sounds he had hoped not to hear.

Soft footsteps, and whispering. He turned to stare at the window, his heart racing. Someone was certainly out there, but whether it was Stephen Gilmore again or an honest-to-goodness intruder, there was no way of knowing. Luisa had said Stephen could not get in by himself because of his wounded hands, but at one o'clock in the morning Michael was not inclined to place any great reliance on that. He thought if something tapped at the window and asked to be let in, he would probably grab his car keys and beat the hell out of Fosse House, trusting to luck that the road would no longer be blocked.

He was just thinking he might do that anyway, when there was a sudden cry from the gardens, either of pain or surprise, he could not tell which. But whatever it was, it made the decision for him, because dashing through the dark gardens and risking confronting whatever was out there was clearly out of the question. Instead, he looked frantically about him for a weapon. It was probably a pointless move, but there was still a chance that this could be some local, enterprising burglar who had heard about Luisa Gilmore's abrupt removal to hospital, and was seizing an opportunity to snaffle whatever treasures the presumably empty Fosse House might contain. Michael glanced at his phone, lying reassuringly on the desk, dropped it into a pocket, and went cautiously to the window. Moving the lamp out of the direct line, he opened the curtains by about two inches so he could look out without being seen.

It took a moment for his eyes to adjust to the shadows, but he could already see that the wrought-iron gate to the walled garden was open, which he thought it had not been earlier. This did not prove anything one way or the other, however. A ghost might not open a gate – it might not need to. But a straight-forward burglar might not do so either, in case it attracted attention. His hand closed around the phone. It would take three seconds to tap out 999, but it might take twenty minutes for the police to get out here.

He was just managing to convince himself that he had imagined the sounds when they came again, and this time he saw dark shapes moving as well. There was a whippy little wind, and flurries of rain dashed against the windows, but through this he could hear whispers. Fragments of words and phrases. At first

he could not make any sense of them, then he recognized one
or two of the words, and realized, with a cold frisson, that the
whispers were in German. *Ruhig sein*, which he was fairly sure
meant quiet, or 'be quiet', and *verbergen*, which he thought was
hide.

Be quiet and hide. Was this Hugbert Edreich's men, creeping
towards the house to capture Stephen? This was a bizarre thought,
but Michael was beginning to think he had already seen so many
bizarre things in this house that the addition of a quartet of
German soldiers from 1917 was perfectly believable.

He leaned forward, and as he did so he accidentally caught
a fold of the curtain, which fell more widely open. The light
from the desk lamp streamed into the gardens, and there, caught
in the ray of light, were two dark-clad figures, apparently
carrying a third figure between them, while a fourth appeared
to be giving directions or even orders. They turned sharply
towards the house and the window, their faces pallid, featureless
blurs, but their eyes wide with shock. For a moment Michael's
curiosity pushed aside his fear, and he leaned over the window
sill, trying to see more. There was an impression of hazy, hasty
movement, the sound of hurried footsteps, and then the iron
gate swung shut, as if of its own accord. Darkness closed down
again and there was only the sound of the rain beating down
on leaves and grass.

Michael realized he was shaking, but after a few moments he
managed to pull himself together sufficiently to close the curtains.
He sat down in the deep chair facing the window and tried to
sort out his thoughts. They've got him, he thought. Those were
the German soldiers and they came for Stephen, and they got
him. That's who they were carrying.

Did that mean there would be no more disturbances? Had the
finale of that long-ago tragedy been played out tonight, and would
Fosse House now sink back into its own brooding half-silence?
It was unexpectedly disturbing to think Stephen had finally been
caught and, presumably, later executed, but it might at least mean
the house would be spook-free for few hours. If so, it might be
safer and more sensible to stay put. And even if the road had
been cleared, he would still have to go outside and walk the
twenty or thirty yards to his car. His mind presented him with a

mental picture of his car, parked on one side of the building, in a small gravel area surrounded by dark, overgrown bushes.

In about four hours – say four and a half – it would be getting light. Could he get through four more hours in this house? He went to the window again and peered out. Nothing stirred. But would those men return? If there was any likelihood of it, Michael would brave the Serbonian bog and hell's scalding pavements to reach the village. But *had* they returned? Was there any way of finding out? How about Luisa's journal?

He made a decision. He would look through the next few pages of Luisa's journal to see if there were any more references to Hugbert's gang of merry men. Depending on what he found – or did not find – he would decide then whether to make a dash for his car and trust to luck that the road would not be blocked.

But, as far as he could tell, nothing moved anywhere, although rain pattered steadily against the windows. If Hugbert Edreich's little band were still out there they would be getting drenched. Michael had a sudden wild vision of himself calling to them to come inside out of the storm, and offering them dry towels and hot toddies. 'And do sit here, Hauptfeldwebel Barth, and tell me about the Kaiser. Is it true he once threw a deed box at Bismarck?'

He reached for Luisa's journal:

> Today I made a slightly surprising discovery. When I opened Father's desk earlier, I found the translation he had made of the German soldier's letter – the one he read to me and that I copied into my diary.
>
> But also in the desk was a second letter from the same man, which Father has also translated. I hadn't known about this letter, but it follows on from the one Father read out
>
> It's another fragment of Stephen, so I'm copying it down here.

Michael spared a thought to wonder why Luisa had been looking in her father's desk – Booth Gilmore had sounded fiercely protective of his work, and Luisa did not seem to have been permitted into the library very often. But perhaps Booth had gone off on another of his research expeditions, and Luisa had simply not bothered to record the fact.

He was aware of pity. Luisa seemed to have written a good deal of this while in her early teens, and she had led a more or less solitary life in a gloomy isolated house, with uncaring parents, and without any of the normal outlets of teenagers. Life in this part of the world in the 1950s would not exactly have been a riot of wild living, but Luisa's situation had been very nearly Brontë-esque. But the Brontës had had their own strange and wonderful fantasy worlds, which they had spun out of the dark moors, and they had had each other. Luisa had had no one. It was small wonder she had succumbed to the slightly eerie fixation on Leonora, and even less wonder that she had focused with such intensity on the mysterious, romantic Stephen.

He began to read the letter she had copied down.

To Hauptmann Niemeyer
Sir,
I regret to report that our first attempt to carry out the sentence passed on Stephen Gilmore has been unsuccessful. You will no doubt wish to know why this was.

It was almost entirely due to the presence of Alexei Iskander in Gilmore's house. We were all very surprised to find him there, although remembering Iskander's friendship with young Gilmore in the camp – more to the point, remembering Iskander's rebellious ways and disruptive influence – perhaps we should not have been so taken aback. He is a rogue and a ruffian, that one, and likely to be always at the epicentre of any kind of trouble.

We had approached the house under cover of darkness, careful to be silent and secretive, in line with all the training we had received. The four of us climbed over a wall and were creeping through the grounds (the house has large gardens – clearly Gilmore's family are prosperous). It was an eerie experience; the gardens are overgrown and filled with thick, nodding shadows and murmuring trees. A bitterly cold and most inhospitable wind blows across this part of the land from the North Sea, and a person of any imagination might suppose the sighing of the trees to be the sighing of the dead. As we went along, a church clock somewhere chimed one, making us all jump nervously. It made

Hauptfeldwebel Barth jump so violently that he tripped over a boulder and sat plump down in a nettle-bed growing untidily against a wall. I am afraid he gave vent to a loud curse of annoyance, which I am sure you will allow that anyone might do in such a circumstance, particularly since it later transpired that he had also stubbed his toe.

But the noise alerted Iskander to our presence. I saw him open the curtains in a downstairs room and look out. There was a lamp shining in the room, and we all saw him clearly – the untidy dark hair which he always wore slightly too long, and the characteristic tilt of the head – a 'listening' air, as if he is intent on absorbing everything he hears, and will be dissecting it afterwards, and writing it into one of his infernal articles. One of the men believed Stephen Gilmore stood just behind Iskander in the room, but opinions are divided on this. I cannot, myself, say I saw Gilmore in the room. I do know that the man at the window was not Gilmore.

We retreated to our inn, in no good order, carrying Hauptfeldwebel Barth as best we could, but making many pauses to rest, for, as you know, sir, the good Hauptfeldwebel is not a thin person.

The innkeeper's wife (a most helpful lady who believes me to be a Dutch tulip-grower from Scheveningen) has been enthusiastic in ministering to the Hauptfeldwebel's injuries, removing his nether garments in the privacy of her own bedroom, and applying suitable lotions to the worst affected parts of his anatomy. She has also strapped up his stubbed toe and feels he should rest in her room for the remainder of the night.

We mean to return tomorrow night, when we hope to outwit the rogue Iskander, and to finally succeed in recapturing Stephen Gilmore. I shall, of course, send you a further report, trusting it will reach you safely.

In the meantime, I send my respectful duty to you.
Hugbert Edreich.

I've copied the letter exactly as Father translated it, and it's certainly full of surprises. I hardly dare hope it means

Stephen could have escaped. But it might. Although, if so, why do I still see him and hear him trying to get into the house? Because I do see him and hear him, and I find myself waiting for him to reach for my hand once again.

I know to think that way is mad, but I do think it.

The greatest surprise – perhaps a greater surprise to me than it was to Hugbert Edreich – is the discovery that Iskander came to this house. Because in my mind Iskander belongs to that mad journey with Leonora – the journey they made across the muddied, bloodied countries sacked by the invading German and Prussian armies, after he got her out of Sacré-Coeur. He has no place here, in this quiet, old-fashioned corner of England, so I'm wondering if those men were right in thinking it was Iskander they saw that night. It's obvious they saw someone peering out of the window – someone who had a lamp burning and who, either deliberately or by accident, let that lamplight shine into the dark garden.

But whoever he was, that man, he was not Stephen.

Michael laid down the diary, his thoughts tumbling.

At one o'clock, those men had seen someone in this house. They had seen someone draw back the curtains, so that light had spilled over into the dark gardens.

At one o'clock, Michael himself had done exactly that. He had not meant to open the curtains by more than a sliver, but they had fallen open and the light from the desk lamp had streamed out. And those figures, those walking shadows that he had seen so definitely, had turned to look at him, their faces startled, their eyes wide with confused alarm. Then, as if an order had been given, they had fled, carrying an injured man with them. Had that man been Hauptfeldwebel Barth, he of the nettle trip and the stubbed toe?

Michael was not going to wonder, even for a moment, if there could possibly be any basis for the wild theory that Booth Gilmore had propounded to the fifteen-year-old Luisa about time bleeding forwards. There was no basis whatsoever, of course. All the todays and tomorrows, and all the tomorrows to come, might creep at their own petty pace, but they crept forwards not backwards.

Michael was prepared to accept – with a great many reservations – that the past could occasionally brush its cobwebbed bones against the present; he had encountered too many odd things not to give that belief some credence. Even Nell, who had shared some of those experiences, now admitted – albeit with even more reservations and scepticism – that past events might sometimes leave a lingering imprint that could be picked up by certain people decades afterwards.

But Michael could not and would not accept that it could work the other way round – that the present could affect the past. The likes of Einstein or Schopenhauer might be able to put forward a Euclidean argument about the concept of space and time or single continuums, and it was an alluring idea to imagine the conversation those two might have. You could even throw in H.G. Wells to spice it up a bit. But even though Michael would probably only have understood one hundredth part of it, if as much, he still would not give it any credence.

That being so, whoever Hugbert and his cohorts had seen standing at the window that night, it had been someone from their own world and their own time.

Having put this tiresome worry firmly in its place, it now occurred to Michael that the soldiers, according to Hugbert's letter, had abandoned their attempt to capture Stephen Gilmore until the following night. That also being so, he could relax his guard for the rest of the night.

As for tomorrow – it would not matter if the entire Prussian Army and the Kaiser himself yomped around the gardens of Fosse House, chasing recalcitrant English prisoners to bring them to grisly justice. Because by tomorrow night Michael would be safely back in Oxford.

SEVENTEEN

Autumn sunlight slanted across Quire Court. Nell, eating an early breakfast in the little kitchen behind the shop, contemplated with pleasure the prospect of seeing Michael this evening, then was annoyed with herself for behaving like a moonstruck teenager.

She was meeting Owen Bracegirdle at half-past nine, and by this evening she might have met Hugbert as well, admittedly only in epistolary form, but certainly more substantially than the fragmented sections in Bernard Bodkin's book. Autumn sunlight slanted across the kitchen, and Nell's spirits rose.

She wrote down the title and ISBN of Hugbert's letters and folded the note into her bag, after which she put the 'Closed' notice on the shop door and set off. It occurred to her that she would be unreasonably disappointed if she and Owen did not find Hugbert.

But they did find him. There he was, neatly catalogued in the Bodleian's customary efficient fashion, the entry sandwiched between somebody's account of the Zeppelin raids and a study of Hindenburg's war strategies in 1915.

'Is it available for actual loan?' asked Nell, peering at the details. She was perfectly prepared to read the entire book in the library, in fact she would happily camp out here for several days if necessary, but she would rather to take Hugbert home and read him in privacy.

'It looks like it.' Owen leaned over her shoulder to see. 'Yes, it is. It'll have to be on my ticket, but if I can't trust you, I can't trust anyone.'

It felt odd to actually walk out of the library with Hugbert's letters stowed in her bag. Nell caught herself beaming every time she thought about it.

Owen insisted on buying them coffee at his favourite patisserie, and over several of the richest eclairs and doughnuts Nell had ever eaten he launched into a progress report of his own contribution to the Music Director's book.

'And J.B. is very pleased with Michael's findings about Robert Graves and Stephen Gilmore,' he said. 'He thinks if Michael can establish that Graves really was at school with Stephen, the two themes – music and Great War poetry – will knit up very neatly, particularly with the Gilmore connection to the Palestrina Choir.' He mopped a few doughnut crumbs from his waistcoat and said, 'But I won't bang on about that for too long, Nell, because I've got to get back to College, and I know you're on edge to immerse yourself in those 1917 letters.'

'Well, yes, I suppose I am.' Nell had been managing not to cast longing looks at her bag, with the book stashed inside.

'The call of the siren,' said Owen, burlesquing the line. 'Or in this case, whatever the masculine equivalent of a siren is.' He grinned sympathetically, and Nell was grateful to him for understanding, although if a history don could not understand the lure of newly found, primary-source research material, there was not much hope for lesser mortals.

She returned to Quire Court, developing hiccups on the way from a surfeit of doughnuts, and made a cup of peppermint tea to quell them. She would sit in the little office at the back of the shop to read Hugbert, so she could keep the shop open and hear any customers who came in.

But Quire Court, with its little shops and mullioned windows and the remains of the original cobblestones, was drowsy and deserted today. It felt as if it might have sealed itself off from the clang of the modern world for a few hours. Michael had often said it was one of the places where time might be paper-thin, and that if you knew the right words, or the right place to reach out a hand, you would find yourself peering at glimpses of the Court's past. Nell, walking under the arched stone entrance, thought this might be one of the days when the veil was particularly thin, although it might simply be that she was absorbed in 1917.

Once inside, she checked her phone messages, hoping Michael might have phoned to say he was about to set off for Oxford. He had not, however. Nell considered phoning him, but thought he might be caught up in the practicalities of Luisa Gilmore's illness. If she had not heard after lunch, she would ring then.

Here was the title page with Freide's dedication: 'In loving remembrance of a dear husband.' How had Freide felt about coming to England after WWI – to a country she must still have regarded as an enemy of Germany – and living here?

For the first few pages Hugbert's writing did not quite achieve the lively style of the letters reproduced in B.D. Bodkin. But perhaps Hugbert had not yet become accustomed to expressing himself with pen and paper. Or perhaps the translator had not got into his or her swing yet. Nell persevered, and by the time she reached a letter sent from France in 1916, Hugbert appeared to have hit his literary stride.

He had written to his Freide that he missed her, but assured her he was with good comrades, and everyone was in cheerful spirits, although life in the trenches was dismal, and there had been outbreaks of illness among a number of the men. 'Details of which I will not embarrass you, my *liebling*, only to say they are distressing and debilitating. I believe the British suffer the same thing. We have much sympathy for them, for it is not an illness to wish on one's worst enemies.'

Dysentery, thought Nell. It was endemic on both sides in that conflict. Poor old Hugbert, I hope he didn't get it.

But although he had spared his *liebling* Freide the finer points of the trench sickness, he had provided her with a description of the trenches themselves:

> It is depressing and dreary, and the fighting is grim . . . We are brave men, but still there have been instances of suicide and madness within our ranks, although there have also been stories of bravery and resourcefulness, of which we are very proud . . . But everywhere is the grey mud of the trenches and the sounds of gunfire and men's shouts, and the screams of horses . . . It is a terrible thing to hear horses screaming, Freide, although it is, of course, far worse to hear men screaming. And it seems as if everything we hear, and see, and smell, is framed in barbed wire like jagged black teeth.

Later, while guarding the *Siegfriedstellung* – the Hindenburg line – at Verdun, he had written that it was bitterly, bone-numbingly, cold, but how, when the freezing mists cleared, they could some-times see the British soldiers.

A curious race, the British, but I find them interesting, although that is something I should not say, since they are our enemies. This week one of our own trenches was captured by a young British Lieutenant, who pelted about fifty of our men with hand grenades. I am sorry to say our men were scared away, although under such an attack perhaps one could not blame them. It is easy to be brave until faced with explosives and spitting fire and showers of metal.

Since it happened, we have heard a strange story about the lieutenant, who is called Siegfried Sassoon. Instead of signalling for reinforcements, as would have been correct after making the capture, he sat down in the trench itself, and began reading a book of poetry. This, you will appreciate, is extremely odd behaviour.

Nell reached for her pen to note it down in case Michael, or Owen, or the Director did not know this small story and might be able to make use of it. She found the brief word picture of the romantic, tormented Sassoon, reading poems in a German trench, touching and evocative.

The next pages appeared to deal with Hugbert's progression through the war. Nell skimmed these. They would no doubt be interesting to a student of the finer points of military history, particularly seen from the Germans' point of view, but she was looking for Holzminden and for Stephen Gilmore and Iskander. But it was rather endearing to read of Hugbert's simple pleasure and pride in his promotions, and also of his obviously genuine sorrow at the death of many of his colleagues.

And then, about a third of the way through, the word Holzminden leapt up from the page. 'My posting for the new prisoner of war camp at Holzminden has been officially announced, and I leave tomorrow,' he had written.

Nell bent eagerly over the page. The letter was not, on this occasion, written to Freide, but to Hugbert's parents, and ended with a brief description of the camp:

... in old cavalry barracks, and specifically intended for British officers. The present Kommandant is a kindly old dodderer, but we hear he is to leave very soon, and his replacement is not yet known. I shall, however, be serving directly under Hauptfeldwebel Barth, who you will remember meeting at that social evening. I am afraid he was very voluble about the food being served, telling everyone that his father, a butcher in Braunschweig, had supplied the bratwurst for the supper, but he is proud of his father's business, and it must be said the bratwurst was very good. Also, allowances must be made for the amount of beer he had consumed that night.

My best love to you both,
Hugbert

Dearest Mother and Father,

Here I am, safely installed at Holzminden, and becoming acquainted with the men in my charge. I should not admit to being glad that I am removed from active duty, but I feel great relief.

I am less pleased at learning the identity of the new Kommandant. He is Hauptmann Karl Niemeyer. He is very much disliked and feared, and is considered a buffoon, but a vindictive buffoon. He likes to think himself very learned and scholarly in English even though he is far from that. Already, some of the imprisoned men are mimicking him behind his back. I beg you will not mention that I have told you that.

Please to take care of my beloved Freide while I am away. I fear she has too vivid an imagination and conjures up all manner of horrors which she thinks I am enduring.

Horrors there have been, of course, and will continue to be. There is a young Englishman here who clearly has seen the worst of them, and he is unable to shake off his memories. He goes in constant terror of being hunted down, and two nights ago I and another attendant found him hiding in the storeroom, crouching in a dark corner, pressing against the walls, as if trying to hide within the very bricks. I fear he is very disturbed.

I have received your parcel with the peppermint draught for dyspepsia and the ointment for bunions. You will be glad to know both are much improved as a result.

My best love to you both,
Hugbert

Dearest Mother and Father,

We heard today that a British newspaper has called Holzminden camp 'the worst camp in Germany'. This is troubling, but sadly not without foundation. The food in particular is very poor and the rations meagre, but in fairness that is largely the result of the economic blockade on our country. It is still the infamous Turnip Winter here, I am afraid. I am heartily sick of turnips, but I eat them for they are filling and nutritious, and are the best that can be obtained at the moment. But if you, Mother, or Tante Mathilde, could find it possible to send me a food parcel, I would be more grateful than I can say. One of your apple cakes, perhaps, and some stollen, which should keep quite well, or even some pickled beet and potato dumplings.

If you can manage this, I would ask that you wrap it very securely, since there is a rumour in the camp that our Kommandant, Hauptmann Niemeyer, steals food from the prisoners' parcels. I do not know how true this is, but he is a greedy and selfish man, much given to petty vindictiveness. He is greatly disliked, and I have occasionally overheard the prisoners making plots against him. Most of the plots are so wild they could never succeed, and involve such fates as dunking Niemeyer in a sewage duct or spiking his supper beer with syrup of figs. I do not think either of these ploys is likely to succeed, but I shall be watchful.

On a more cheerful note, I and several others have organized games for the men – football, hockey and tennis – and next week there is to be staged a concert, which the men have written and rehearsed themselves. This I shall attend and anticipate enjoying. Unfortunately, Hauptmann Niemeyer's twin brother is to pay us a visit, and will form part of the audience. That I shall not enjoy, for he is reported to be as humourless and greedily inclined as the Hauptmann himself.

The Englishman who is so plagued by nightmares seems to have found a friend, which I am hoping will help him a little. It is a Russian journalist who was captured in France – a dangerously charming young man, the kind that I should not like my dear Freide, or any of my sisters, to encounter. He is, however, teaching me a little Russian, although it is a difficult language. But with that, and the smattering of English learned from some of the other prisoners, I feel I am adding to my knowledge. This pleases me.

    Fondest love,

    Hugbert

The next letters were the ones Nell had read in B.D. Bodkins' book, and talked about Iskander and the young British officer. Hugbert still had not named the officer, but she was starting to hope very much that it really was Stephen Gilmore.

But in the summer of 1917, Hugbert had written to Freide:

I am becoming more and more uneasy about the Russian newspaper man, Alexei Iskander. I sense that he is planning something outrageous, and certainly he dislikes the confines and the authority of the camp. You remember I wrote to you of how he argues against everything and regularly challenges the regime here and the conditions. He is a scoundrel, that one, and I would not trust him with anything, but he is such entertaining and lively company, I can forgive him much. One night recently I asked him what he had done before writing for newspapers. He eyed me coolly and with complete self-assurance said, 'I was a burglar. And I was a very good burglar indeed.'

I must have looked disbelieving, because he said, 'It is perfectly true. I was successful and prosperous and I was never caught. When I am finally freed from this hell-hole, Herr Edreich –' (he will never use my rank no matter how often he is ordered to) – 'I shall return to my apartment and the beautiful things in it.'

Against my will, (Iskander has the effect of making people say things they know to be unwise), I said, 'And is there a beautiful lady waiting for you?'

The curious thing is that with the question his self-possession seemed to vanish for a moment. His eyes suddenly seemed to look inwards, as if at some cherished memory, but then he blinked as if to dispel an image, and said, lightly, 'Ah, there are so many of them, Herr Edreich. So many ladies, and so little time.'

I do not believe any of it, of course. What I do believe is that he will cause trouble, although I do not, as yet, know what that trouble might be.

He has befriended the young Englishman, and I think they communicate mostly in French, although I believe Iskander is already able to make himself understood in English. He is also becoming proficient in some basic German – he has a magpie mind and devours all information with immense energy. I do not worry about him, for he is a survivor, but I do worry about the English boy. Sometimes, often during mealtimes, he rocks back and forth, whispering to himself, almost like someone praying. '*Let me not be mad,*' he says, over and over again. '*Not mad . . . Let me keep hold of my sanity, then I shall survive.*'

Recently, he said, in a perfectly normal tone, '*He* is with me most of the time now.'

He has quite good German – I believe he learned it at school, and I have a little English now, so we are able to understand one another fairly satisfactorily.

'Who?' I said. 'Who is with you most of the time? Iskander? Is that who you mean?'

He looked at me from the corners of his eyes. 'Don't you see him?' he said. 'I didn't, not at first. I thought he was a shadow. But he's there, waiting his time. Sometimes he reaches into my mind – he deforms it so that I'm different inside. When it's like that, I mustn't ever look in a mirror, because it wouldn't be me looking back.'

I find this kind of conversation deeply distressing, and I shall talk to our medical officer, to see if there is any help that can be given. Hauptfeldwebel Barth says it is not for us to worry about any of the men's minds, only to keep their bodies securely confined. He maintains the Englishman is shamming in order to get better treatment. Personally, I do not believe this, in fact I do not think Hauptfeldwebel Barth would know a wounded mind if it bit him on the behind. You will excuse my mentioning such a part of the anatomy.

You will remember meeting Hauptfeldwebel Barth at a social gathering last year, which my parents also attended. I recall you found him somewhat over-gallant in his manner, as well as having strong onion breath. I am trying to persuade him that young ladies do not care to be complimented on the proportions of their bosoms in the explicit way he complimented you that night. I am hopeful he will not do it again. About the onion breath, I can do nothing.

A couple of weeks ago, I found out that the English boy was a keen amateur artist, so I mentioned this to Iskander.

'I know it,' he said. 'And perhaps if he could draw his fears it would exorcize them. The Roman Church, Herr Edreich, has a belief that in order to exorcize a demon, it's first necessary to name it.'

'Would drawing his demons exorcize them?'

'It might.'

I was just wondering whether a requisition for drawing or even painting materials would be viewed with approval, when Iskander, who sometimes has the uncomfortable trick of reading people's minds, said, 'You may leave matters to me, Herr Edreich. All I say is that you do not ask questions.'

And, incredibly, he has somehow managed to get his hands on a sketch pad and pencils, and sticks of charcoal. I have not asked questions, but I begin to believe his story about having been a thief in peacetime.

The English boy did not, at first, seem interested in the sketching materials, but then one day, when he thought no one was watching him, he reached for the sketch pad, and ran his hands over the surface of the paper. The next day I noticed him drawing the view of the courtyard beyond the refectory, doing so with fierce concentration and absorption. I shall ask, tactfully, if I may see his work sometime.

We are currently engaged in scrubbing the entire camp to within an inch of its life for the impending visit of Hauptmann Niemeyer's twin brother, Heinrich. Niemeyer says all must be in precise and immaculate order, but we have exhausted the entire stock of lye soap and he still barks that everywhere looks like a pigsty and to do it all again.

The kitchens are at their wits' end to provide a respectable
series of meals. You would think royalty is coming, instead
of a jumped-up popinjay with the manners of a rutting goat.
Do not, please, allow anyone else to read that last sentence.

This seemed to end that particular section of letters and made a
good place for a break. Nell took a breather to make herself
a cup of coffee. Drinking it, she wondered how Michael's morning
was going and hoped that he might ring soon to say he was on
his way home.

EIGHTEEN

Michael had woken to rather watery autumn sunlight filtering through the latticed windows of the library, and the realization that he had fallen asleep in the deep old wing chair. So either the night had passed without further disturbance, or if any manifestations had taken to floating around Fosse House or its grounds he had slept through them.

The chimes of the church clock came faintly across the morning, and he saw with immense relief and slight surprise that it was eight o'clock. This was so gratifying and welcome that he bounded out of the library, without giving a thought to what might lurk in the hall, and went up to his room to collect clean things. He showered happily in the old-fashioned bathroom, not caring that the pipes clanked as if something was trapped inside them, then made a pot of tea and ate a bowl of cereal and some toast and marmalade. After this, he remembered his obligations to the hospital, and ventured into Luisa's bedroom to search for some kind of contact for them. The big wardrobe held clothes and a faint scent of lavender, and shoes neatly ranged on racks. He tried the drop-front bureau in the window alcove and was relieved to find a small address book. Was there a solicitor in here? Yes, here it was: Mr Josiah Pargeter and an address in Walsham. Thank goodness. He went back downstairs and phoned the hospital.

'I haven't found any family,' he explained to the ward sister who had just come on duty. 'But I've tracked down what looks like Miss Gilmore's solicitor. A Josiah Pargeter of Walsham. I don't know how recent an address it is, but it'll give you a starting point.'

'That's really helpful,' she said. 'Look now, is there any chance you could telephone him for us? I know it's a bit of a cheek to ask, but what with you being actually in the house and knowing exactly what happened last night— Somebody needs to establish that he does act for the family, you see. Once we know that, we can get things moving here.'

'Yes, all right.' Michael felt this was the least he could do for Luisa, and a phone call or two would not take very long. 'I'm hoping to leave today, but I'll sort that out right away and call you back.'

'We'd be very grateful,' she said.

By this time it was half-past nine, an hour when a solicitor might reasonably be expected to be in his office and at his desk, so Michael made the call.

'Mr Josiah died a few years ago,' said the receptionist. 'But Mr John Pargeter – his nephew – took over his clients. I'll put you through to him.'

John Pargeter expressed conventional regret at hearing of the death of a client and was slightly acquainted with the family details. 'Although there hasn't been a great deal to do on their behalf for some considerable time,' he said. 'With Miss Gilmore being elderly and so on. I don't know about a next of kin, though. I'm not even sure if there is one. But I'll look out the file and ring you back.'

'Can it be this morning?' asked Michael. 'The hospital do need to have some details as soon as possible, and I'm hoping to leave later today.'

'I should think so.'

Michael gave him the Fosse House number and also his mobile as back-up. After this, he rang the police station and was relieved to hear the tree was being cleared even as they spoke.

'Give it a couple of hours,' said the sergeant. 'It should be fine by midday.'

This was all very satisfactory. Michael started to dial Nell's number, then thought he had better keep both phones free for Mr Pargeter to call back. Also, Nell had mentioned meeting Owen at the Bodleian this morning, so she was likely to be out until at least lunchtime. He would wait until he knew what was happening, then he could tell her the whole story.

John Pargeter phoned back half an hour later. 'We've found the Gilmore file,' he said. 'And, as I thought, there's no known family. In fact this firm is named as executors.' He hesitated, then said, 'Dr Flint, I have no right to ask you this, but we would be extremely grateful if you could stay at Fosse House until we can get someone there.'

'I don't think that's possible,' began Michael. 'I was hoping to leave quite soon—'

'We'd hope to make it today, and it's only about an hour's drive from here. But I can't promise we'll manage it,' said Pargeter. 'There are several appointments with clients in my diary and my partner's. But we do need to collect keys and assure ourselves that the place is secure, and – well, put the preliminary wheels in motion.'

Michael tried to think if there was any way of getting keys to Pargeter's office in Walsham without remaining in the house – always supposing he could find keys in the first place. But before he could say anything, John Pargeter said, 'There is another thing, Dr Flint.'

'Yes?'

'The main bequest in Miss Gilmore's will is actually Oriel College's Faculty of Music.'

Michael had not expected this. He said, 'What kind of bequest? Or can't you tell me?'

'There's no reason why you can't know the general outline. She's left what she calls the Palestrina papers to the college, and— Sorry, did you say something?'

'That's what I've been working on,' said Michael. 'They're extremely interesting, those papers. I should think the Music Department would be over the moon to have them.'

'Ah. Good. Well, now, she's also left a very substantial sum of money – really a *very* substantial amount – to endow the college's choral scholarship. Or even to create a new one if it's thought possible and if Oriel wants to set one up.'

'That's immensely generous of her.'

'The house will have to be sold to pay out, but we'll deal with all that.'

'Yes, I see,' said Michael, rather blankly. And then he did see; he saw that this placed a degree of responsibility on him. He was not part of the Music Faculty, but for the moment he was probably Oriel's representative, or the nearest thing to it. Because of the last two days, he could even be regarded as some kind of custodian or guardian of the Palestrina papers. A sly little voice in his mind reminded him that if he stayed in the house, he could make an open search for Stephen and Iskander.

To quell this last thought, he said, 'I think I could stay at the house until you get here. I could book into the local pub and stay until tomorrow if necessary. That might be preferable. But there is another thing— It's only a half-idea, and it might not be practical, or even ethical. But you mentioned selling the house. Presumably, you'll have to sell its contents as well?'

'Yes.'

'Well, then, my—' He stopped.

'Dr Flint? Are you still there?'

'Yes, I'm here. My partner runs an antiques business in Oxford,' said Michael firmly. 'I'm not putting her forward for the appraisal of the furniture, and I'm certainly not touting for business on her behalf at any level. But there are a couple of things in Fosse House that I think ought to be looked at by experts. She might be able to point you in the right direction.'

'What kind of things do you mean? Furniture? Silver?'

'Well, there's certainly some nice old furniture and probably silver and china stored away as well,' said Michael. 'But specifically there's a sketch which I think might be what's called a prisoner-of-war sketch. Done in one of the camps during the Great War. Apparently they can be quite valuable.'

'Really? I don't know much about that kind of thing,' said Pargeter. 'But if your – partner, did you say? – could spare the time to take a look—'

'I can ask,' said Michael, uncertain if Nell would want to become involved, or even if he would want her to be. 'I don't think it's the kind of thing she would deal with herself – it's a very specialist field, I believe. But she could probably recommend someone.'

'I think we'd be very grateful for that,' said Pargeter. 'So I'll find out what we can do about coming out to Fosse House – if I can do it myself, I will. I'll call you back.'

'In the meantime, I'll phone Nell to see whether she can help with the sketch,' said Michael.

As he dialled Nell's number, he considered that hesitation before referring to Nell as his 'partner'. Why had he done that? But he knew already. It was because the word, perfectly accept-able as it was, somehow no longer seemed right or even adequate to describe what Nell had become to him. Partner, probably from the old French word *parçonier*, meaning a sharing, which was fine, but not when you remembered that the word also had as its root the Latin *partire*, to divide. Any kind of division from Nell was an appalling prospect. But how would she feel about forging a permanent link? He put this idea aside, to be dealt with later, and dialled her number.

She answered almost at once, but Michael had the impression that she had been deeply absorbed in something and was mentally blinking to adjust to a sudden ingress of light from a different world.

But she said, 'I'm glad to hear you. What's been happening?'

Michael explained about Luisa and the request that he stay until the solicitor could get to the house and seal it up.

'I'm sorry about Luisa,' said Nell. 'But I'm glad you were there and that she didn't lie helplessly on her own.'

'Yes. But Nell, the thing now is—'

'—you want the Holzminden sketch appraising.'

'I mentioned you to the solicitor – just saying you might point them in the direction of someone who specializes in that kind of stuff.'

'I expect I could dredge up a couple of names. Or – do you want me to come out to the wilds of Norfolk to take a preliminary look?'

'Yes. No. Hell's teeth, I don't know. It's a bit far. Obviously, you couldn't come just for a couple of hours, then go straight back. But I don't know if this solicitor will be able to get here today, and I might have to stay until tomorrow—'

'Would you like some company?'

'It's a gloomy old place,' said Michael evasively.

'But if I were to come,' said Nell, 'we wouldn't need to actually stay in the house, presumably? Is the road clear yet?'

'It was supposed to be cleared by midday, so it should be all right now.'

'All right,' said Nell, in the voice that indicated she had made a decision. 'Here's a suggestion. I could travel out there straight after lunch. But I won't drive – I should think the train will be just as fast, or equally slow, and it would mean I could travel back with you tomorrow.'

'Sounds good.'

'Also—'

'What?'

'Also,' said Nell, and Michael heard the smile in her voice, 'if I'm on a train I can carry on reading some letters written from Holzminden camp in 1917.'

'Is that what Owen helped you find in the Bodleian? It's not Hugbert Edreich by any chance, is it?'

'Yes. *Yes.* How do you know about Hugbert?'

'I won't tell you now, it'll take too long and my battery's running a bit low. And *don't* chuckle like that, you shameless hussy, you know quite well I mean the phone battery. Would you really travel today, though? What about the shop?'

'Henry Jessel or Godfrey at the bookshop could have the keys and deal with anything urgent.'

'Ah, the quaint old system of barter, still practised amid the timeless cobblestones of Quire Court.'

'Don't knock it. I sold two first editions for Godfrey last week when he went to that antiquarian book fair in Cambridge. And a set of silver Victorian photograph frames for Henry the week before that. So I'll find out train times and phone you back,' said Nell. 'Then we can decide how practical it's looking.'

'While you do that, I'll make sure the tree's been cleared.'

She rang back within ten minutes, saying there was a train that would reach Norwich shortly before six o'clock. 'It's a bit of a circuitous route, and I have to change trains in London which is slightly irritating, but the journey's no slower than driving would be.'

'I could pick you up in Norwich. I think it's about forty minutes' drive from here.' Michael supposed the satnav would take him from Fosse House to Norwich without too much difficulty.

'No, it's all right, there's apparently one of those little local trains that bumbles out of Norwich and into a tiny local station,' said Nell. 'I don't think it's much more than fifteen minutes from your village.'

'I'll pick you up at the bumbly station, then.' Finding that would probably be a lot easier than finding Norwich, but Nell was ahead of him.

She said, 'Why don't I just hop in a taxi when I get there and come straight out to Fosse House?'

'Better still, why don't I book the taxi from here,' said Michael. 'If it's one of those minuscule stations there isn't likely to be anything as grand as a taxi rank. I can easily find a local firm in the phone book.'

'Good idea. I'll give you the train times.'

'And you may as well go straight to the local pub – it's called the Bell.' There was no need to tell Nell yet about seeing Hugbert last night, or about the letter he had found with Hugbert's plans to return the following night. He would tell her later, but in the meantime, he would definitely prefer to be out of the house before night fell. He said, 'I was booked in there anyway, so there'll be a room available.'

'So we won't be spending the night with the ghosts?' said Nell. 'What a pity. I quite wanted to meet them.'

'Not these ghosts, you don't,' said Michael. 'At least, not unless it's broad daylight. Oh, and Nell—'

'Yes?'

'I've missed you.'

'It's mutual,' she said, and Michael heard the smile in her voice before she rang off.

NINETEEN

Nell liked train journeys. She liked the feeling of being in the no-man's land between one place and another, and she liked seeing the countryside slide past, and speculating about other travellers and their journeys, and if they were looking forward to reaching their destinations.

It had been a bit of a scramble to catch the early afternoon train, but she had thrown a handful of things into an overnight bag, left the shop keys with the obliging Godfrey, and managed to reach the station with ten minutes to spare.

The carriage was not very crowded, and most people were travelling in twos and threes, all of them absorbed in their travelling companions. Nell found a seat by herself, stowed away her case, and contemplated with pleasure the fact that she had her own travelling companion. Hugbert Edreich.

She had left Hugbert established in Holzminden, helping to organize concerts, making the best of the meagre rations, and dealing with the recalcitrant Iskander, while at the same time trying to help the Englishman with sketching materials.

The letters recommenced with one to Freide written in 1917.

My dearest Freide,
You will think it strange that I tell you how shaken everyone at Holzminden is by an episode of violence, particularly since all of us here have been on active service and seen the nightmares of this war. Mercifully, though, the memories fade, and at times I think the war has even receded a little for some of us.
It did not recede for Stephen Gilmore though.

The name leapt off the page, and Nell stared down at it. Stephen Gilmore. Michael's elusive, shadowy Stephen. It had sounded likely all along and she had hoped for it, but it still came as a shock to see it written down. Hugbert wrote:

Gilmore took to hiding himself away more and more frequently. Often at meals he would half-close his eyes and murmur the words that had begun to seem almost like a private prayer.

'*Let me not be mad . . . If I can keep my sanity all will be well . . . If I can remain sane I shall be safe . . .*' Sometimes he would make clawing movements at the air, although whether he was fighting off an invisible enemy, or fighting to break free of some imaginary prison, it was impossible to tell.

Hauptfeldwebel Barth still insists Gilmore is perfectly sane, and says he most likely got the idea about clawing the air from the Bible, from the *Book of Kings*, where David scrabbled on the prison walls.

'It's all a pretence,' he said to me, over lunch. 'You mark my words. Please to pass me the pickled cabbage.'

If Hauptfeldwebel Barth were not my senior officer I should probably tell him he is a pudding-head.

It all began two weeks ago on a normal morning. I was on breakfast duty – breakfast was a bit sparse because all the eggs had been commandeered for Niemeyer and his brother. (Eggs are a rarity at the moment, anyway.) The brothers had already walked around the camp like two fat, moustached trolls, and a number of the prisoners had jeered at them and shouted rude comments, resulting in their being sent into solitary confinement on bread and water.

Iskander and Gilmore were at breakfast. Iskander is impossible to miss in any gathering, merely because he has such a forceful personality that he makes everyone else seem rather colourless. If he really was a burglar, he must have found it very difficult to pass unnoticed when he was a-burgling. Stephen Gilmore is noticeable as well, not because of his looks, but because he has the air of constantly listening and watching, as if he fears his nightmares are crouching nearby. He is, in fact, what you would call a well set-up young man, fairish of hair and complexion, and with a tiny scar or perhaps a birthmark on one cheek. This mark, rather than disfiguring him, actually draws attention to his good bones, in the way eighteenth-century ladies used to place a beauty patch on their faces to enhance an attractive nose or a dimpled smile. (You, my *liebling*, have no need of such adornments, being pretty enough to rival any famous beauty in any time and in any country. I know I am not the only one to think this, and I hope you are not succumbing to the blandishments of others while I am away.)

On that morning Gilmore seemed more distressed than usual, but I had to deal with a shortage of soda crystals for washing-up and could not spare him much attention. The men were clearing the tables and carrying plates and dishes to the sculleries – this is a task they all dislike, but we have in place a rota system, and it is important to clear the dishes used for pottage straight after eating.

[*Translator's note: It is likely that by 'pottage' Hugbert is referring to a scaled-down version of Bauernfrühstück, a kind of breakfast hash.*]

It was not until I returned to the dining room that I realized Gilmore and Iskander were no longer there. This was not immediately alarming, and one does not question too closely where a man might have gone after a large helping of Holzminden's pottage, for, as well as the ubiquitous turnips, it also contains many onions. But I was just thinking I must make sure of their whereabouts, when the alarm sirens ripped through the camp. They are like giant wailing monsters, those sirens, they tear into a man's eardrums, and they demand instant action.

We have had a few escape attempts here, and we usually recapture the men. But it means we are not unfamiliar with the screeching clamour of the alarms, which only ever signals one thing, and that is an escaped prisoner.

Well, Freide, I am not a person built for running, even with the sparse rations we have had for the last two years. But when the clamour started, I responded at once, and along with the rest ran around the camp, all of us scurrying hither and yon, searching the perimeters, looking at the walls and gates, and peering into ditches and sewage ducts and all manner of dark and unsavoury places.

Hauptmann Niemeyer came out as well, along with his brother, Heinrich. We could have managed perfectly well

without them, in fact a sight better. But Niemeyer was
determined to show Heinrich how efficient and authoritative
he is, and he barked orders at us, most of which went
unheeded because we did not hear them properly. Heinrich
barked a few orders of his own, so it was all very muddling.

Then a cry came from the main gates, and everyone ran
along to see what was happening. I was bringing up the
rear by that time, but I got there. And there were Iskander
and Stephen Gilmore, Iskander leaning negligently against
part of the gates, arms crossed, eyeing the sentries with cool
insolence. Gilmore was cowering behind him like a trapped
hare.

Iskander's escape plan was all of a piece with the rest
of him. Daring, arrogant, and so outrageous it might have
succeeded – well, it nearly did succeed. Somehow – I still
have not found out how – he had acquired two officers'
uniforms, which he and Gilmore donned in the latrine block
after breakfast. Thus clad, they simply walked openly across
the courtyard, and Iskander gave an order in German for the
gates to be opened. He even had the effrontery to salute
the sentries, two of whom saluted him back. (Those two
hapless sentries are now awaiting court martial.)

Iskander himself was philosophical about being caught;
he shrugged and made some remark about it being worth
the attempt, but perhaps not one of his better plans. Gilmore,
on the other hand, was devastated. He seemed to become
almost possessed at realizing he had not achieved freedom,
for he rounded on the guards like a trapped animal. I do
not think I shall ever forget the sight of his face, white and
utterly terrified, but with such desperate anger blazing from
his eyes it was as if his mind was on fire. Then, before any
of us realized what he intended, he sprang at the nearest
guard and snatched his rifle from him. The sentries at once
levelled their own rifles, and Gilmore would certainly have
been shot, for the orders regarding treatment of escapees
are very clear, but he managed to dive into the nearby
gatehouse. Within seconds a shower of bullets came rat-a-
tatting out. They were fired wildly, though, and none found
a mark.

'Shoot him!' cried Niemeyer, although it was all very well for him, standing half behind a stone arch. His brother, hiding behind the arch's fellow, joined in, calling for the soldiers to advance. 'Storm the place and shoot him!' he cried.

The sentries did not immediately obey either of the commands, for Gilmore had the gatehouse walls for protection, and they were in an open courtyard. Then a second shower of bullets came sizzling out and most of the soldiers dropped instinctively to the ground. But – and here is the cause of our upheaval – a stray bullet hit Heinrich in the stomach. He fell to the ground, screaming and writhing, giving vent to a series of curses the like of which I have never before heard from an officer's lips.

That was when Karl Niemeyer shouted to the soldiers not to fire.

'Shooting is too good for him,' he cried as people scuttled to help the wounded Heinrich, most of them keeping a wary eye on the gatehouse occupant. Niemeyer's face was as red as a beet, his eyes were popping, and his moustaches quivered. He should have been a comic figure, but he was very terrible. By that time I had managed to edge forward, working around the edge of the courtyard, and I could see Gilmore through a narrow window of the gatehouse. He had collapsed on the ground in a boneless heap, as if something had pulled the core out of his body. The rifle was no longer in his hands. Bullet holes showed in the low ceiling and parts of the walls, and I had the strong impression that Gilmore had not even aimed at the soldiers, but had simply fired the rifle into the gatehouse stones, almost as an expression of his bitter despair – even as an outlet for it. I glanced back to the courtyard. Someone had pressed a wadded jacket against Heinrich's wound, and three men were lifting him, obviously preparing to carry him to the medical block.

What I did next probably appeared quite brave, but it was not, because I could see it was perfectly safe. I walked up to the gatehouse and went through the open door. Gilmore stared up at me, his eyes wide and wild.

'Is he dead?' he said. 'But I didn't kill him. I didn't—'
He clutched at my hands, and his fingers felt like twigs,
frozen in the depths of winter, so cold and brittle that they
might snap off. The light had gone from behind his eyes,
and he was shivering. 'I didn't fire those last shots,' he said.
'*He* did it.' I glanced round, but there was no one in the
room with us. The rifle still lay by the far wall.

I said, 'Who did it?'

'The one who waits to take hold of my mind,' said
Gilmore.

This, clearly, was not the time to come to terms with
Gilmore's madness, real or pretended. I said, very firmly,
'Stephen, you must come with me.' And, may God forgive
me, I added, 'Do what I tell you and it will be all right.'

'Iskander—? Where is Iskander?'

'Iskander is outside. Stand up, Lieutenant.' I thought
using his rank might bring him to a sense of order, and it
seemed to do so, for he got up, brushed down his tunic,
and obediently came with me into the courtyard.

Two of the soldiers were spreading sawdust over the
spilled blood. Two more stepped forward, their rifles lifted,
but I held up a hand. 'He is not armed. He won't harm
anyone.'

'Imprison him,' screamed Niemeyer, and I promise you,
Freide, the man was almost dancing with rage. 'Throw him
into a cell and leave him in the dark. And if my brother
dies, I will see that real justice is done. As for the other
one—' He broke off in a spluttering access of fury, and
Iskander, who was being held by two of the sentries, said,
cool as a cat, 'If you take Lieutenant Gilmore, you take me
as well.' Even held captive, his stolen uniform disarrayed
and his hair tumbling over his brow, he managed to dominate
the entire situation.

'I organized this escape,' said Iskander. 'Therefore I
should take the blame.' He turned to the soldiers holding
him. 'Well? Why do we wait?'

After Iskander and Gilmore had been taken away, there
was much rounding up of various men who would have to
explain how the miscreants could have got as far as the

gates without being recognized, and how the two uniforms
had been obtained. We never did find that out, but thinking
about it, I am inclined to give more credence to Iskander's
claim to have been a burglar in peacetime, for only an
accomplished thief could have got into the officers' quarters
and out again without being seen.

But now comes the distressing part.

Nell came out of 1917 to a droning announcement that they
were approaching Paddington where she had to switch trains.
This was infuriating; it was almost as if the rail network was
deliberately interrupting Hugbert's story on the brink of a
denouement. But it could not be helped. She stowed Hugbert
away, grabbed her bag, and prepared to battle with London's
crowds.

The battle was not, in the event, so bad, and Nell reached the
new train smoothly. This time the carriage was almost empty,
and she was back into Hugbert's story before the train had gathered speed.

Iskander and Gilmore were taken to the solitary confinement
cells. I was commended for my brave action in entering
the gatehouse, which is very gratifying, but was not really
brave in the least. I could see Gilmore was not holding the
rifle.

We all thought Niemeyer would wait to see if Heinrich
recovered before pronouncing sentence, but the following
morning, with Heinrich still hovering between life and death,
he called for the miscreants to be brought before him. I was
ordered to be present as well, along with Hauptfeldwebel
Barth. We had a translator there, but I will relay the details
to you without the interpreter's interjections, so as to make
a smoother, more understandable account.

Iskander remained disdainfully courteous throughout the
proceedings. Questioned, he said that of course he had tried
to escape. It was the duty of every prisoner in every prison
camp to do so.

'You would yourself,' he said, eyeing Niemeyer.

Niemeyer said he would not be so foolish as to be

captured in the first place, to which Iskander promptly replied that it was unlikely that Niemeyer would venture himself into any dangerous situations anyway. I wanted to tell him to be quiet, for to enrage Niemeyer was to weave his own noose.

In contrast, Gilmore was in a pitiable state. He was shaking, causing the fetters around his ankles and wrists to scrape teeth-wincingly. Asked to give an account of himself, he said, 'I am innocent. I was not the one who fired that shot at the commandant's brother.'

'Then who did?'

At first I thought Gilmore was not going to answer. Then, in a strange, hoarse whisper, he said, 'The one who tries to take my mind. I have never seen him, but I know he is there. He fired the shot. I am innocent.' Despite the fetters he cowered back, huddling into a tiny ball, covering his face with his hands, then making clawing, scrabbling gestures as if fighting something off.

Niemeyer and the others stared at him, then Iskander said, 'Hauptmann Niemeyer, you must see that Lieutenant Gilmore is not entirely sane. He is certainly not accountable for his actions over the last twenty-four hours. I know it, and I think your soldiers know it—' He glanced at me, then away again.

But Niemeyer was so incensed at the interruption, he leapt to his feet, overturning the chair. His face was scarlet with rage, and he shouted, 'Be silent. This man is entirely sane.'

Iskander leaned forward, his expression more serious and earnest than I had ever seen it. Speaking quietly, he said, 'I will not be silent. Stephen Gilmore is a damaged human being. His mind is deeply wounded by the horrors he has seen. If you would bring doctors to him – men trained in the sicknesses of the mind—'

'We will do no such thing,' cried Niemeyer. 'In Holzminden we do not pander to weakness. Soldiers are not children.' He glared at Gilmore, still huddled in his own helpless misery. I thought: now he will pronounce the death sentence. They will both face a firing squad, although Gilmore may hang if Heinrich dies.

Hauptmann Niemeyer said, 'You, Iskander, you will be shot. A firing squad. You, Lieutenant Gilmore, will also die. But your sentence will be a darker justice in line with the darker crime you committed. In one week's time you will be bayoneted to death.'

Nell felt as if she had been dealt a blow. Bayoneted. Stephen, that gentle, bewildered young man – the boy who had clung desperately to the memory of lights burning in the windows of his childhood home. The frightened boy who crouched in corners, trying to fix his gaze on a horizon far beyond the nightmares of a dreadful war. He had been sentenced to that brutal death.

Bayoneting. Repeated and vicious stabbing of the victim with a long blade attached to the muzzle of a rifle. Over and over again, until the blade finally pierced a vital organ – heart, lungs, liver. Oh, Stephen, thought Nell, leaning her head back for a moment, and watching the landscape slide past. Did they really do that to you? Or did you manage to escape? Did you finally manage to see again the lamps burning in Fosse House?

There was still more than an hour before they reached Norwich. She collected a cup of coffee from the buffet car, and resumed reading.

I do think, Freide, that the cruellest part of the sentence is that it has been set for one week ahead. If Gilmore could have been taken out immediately after the enquiry and executed at once, the matter would have been over and done with. But Niemeyer would not permit it. And that, I think, was when the last rags of Stephen Gilmore's sanity deserted him.

Some of the officers have tried to talk to Niemeyer, but he will not be swayed. The sentence stands, and anyone refusing to carry it out will be court-martialled, and probably shot for treason in the face of the enemy. I begin to think if anyone is mad in this camp, it is Niemeyer himself.

Today he decided he will not risk solitary confinement for either prisoner, in case they cheat their executioners by some means of suicide. Instead, they have been locked away

in the dormitory they share with six other men, and two
armed guards have been posted at the door day and night.
The other prisoners have been told that to assist Iskander
and Gilmore in any way will result in their own deaths.

Iskander seems unruffled by his approaching execution,
although he is clearly frustrated at being confined to the
room, for the sentries report that he paces to and fro, as if
seeking a chink in the structure through which he might
escape.

Gilmore is retreating deeper into his own haunted
darkness. He sits on his bed for long hours, sketching –
some of the sketches he tears angrily to shreds, but others
he places with great care between sheets of card. One is of
the dormitory, with the men playing cards or chess, and
several of our own men peering in at him. Curiously, Gilmore
has drawn himself in the picture, but he has drawn himself
as seated apart from the others. I do not have the knowledge
to interpret this, but I find it immensely sad.

Last evening I asked him if I might have one of the
sketches – not the dormitory one, which disturbs me, but a
drawing of the courtyard beyond the dormitory's windows.
Gilmore has caught the brooding shadows, but has woven
into them the suggestion of a watching, waiting figure. The
face is barely discernible, but it is very clear that seen in
light it would not be a pleasant face. And yet the sketch
has such intensity that I cannot stop looking at it.

Gilmore said, 'You can have it if you want. I don't care.'

'I shall treasure it,' I said, and meant it, but, Freide, when
we finally have our own house together, I don't know
whether we would want to hang it on our walls.

When Gilmore is not sketching, he walks back and forth
to the same corner of the room, and stares down at a
particular spot on the ground, like a man watching the slow,
crawling progress of an insect. There is no insect there, of
course, but he constantly peers down at something which
he can see, but the rest of us cannot. At times he retreats
quietly to a corner and huddles there, wrapping his arms
around his body, staring at nothing.

Today both men were permitted to write a final letter to

their families. I took them when they were finished, ready to post. Gilmore's is addressed to a place called Fosse House in a village on England's east coat. Iskander's is to the Netherlands – a small town which I think is just outside Amsterdam. I did not read the letter, but before I placed it in an official envelope I could not avoid seeing that it was written in French, and that it began, '*Ma trés chére, fille. Ma bien-amié*, Leonora.'

I have not pried, but I cannot help remembering asking Iskander if there was a lady somewhere who was waiting for him, and his sudden defensive look, as if he was guarding something too precious to speak of.

Whoever had edited the letters – presumably Freide Edreich – had inserted the equivalent of a chapter break here. But there was still a good forty minutes left of the journey, and there did not seem to be many more pages, so Nell read on.

TWENTY

Dearest Freide,

I write in some haste and not a little turmoil.

Stephen Gilmore and Iskander have escaped. Incredibly, they walked out of Holzminden wearing the same officers' uniforms as they did the first time, and even more incredibly no one realized they had gone until it was too late.

We have pieced together as much as we can. It seems that Iskander acquired from the medical block (I dare say we will never know exactly how he did it) a strong opiate, which he used to drug not only the two soldiers guarding him, but also the other prisoners in the dormitory. Or, if he did not drug them, they made an extremely good pretence of being deep in drugged slumber for twenty-four hours, until Iskander and Gilmore had got away. This is either very devious of them, or loyal and courageous, depending on how you look at it.

And this time, no amount of wailing of sirens and wailing of Kommandants has recaptured Iskander and Gilmore.

The camp is in an uproar. Niemeyer is reported as being on the verge of an apoplexy, and he has stamped furiously around the camp confines, ordering arrests more or less at random, and court-martialling anyone who gets in his way. He cannot be dissuaded from sending a small party of men after Iskander and Gilmore, in order to ensure that his brand of black and bitter justice is carried out to the letter.

And I, Freide, am to be one of that party. It is partly because I have gleaned some knowledge of English, and partly because it is known I am a frequent correspondent to you and my family, and therefore thought able to send proper reports of our journey.

So now I have told you of my mission, which I should not have done. But I find such solace in knowing you will read this and that you will know what is happening, although I entreat you not to worry about me. It is true we are going

to England, to Stephen Gilmore's home on the east coast
– it is believed this is where he is most likely to go, and
we have the exact direction from the letter he wrote – but
please be assured that the danger to us is very small.
The journey has been meticulously planned, and I think the
arrangements are safe and good.

But as to the purpose of the journey – oh, Freide, I am a
loyal subject of our country and I will do what has to be done
and obey all orders, but I am unhappy and more reluctant
about this task than I have ever been in my entire life. There
is such brutality and vindictiveness behind the Hauptmann's
actions. I know this is a time of war, but I believe, with
Iskander, that Stephen Gilmore's mind has been damaged by
the horrors he has seen; I do not think he is in his right mind,
and he should not be held accountable for his actions. Also,
I cannot think it is right for such a senior-ranking officer (for
anyone of any rank) to behave with such calculating cruelty.

This evening I bade farewell to my colleagues in the camp.
They all wished me good fortune, and embraced me (in a
perfectly manly and soldierly fashion, you understand).

I and two other soldiers are to be under the command
of Hauptfeldwebel Barth. He is in high glee at being
entrusted with such an important mission and has told me
very solemnly that he is resolved to carry out Hauptmann
Niemeyer's orders to the last detail, and talks of how best
to do so. I fear he has no imagination and precious little
sensitivity. I should not say this – I certainly should not
write it down – but if I am able to find a way of avoiding
the vicious fate Niemeyer has decreed for Stephen Gilmore,
I intend to do so. Even in the midst of this war, I can not
believe that Niemeyer's sentence is justified.

Hauptfeldwebel Barth has advised me on items I should
pack, but since he has never travelled outside Germany in
his life, and appears to regard the inclusion of a fresh
consignment of bratwurst and six jars of pickled cabbage
as necessities, I do not think I will pay his advice any regard.
I have packed my woollen socks and also some flannel vests
and bodices since England is known to be a chilly country.

We are to pose as Dutch émigrés (my own ancestry

apparently suggested that to Niemeyer), although it is all very well for Niemeyer and Hauptfeldwebel Barth to say, airily, that the two languages are similar and the English will not know the difference. There is a considerable difference, I know that perfectly well from my Dutch grandfather. German and Dutch are two different tongues.

It is to be hoped the bratwurst will not go bad during the journey, because the smell will betray us to the enemy far more thoroughly than incorrect Dutch or English speech.

I have no idea when or how I will be able to write to you again – or if any letters will reach you – but I will do my very best to send you news. In the meantime, do not worry about me, for I shall be perfectly all right.

Your loving Hugbert

Dearest Freide,

This is a mad journey across Europe, and fraught with difficulties – although not, so far, with any dangers.

We are able to follow Iskander's trail surprisingly easily, and this is because his wild story about having been a burglar appears to be true. In each town along our way, we have met stories of some great house in the area having recently been plundered. The plundering does not seem to have been done with any violence – all the burglaries have been executed with finesse and what might even be termed consideration. In Osnabruck and Munster two large houses had been broken into and various pieces of silver jewellery taken. (In both cases, the owners described the jewellery as 'exquisite'.) In Düsseldorf, Iskander had romped through three museums, who were still mourning the loss of some seventeenth-century miniatures (described as 'priceless'), a notebook reputed to contain original jottings of Goethe ('unique'), and some early sketches by Theodor Hildebrandt ('irreplaceable').

Niemeyer and Hauptfeldwebel Barth were of the opinion that we should catch up with our escapees long before they reached England; they would have no money for travelling or food, said Niemeyer, as if this settled the matter. The Hauptfeldwebel agreed. I did not question them, but I suspected that Iskander would revert to his former profession to fund his and Gilmore's flight, and it seems I was right. It is deplorable behaviour on Iskander's part, but at least it is making the trail easier to follow. We have even been able to find out the trains on which the two travelled, and it is typical of Iskander's careless arrogance that he always used the first-class services. For us, issued with carefully calculated funds, that is not possible, and jolting across the border into Holland in a third-class carriage with wooden seats, no sanitation, and a pervading smell of stale onions, I began to think much might be said in favour of burgling as a career.

We had expected them to travel in a more or less direct line east across Holland, to The Hague, and from there to cross the English Channel. We found, though, that they headed a little further north. The trail led us to a small town outside Amsterdam, and it was then I remembered Iskander's letter, addressed to someone called Leonora. I explained this to Hauptfeldwebel Barth, who thought it more than probable that Iskander had made a frivolous detour to see a lady friend.

'We should follow him,' he said determinedly, so off we went again. (Trains for the relatively short journey were a little better this time.)

Infuriatingly, we missed our quarry by a mere two days, but I was able to discover that Leonora's last name is Gilmore, and that she had left Amsterdam in Iskander and Stephen Gilmore's company. The name cannot be coincidence; if Leonora Gilmore is the lady about whom Iskander was thinking that day – that precious private memory I glimpsed in his eyes – it is very believable that he would have befriended a man he believed to be from the same family.

The gentle Dutch couple with whom Leonora had apparently been lodging regretted that they did not know where the trio were bound; Miss Gilmore had boarded with them for about a year, they said. A generous payment for her keep had been made in advance by a very charming foreign gentleman – they did not know his name, but he had been courteous and considerate. (This is Iskander in his more gentlemanly role, of course.)

As for Miss Gilmore, she had been a most charming guest in their house. Polite, ready to help with household tasks. She had attended church every Sunday, and often during the week, and she had joined in some of the church activities – she had sung with their choir as well. She had a truly beautiful voice.

But there had always been what they would call an air of waiting about her, they said. As if she was daily expecting to be collected and taken to another destination – even another country, perhaps.

'England?'

Ah yes, that was entirely possible.

So now we are heading towards the coast where we hope to find a suitable craft to take us to England ourselves.

Ever your devoted,

Hugbert

Dearest Freide,

So finally and at last we are in England and I send this in the hope of its safe arrival.

The journey was not as bad as we feared, although the crossing of the English Channel was fraught with difficulties, and Hauptfeldwebel Barth was in constant fear that we should be shot at or sunk, for the English, say what you will of them, have a very good navy, and we had all heard stories of the Dover Patrol. I am still not sure how we avoided the miscellany of Royal Navy crafts – the armed cruisers and drifters and paddle minesweepers, not to mention the submarines – but somehow we did. Perhaps we were too small and too insignificant a craft to attract attention.

Halfway across, the Hauptfeldwebel stopped worrying about being captured on account of falling victim to violent seasickness which appeared to attack him from both ends, if you take my meaning. He confided to me afterwards that he felt it could not help a senior officer's authority over his men for them to see him crouching over a pail in a sheltered corner of the deck and retching into a pan at the same time. I was forced to agree, although I feel it was unnecessarily harsh of the two men with us to dub him Chunder Guts [*translator's note: this may not have been Hugbert's precise word, but is the nearest term that can be found*], and it has to be said that the Hauptfeldwebel's energetic consumption of some of the bratwurst was probably to blame for his condition. As I feared, it had started to go unmistakably off, and the pickled cabbage had turned a very suspicious colour as well.

After alighting from the boat and starting our journey to our destination, we were, and still are, uncomfortably aware of being in enemy territory. Hauptfeldwebel Barth says if we are recognized as Germans we will be shot against a wall at dawn. I suppose this is true, but, for myself, I find the people we meet to be incurious and even cautiously friendly. They are remarkably resilient and much given to their own brand of humour. We visited one tavern where what I recognized as very rude songs were being sung about the Kaiser. Fortunately, I got the others outside before they could try to join in.

We are a cheerful quartet as we go along, usually in the guise of itinerant hop-pickers or something of the kind. We occasionally risk accepting offers from passing draymen or carters, which covers the miles more easily. I am able to talk about bulb-growing in Holland, which reinforces our disguise, and is also unexpectedly pleasant. I remember so much of the stories from my grandparents, and the holidays I spent with them. My health is good, although I have developed corns on both feet from walking, but we have slathered on goose fat from a very accommodating farmer's wife, which has helped.

Much of the food contains what the English call stodge, which is not good for the digestion, so I am glad of my mother's peppermint cordial. But I am finding the famous English roast beef excellent, and also dumplings, and there is something described as jugged rabbit. I am uncertain whether the rabbit is actually placed inside a real jug, but it is stewed in cider, which is a local apple-flavoured wine, and very delicious. On the other hand, last night we were offered a dish of tapioca pudding which I would not inflict on anyone.

Your always loving,
Hugbert

Dearest Freide,

Yesterday we arrived in the village of Stephen Gilmore's home. Earlier this evening I walked along a lane by myself, to make sure of his house's exact whereabouts. And now comes a curious fact. You will remember I wrote to you of how Gilmore talked of lamps being lit for him within the house, when he or his family returned from any journey. Like seeing a beacon, he said, welcoming the traveller home and guiding him through the twilight.

Freide, tonight I saw those lamps burning for myself. I stood at the gates of Fosse House and I looked down the long drive, with its dark trees lining it all along, and I saw the lamps flaring against the darkness. They are warm and welcoming, and I understand now why Stephen Gilmore clung to this memory above any other. They beckoned to me in a way I cannot explain, even to you. I think Stephen is here – I think he is hiding in that house.

So now comes the difficult part of our mission. Our orders are to execute Stephen – and also Iskander. But I believe he acted under extreme distress – that he was not sane when he fired those shots. If, indeed, he did fire them, for he was so vehement in protesting his innocence.

Even if he is guilty, I have resolved that if I can find a way to sidestep Neimeyer's command and cheat Hauptfeldwebel Barth's resolve, I shall do so.

If I fail – if Stephen dies – I believe the memory will be with me all my life.

My dearest love to you,

Hugbert

Nell had read the section about Leonora Gilmore with faint surprise. Having found Stephen in Hugbert's letters, she had not been expecting a second Gilmore to turn up. As Hugbert said, though, if Iskander was romantically involved with a member of Stephen's family, it was natural that he had been drawn to Stephen. But Nell would still like to know what had happened to Iskander, and also his Leonora.

There were only a couple of pages left, and she saw with a sharp sense of loss that Hugbert's letters had ended, and that the final brief section was taken up with a note from Freide Edreich. It was dated the year of the book's publication.

My husband, Hugbert Edreich, never spoke of what happened in Fosse House that night in 1917, even to me. I believe, though, that the memory stayed with him all his life.

I never knew Stephen Gilmore's eventual fate, and I never tried to find out. My husband said to me once that some parts of the past were better left sealed up, and I believe that night in 1917 is one of those parts. I always respected his deep reserve on that period of his life, and I did not ask questions, but I believe he was still haunted (if that is not too dramatic a word) by his memories of the place.

I understood and respected his feelings, for I, too, had my ghosts from those days – the ghosts of gnawing anxiety for my husband-to-be who had come through the horrors and dangers of active service, and had then been sent on a difficult and uncertain mission into a country with whom Germany was at war. For me, those fears and those ghosts were somehow bound inside a charcoal sketch, drawn by a young man who had been in extreme fear of a brutal death sentence. Stephen Gilmore's sketch of the Holzminden courtyard hung in our house for many years – my husband had carried it with him from Germany – and I sometimes stood beneath it, staring into the dark shadows so deftly drawn, so cunningly suggestive.

'Who is that figure within the shadows?' I once asked my husband.

'I don't know. But I believe the young man who drew the sketch saw it as the symbol of his own insanity.'

The sketch's macabre qualities seemed to deepen over the years, although I repeatedly told myself that it was no more than a sheet of paper with pencil markings. But the mind is a strange thing and at times it operates at curious levels. There came a night when, from nowhere, a thought formed: supposing that figure – what Hugbert had called the 'symbol of insanity' – escapes? That was the night I took the sketch down from the wall and burned it.

My husband stood with me, watching it curl and brown in the flames. Then, very quietly, he said, 'Sometimes, in dreams I still walk along that tree-lined drive to Fosse House. I see the house through the trees and I see the lights glowing faintly at the windows – the lights Stephen longed to see,

that he thought of as a symbol of his home. Only, in my
dream they aren't quite real, those lights. It's as if they're
flickering ghosts, or the goblin lamps of some lost world.
And, in those dreams, something always comes out of the
house to meet me. I never quite see it, but I know it's there.'

'Stephen,' I said, for I had always known that Stephen
Gilmore's ghost had never quite left my husband.

'Yes,' he said. 'I think it's Stephen who comes to meet
me in those dreams. Who walks with me along that drive.
Because I think he's still at Fosse House, Freide. I know
that is a strange statement to make – a fanciful statement
– but I believe it to be true. And it's a bad feeling to think
of him in that lonely, dark old house.'

The book ended there, and Nell closed it with a sense of loss and
also an awareness that there were too many loose threads – the
loosest being what had happened to Stephen Gilmore. Did Hugbert's
silence about that long-ago night mean the execution had gone
ahead? That it had affected him so deeply, he had never been able
to speak of it? Or did it mean he had found some way to sidestep
Niemeyer's order, but had done it in some way he dared not disclose?

There was also no clue to Iskander's fate, or Leonora's. It was
unreasonable to expect Hugbert to have reported an idyllic, hand-
in-hand into-the-sunset conclusion for them, but Nell would like to
believe Iskander and Leonora had had some kind of happy ending.

But life did not always give people happy endings.

The bumbly local train out of Norwich was on time and painted
bright scarlet with green trims, like a picture from a child's
storybook. This pleased Nell, who spent the first ten minutes of
the short journey pretending she had stepped back into a 1940s
film. Will Hay, perhaps, or Arthur Askey in *The Ghost Train*.
She amused herself by imagining what the station would be like,
and whether she would be greeted by the shade of some old
station master who had died fifty years earlier but who could
still occasionally be seen wandering through the dark tunnels,
his lamp still burning in his hand.

There did not seem to be any shadowy station masters or
spectral ticket collectors at the station; in fact, the station was

little more than a platform with two small seats, a flower bed, and a narrow exit. It was dark by now, but Nell saw that Michael's taxi was waiting on the roadside. This was good, because the train had been more than ten minutes early.

'A good journey?' asked the driver, companionably, stowing away her small case.

'Very, thanks. We're going to the Bell, I think?'

''s right,' he said. 'Dr Flint phoned the details through. He's been doing some work out at Fosse House, seemingly. Shame about Miss Gilmore going like that. News got round pretty fast. Bit of a local legend, Miss Gilmore.'

'I'm sure she was. Do we go past Fosse House on the way?' Nell would quite like to see Michael's House of Usher from the security of a car.

'We don't,' he said. 'It's on a road to nowhere, as they say. But if you want to see it I can take a detour. Take us about fifteen minutes.'

'Will you do that, please?' said Nell. 'We're earlier than I was expecting anyway.'

'Lonely old road, it is.'

This turned out to be an understatement; the road that led to Fosse House was very lonely indeed. There were no street lights, and the taxi's headlights picked out trees and fields and little more. The roads were strewn with branches, which must be from the storm that had uprooted an entire tree and trapped Michael.

Nell tried to imagine living out here, especially in the depths of winter, and found it a rather depressing prospect. But these would be the lanes Hugbert and the others had walked all those years ago, spying out the terrain for their assault on Fosse House. She remembered again the sentence pronounced on Stephen Gilmore and repressed a shiver.

'All right in the back?' asked the taxi driver, half turning his head.

'Fine. Are we coming to the house now?'

'Just along here on the right,' he said. 'There's a bit of a wall – see it now, can you? The gates are just coming up.'

'Yes,' said Nell, leaning forward. 'Yes, I see them.'

He slowed down, and Nell peered through the windows at the gates and the clustering trees. This would be where Hugbert had stood that night in 1917, looking towards the house.

'You can't see the house at night, unless the lights are on in the front,' said the driver.

'Actually, there are lights on,' said Nell, suddenly.

'Are there? So there are. I thought Dr Flint was going off to the Bell?'

'It looks as if he hasn't left yet.' Michael was quite likely to have become absorbed in some esoteric piece of research and not noticed the time, so Nell said, 'Could you drive me up to the house? If Dr Flint's there you can drop me off here, and I'll go along to the Bell with him.'

'OK.' He turned off the road and drove through the gates.

The drive was quite long and rather dark. Had Hugbert crept along it, keeping to the concealment of the trees, dodging out of sight at every sound? But the lights were still glinting through the darkness. Were they Hugbert's ghost lights? No, of course they were not.

The taxi driver pulled up in front of the house, and Nell got out. The house was all that Michael had said, and it was rather daunting to think he had been forced to spend last night here by himself.

The taxi man got Nell's case out and hesitated.

'I'll see you in, shall I?'

'It's fine,' said Nell. 'I can see Michael through that window.' She indicated the long, low window on the right of the main door. The curtains were closed, but a light shone through them, and they were certainly not ghost lights, because there was a clear silhouette of a man seated at a table or a desk, his head bent. Nell smiled, because it was such a characteristic pose for Michael; he would be lost in reading something or tracing some reference, and he would not have realized the time. It did not look as if he had even heard the taxi draw up, although the walls of Fosse House were probably thick enough to blot out noises. She reached for the heavy door knocker, while the helpful driver deposited her case at the door. He accepted his fare and the tip with thanks, then paused again, as if wanting to be sure she went safely inside.

The silhouette in the window stood up and Nell heard footsteps coming towards the door.

The taxi man heard them as well. He smiled and nodded, then got back in the taxi and drove away down the dark drive.

TWENTY-ONE

Michael had worked in Fosse House's library until the middle of the afternoon. He found several old newspaper articles about the Palestrina Choir and two concerts it had given in Paris in 1904 to celebrate the Entente Cordiale.

The article listed some of the music performed – mostly Vivaldi and Bach – and also several of the more notable guests. These apparently had included the Archdeacon of Lindisfarne, the Venerable Henry Hodgson, together with his young son, William.

William Hodgson, thought Michael. That's surely W.N. Hodgson – better known as Edward Melbourne. I'm sure his father was in the church; in fact, I think he ended up as a fairly eminent bishop. He transcribed the details on to the laptop. Melbourne had not been one of the most famous of the War Poets, but he had written the deeply moving 'Before Action', and Michael was pleased to find this report of him listening to Vivaldi and Bach as a young boy, and perhaps being influenced by them in his later work.

Around three o'clock, the solicitor, John Pargeter, phoned to say he was very sorry, Dr Flint, but they would not be able to make the journey that day. Could they meet at the house tomorrow morning, though? Say around eleven? Most grateful – he would look forward to that.

The distant church clock was chiming the half hour, and Michael saw that the shadows were already starting to crawl out from the corners. He was meeting Nell at the Bell around six, so he might as well pack his things now.

He tidied away the papers he had been working on – the newspaper cuttings of the concerts, and some correspondence between Luisa and the present incumbents of the revived Liège convent, which was not yielding very much – and made a quick check of the rest of the house. The rooms were orderly and neat; there was a large drawing-room at the front of the house, which Michael had not yet seen, and which looked as if it was hardly ever used.

It contained large old-fashioned furniture, and several paintings hung on the walls, dim with age. Michael paused to study them. Stephen, are you in any of these? But the paintings were all rather turgid landscapes, except for one lady in elaborate Victorian dress, and two small oval-framed images of rosy-cheeked, ringletted little girls. It did not look as if there were any papers or anything private in here, so Michael, finding it rather a sad room, closed the door.

In the kitchen he was relieved to find a set of house keys. Taking them from their hook, he went diligently round the house, locking everything that could be locked, bolting the garden door and a little door off the scullery, and making sure all the windows were closed and the lights switched off. He would leave the various files and papers until the solicitor gave permission for him to take them, but rather guiltily he dropped Luisa's journal into his case. Then he set off for the Bell. He was relieved to find, when he reached the end of the drive, that the tree had been cleared. The road was still in a bit of a mess, with large branches and debris everywhere, but it was easy to negotiate this, and Michael would not have cared if he had to drive through the ditches and dykes if it meant getting away from Fosse House.

The Bell, when he reached it, was warm and friendly, and the room he had originally booked was still available – it was chintzy without being twee and oak-beamed without being self-conscious. Michael thought Nell would like it, and he thought she would like the Bell. Their tastes coincided on most things.

He unpacked his few things, then went downstairs to wait for Nell's arrival. It was just on five, which was much too early for her to get here, but he would prefer to be in the normality of the Bell's bar for the next couple of hours. He bought a drink at the bar and carried it to a quiet corner table. He had brought Luisa's journal downstairs with him, and there were only a handful of people in the bar, so he could finish reading it without interruption.

A faint, appetizing scent of cooking came from the direction of the kitchens, and Michael remembered he had not eaten a conventional meal for what seemed a very long time. Providing Nell's train was on time they could enjoy an early dinner together. And an early night afterwards? He remembered the deep, wide bed upstairs and smiled slightly. But in the meantime, there was Luisa.

He found the page he had reached last night, which was Luisa's description of finding Hugbert's second letter, describing how he and the others failed to get into the house because they had seen someone they thought was Iskander at the window. Michael began to read. Luisa had written:

It's late at night. I'm in my bedroom, seated at my writing desk, and I know I have to set down what happened the night my father invited Stephen in.

Leonora says I should do so. 'Write it all down, Luisa,' she says. I can hear her voice as clearly as if she's in the room with me. 'Your diary is the place where you should always tell the truth, and confession is good for the soul . . .'

That's her convent training, of course. But will I feel better for having written it down? And what if someone finds it?

'Then keep it a secret – keep it so well hidden no one will ever read it . . . Unless one day you decide the truth should be known . . . Because one day you might meet someone you feel you can trust with it . . .'

I don't believe this particular truth will ever need to be known, or that there will ever be anyone I will be able to trust that much.

But there was someone, thought Michael, coming out of Luisa's world for a moment. She met me and for some wildly incredible reason she thought she could trust me. It might only have been because she was dying – she might have trusted anyone in that situation. But he still found it moving that she had trusted him.

I'm terrified that this might be another of Leonora's tricks to take over my mind. Is that what she wants to do? Did she live in this house once? With Stephen? That thought makes me rather jealous, but I believe Leonora is a friend rather than an enemy, so I'm going to do what she says. It will be difficult, but I'll follow the advice from *Alice in Wonderland*: 'Begin at the beginning, go on until you reach the end, then stop.' I know when the beginning is. It's three nights ago when I let Stephen into the house.

'He's here,' my father had said, pointing to the faint

footprints across the floor, and I had felt such a mixture of
fear and excitement that I had not been able to speak.

My father left the room, and I heard him cross the hall.
There was the sound of a door opening somewhere with a
slow creak, although I had no idea which door it was. I
stayed where I was, huddled into the chair, wrapping my
arms around my body, watching the wet footprints gradually
fade, as if Stephen was fading out of my reach. Or was he?
Father had seemed so sure he was in the house. And the
memory of Stephen's hand closing around mine was still
vivid. It's vivid now as I write this.

At last I went out into the hall. It looked different, as if
something had been altered. I looked round, trying to see what
it could be. It was a large hall, nearly always dark because
of the panelling and the narrow windows on each side of the
door which did not let in much light. Then I saw that a small
section of the panelling seemed to have come away from the
wall, but when I went closer, it was a small door, set so deeply
and so cleverly into the surrounding oak that unless you knew
it was there you would never have noticed it. I certainly had
never done so. It was slightly ajar. Was it the door I had heard
being opened earlier? Was Father in there?

Mother was in the small sitting room at the back of the
house – I could hear the faint murmur of a wireless and I knew
she would be there for the rest of the evening. She always
pretends to despise the wireless, but she listens to it avidly.

I walked towards the panelled door and pushed it wider
open. It gave a faint groan, and stale air gusted into my
face. Beyond was a flight of stone steps leading down. I
glanced behind me, then went down the steps.

To describe what I saw at the foot of those steps is easy
enough. A low-ceilinged room, with floors and walls of
thick old stone. There was a wavering light from an oil
lamp placed on the ground, and there were a few pieces of
furniture – a small table, one or two broken kitchen chairs,
a jumble of household rubbish in one corner.

But there was one other object in that room, and although
I can describe it, I don't think I can put into words how it
affected me. It was a massive oak chest, carved and elaborate,

a little like those stone structures you see in paintings of Egyptian tombs. To me it was exactly like a deep old coffin. It was repulsive and frightening, but somehow it was also sad.

My father was kneeling in front of the chest, but he turned at the sound of my footsteps, his eyes wild and strange – wilder and stranger than I had ever seen them.

'It's all right,' he said, in a conspiratorial whisper. 'I'm going to save him. I've found a hiding place for him.' He was unwinding a thick length of chain that had been around the chest.

'Father, what's happening? Please tell me. I'm scared.'

He lifted a finger in the traditional hushing gesture. 'You must never tell anyone about this,' he said. 'Never. Niemeyer's butchers are nearby. I can hear them whispering to one another, creeping towards the house. But even if they get in, they can ransack the entire house and they'll never find him down here.'

He terrified me. I saw that he believed himself to be back in Stephen's time – the time when the German soldiers had come here to kill him. It was all in the letters he had found in Belgium. And after all the years, my father could still hear those men . . . But if I listened intently, couldn't I hear them as well? As for Stephen— The logical part of my mind knew Stephen was just an echo of the past, a fragment of an old memory blown forwards to the 1950s, like a dry leaf.

And yet . . . And yet I could still feel the pressure of his hand against my palm. I could still see his eyes looking imploringly into mine. *'You must let me in . . .'*

'I'm going to open this and let him get inside,' my father was saying. 'Then I'll chain it and lock it – you see there's a padlock, Luisa? Then I'll lock the door upstairs and they'll never know this room is here. You didn't even know it was here, did you, Luisa?'

'Well, no, but—'

'All I've got to do is wait for him,' he said, looking back at the chained chest. 'Then he'll be safe.' He was nodding to himself, murmuring the word 'safe' over and over again. But the dreadful thing was that he didn't just nod once or twice, he went on and on nodding, as if he had forgotten what he was doing or how to stop. I moved towards him, and that was when

I saw the Holzminden sketch propped up against the wall behind him. In the flickering lamplight it looked different – the eyes of the people seemed to have come alive.

I reached for my father's arm, intending to take him back up the stone steps, and that was when the strangeness in his eyes erupted into something far worse, something that reared up and came towards me, hands clenched and curved into claws. I backed away and made for the stone steps, but my father came towards me.

'You must never let anyone know about this room,' he said. 'I can't let you go until I have your absolute promise, Luisa.'

'I promise,' I said, in a gasping sob. 'I truly promise.'

'Good.' He stepped back. 'I have to stay here, though. I must wait for him, you see. I must be here, ready to help him. Do you understand that?'

'Yes, I understand.'

This time I managed to get away, and I scrabbled to get up the stairs, tumbling through the door in the hall. I was gasping and sobbing, and I had no idea what to do. Then I heard him come up the stairs behind me. He closed the door, and I heard a key turn from within.

The mind is a curious thing. At times it works at levels that we don't understand. I didn't understand my mind that night. I waited in the hall until I could be sure I had stopped shaking and I thought my voice would be firm, then I went along to the little sitting-room and called to Mother that I was going to bed early to finish my book.

'Don't lie reading too long. It's bad for your eyes. Is your father still working?'

In a perfectly ordinary voice, I said, 'Yes. He's in the library. He said he might be there until late, and we aren't to disturb him.'

I sat in my bedroom for a very long time that night. I didn't even attempt to sleep.

My mind was filled with the thought of my father locked into that room, locked in with that oak chest, so like a deep, dark coffin. And Stephen . . .? Was it really possible that Stephen could be lured down there and that my father could chain him inside the chest and so save him from the German soldiers? Written down it looks utterly mad. In reality, mad is exactly what it is, of course. What I also know is that a lot of it is my fault. I let Stephen in – it didn't matter that father told me to do it, I was the one who opened the window so he could come in. I fed my father's madness. Perhaps I even caused it.

I lay listening to St Augustine's church clock striking the hours. When the wind is in a certain quarter, you can hear the chimes quite clearly. It's a cold, lonely sound at any hour, though, and on that night it was the coldest, loneliest sound I had ever heard.

At half-past six I got up and went down to the hall. The house was shrouded in early-morning light – thin and grey, not hopeful like the start of a new day should be.

For a wild moment I thought the door in the panelling might have vanished, like a door in a fairy tale that isn't always there. It had not, of course. But it was still locked, so I tapped on it and called out softly. At first I thought he was not going to reply, but then I heard him come up the stairs.

'Luisa?'

'Yes. Please unlock the door.' There was silence. I tried again. 'Come out and have some breakfast. You can go back in there later. Please, Father.'

'Bring my breakfast here,' he said. 'I must wait for him. If it takes months – years even, I must wait for him.'

Him. Stephen. The young man with soft hair and that beseeching hand-clasp who had been dead for more than a quarter of a century.

I thought if I could at least get Father to open the door, I might be able to reason with him. He might snap back to sanity, and we could go on as we had before, and no one would have to know about this. So I went along to the scullery and made coffee, strong and sweet, the way father liked it, and I made toast and spread it with butter and his favourite Oxford marmalade, and I took a small tray to the panelled door.

He opened it a very little, and his face appeared in the narrow gap. For a terrible moment I thought it was not my father – that it was some wild-eyed madman who had got into the house. Then I saw he was wearing the shirt and cardigan he had on last night, and as his hands came out to snatch the tray from me, I saw the signet ring he always wore. Before I could say or do anything, he retreated and I heard the lock turn again. Footsteps went back down the stone steps.

I had no idea what to do. I did not even know if anyone would believe me if I told them – I did not think Mother would. And without the key it would be impossible to open the door – no one had known it was there anyway. Even Mother's cousin, my Uncle Charles, had never noticed it, and Uncle Charles liked exploring the house. He usually came for Christmas, and he was apt to organize boisterous games after Christmas dinner – treasure hunts and hide-and-seek and something called Sardines, which he always said was a corking game – they had played it when he was a young man and it would liven up our guests splendidly. Our guests were generally the vicar and his wife, and their two unmarried daughters, and none of them were the Sardines type, but that never bothered Uncle Charles.

Uncle Charles.

I took a deep breath and went into the library and picked up the phone.

Michael saw that someone – and presumably it had been Luisa herself – had folded a small piece of paper into the diary at this point. Unfolding it, he saw the familiar writing of Chuffy Chiffley. Luisa's Uncle Charles.

Dear old Tommy,

I'm in need of a rather large favour. I know it's a frightful imposition, but I'm wondering if you might be able to help us out over a cousin who's become a trifle unhinged.

It's nothing too serious, I shouldn't think – probably down to the war, you know – but he's taken to locking himself away in a cellar and refusing to come out. Awfully upsetting for the family – there's a wife and a young daughter. I'm anxious to help, but I don't mind telling you I was absolutely at a loss until I remembered you and that you treated a few chaps who'd been in Intelligence in the 1940s, and who'd come out of it a bit battered mentally. I remember how grateful they were. Also, I think you were at that Scottish place – Craiglockhart, wasn't it? – during the Great War. I'm sure you once told me you'd helped look after those poor blighters who suffered shell-shock.

My cousin has been looking into the life of one of his relatives who went through all that grim 1914–18 stuff, and it's my idea that he's got a bit fixated on it all – I think that's the right word. So if you've got a spare room in one of your nursing homes where he could be kept quiet and safe, with a few trained people on hand to help sort him out, the family would be most awfully grateful. I don't know how these things work, but I can give you my personal assurance that the wherewithal will be forthcoming.

How are things with you? I wish you'd toddle along to join us at the next regimental reunion. They always put on a pretty good show, and it would be splendid to see you again.

Hoping to hear from you soon,

Affectionately,

Charles (Chuffy) Chiffley

It was like meeting an old friend. Michael thought Chuffy's anxious generosity came off the page vividly and endearingly.

He reached for his drink and glanced at his watch. It was quarter past six. Nell would probably not be much longer. There seemed to be only a brief entry left in the journal, so Michael took a sip of his drink, and read on. Luisa's next entry sounded just a short while after the previous one.

Today Mother was more angry and snappish than I have ever known her. At lunch she talked about inconsiderate people, and how some men become so caught up in their own concerns they have no thought for others. She added the usual comment about wishing she had married her cousin Charles.

I wish she had married her cousin Charles as well, because Uncle Charles is a cheerful person, and that morning when I phoned him, he drove out here the same day. My life might have been a lot different if Mother had married him.

The doctor has been again. He gave Mother a bromide to help

her sleep. He offered me a half-measure of it, as well. It was important I remained strong and calm, he said, to help my poor mother. I accepted the pills he gave me, but later I threw them away. If I let my mind be taken over by pills, Leonora might find a way in. She's dead of course, I know that. The Palestrina Choir is dead as well, it died in 1914 . . .

But I can't rid myself of the feeling that Leonora is still here.

Everything is so quiet, and there are long, empty hours to fill. Ordinary activities don't seem to be thought suitable. Mother keeps saying things like, 'I would have thought you'd have found something better to do than read those rubbishy books, Luisa.' And, 'Turn off the wireless, those droning voices make my head ache.'

Late last night, after she was in bed, I got an electric torch from the scullery and went to open the panelled door. The broken lock has been repaired after they broke it down – Uncle Charles had a carpenter here within two days – and there's a new key in the drawer of the hall desk.

'Best leave that room locked up,' Uncle Charles said firmly. 'No need to go down there. Unpleasant places, cellars, anyway. Best forgotten altogether.'

But I couldn't forget it, so last night I crept through the house, which was dark and silent – at least, it was as silent as it ever is, which is to say it was filled with odd whisperings and creakings.

The new lock turned with a slight grating sound, then the door swung open. The steps were in darkness, and it was like facing a climb into a deep old well, but I went down them and shone the torch cautiously around. Everything was exactly as I remembered it.

The oak chest was exactly as I remembered it as well. Without realizing what I was going to do, I knelt down and placed my hands on the domed lid. Oak is a lovely thing – oak trees are beautiful and friendly, and furniture made from them is beautiful as well. Solid and sturdy and with a satiny gloss. But the oak of the ancient chest felt dull against my skin, as if it had been torn from the tree, and left raw and untreated. I laid my cheek against it.

Stephen, are you there? Did my father succeed in hiding you in there? I think I even held out my hand, hoping – longing – to feel those poor sounded fingers close around mine again. But there was nothing. If Stephen or that strange fragment of him still lingered in this house, it did so invisibly and soundlessly.

The Holzminden sketch lay against the wall, and I had the curious impression that it did not like being down there in the dark— No, that's absurd, I shouldn't have written that.

I've brought it back upstairs, that sketch, and I'll find a space to hang it on a wall somewhere. In the meantime, I've left it in Father's room.

Going into his room upset me, which I hadn't expected. I don't think I love my father, and I don't think he's ever loved me. But entering his bedroom, I smelled the bay rum he rubbed on his hair and the wintergreen he used for his chest in cold weather. And I remembered that he was shut away in a place where the smell of sickness and insanity is everywhere, and where there are long, bare corridors that need painting, and that ring with people's hurrying foot-steps, and scrape-wheeled trolleys bearing nameless pills and injections for all the poor bewildered people who will never again see the outside world. I don't think my father will ever see the outside world again, either.

I stood there in his bedroom, and I thought: I'm the cause of him being in there. His mind cracked because of Stephen, and I was the one who let Stephen in. Then I sat on the edge of his bed and cried for a long time over the pity of it all.

But later I hung the sketch on the small landing. It feels as if it's a little piece of Stephen, and for that reason alone I'd like to be able to see it each day.

It looks quite nice. I think I'll hunt out some of the photo-graphs of Fosse House from the war, to hang with it – some of the nurses took photos of the men who were here convalescing.

Next week we have one of our permitted visits to see Father.

They seem to think it's unlikely that he will ever improve.
He has created a hiding place in his room – a wardrobe –
and he sits in front of it, watching and waiting. Sometimes
he crouches on all fours, like an animal waiting to pounce.
The doctors say they can't find out what he waits for. I know,
of course, but I can't bring myself to tell them. I can't bear
to think of them discussing Stephen, analysing his life,
making judgements about him. It wouldn't make any
different to Father's treatment if I did tell them, so I shan't.

Mother says she does not know what we will do for the
fees of the nursing home, but Uncle Charles says we are not
to worry about that; he will see everything is taken care of.
Dear Uncle Charles.

When we get home from the visit, I think I might go
down to the stone room again. I feel close to Stephen there
– I feel Leonora would like prayers to be said for him. I
can do that. Leonora grew up knowing about prayer, and
I know about it as well.

The more I think about it, the more I think I shall go
down there from time to time.

Michael turned the page. There were a few more entries – brief
notes about ordinary day-to-day life at Fosse House. Luisa, having
recorded the traumas and tragedies of those years, seemed to
have lost interest in keeping the journal.

But there was one entry right at the end, and although Michael
thought it was in Luisa's hand, it was no longer the writing of
a fifteen-year-old girl. This was something she had written very
recently.

I had not thought I would want – or need – to write in this
private book again. But once, all those years ago, Leonora
said I might one day meet someone I would feel I could
trust with the contents of these pages. I never thought so
myself, but I was wrong . . .

Because yesterday I believe I met that person, the one I
can trust with the truth—

The final word trailed off, and Michael, staring at it, thought:

that's when she had the heart attack. His mind presented him with a picture of Luisa writing that entry, then feeling the heart pain, and falling. But at least I heard her, he thought. At least I could summon help. He reread the last sentence. *Yesterday I believe I met that person, the one I can trust . . .*

He closed the diary and put it into his jacket pocket. He was scarcely aware of the modern surroundings – the buzz of conversation from the drinkers at the bar, preparations at the far end for what looked as if it might be a pub quiz.

Nell's train had probably reached the local station now. He would try phoning her to find out. He felt in his jacket pocket for his phone, then realized with annoyance that he had left it up in the bedroom. He was just getting up to fetch it, when the barman called out to ask if he would be having dinner there that evening.

'Because if so, I'll reserve you a table, Dr Flint. It's a quiz night, and we get fairly busy.'

'Yes, please,' said Michael. 'There'll be two of us. At least, if the trains run to time there will be.'

At this a man who had just come in and was helping with the tables for the quiz, looked sharply round.

'Dr Flint?'

'Yes.'

'The same one as booked a taxi at the station earlier?'

'Yes. You were going to pick up my partner and bring her here. Was the train delayed or something?'

'As a matter of fact, it was early,' said the man. 'Which is a miracle these days. But your lady wanted to be driven past Fosse House, and we saw lights on, and we thought you were in there, so— You were in there,' he said, half accusingly, half puzzled. 'We both saw you. So your girlfriend said she'd go in and drive out here with you.' He was starting to look more than puzzled. 'I saw her go up to the door,' he said. 'I waited and saw her knock on the door.'

Michael said, 'I've been here since about half-past four. I locked up the house and switched off all the lights.'

'Then,' said the man, 'who was it I saw at the window?'

TWENTY-TWO

Nell thought Michael was taking a long time to come to the door and let her in. She had seen him cross the room on the right-hand side of the front door, and she had heard him walk across what was presumably the hall. Then nothing.

She tried the knocker again and heard it reverberate in the house. Surely no one could have missed hearing that? She pressed her ear against the door, to listen, and for a dreadful moment had the feeling that someone was standing on the other side, listening to her. This was absurd. Probably the house and the darkness was affecting her. She delved into her bag for her phone to ring Michael's number, but it went straight to voicemail. Clearly, Michael had switched it off for some reason and forgotten to switch it back or he had let the battery run down. Either of these would be like him. Nell left a message on the off-chance he would pick it up, then walked to the lighted window and tapped on it.

'Michael? Are you in there? It's me – Nell. For heaven's sake let me in, it's freezing out here.'

Still nothing. She stood close up to the window, trying to see inside, but the curtains were drawn tightly and there was no chink. She thought the room was empty – the silhouette she had seen earlier was no longer there, that was for sure.

A tiny beat of apprehension began to tap against her mind. She was not going to recognize, even for a second, any thoughts about spooky goings-on. What she was going to think was that Michael had not, after all, heard her knock. He could have had a radio on – headphones plugged in, maybe. He might, by pure coincidence, have walked across the hall just at that minute. She would walk round the side of the house; there was bound to be another door at the back. Tradesmen's entrance. And very suitable too, thought Nell.

The lighted window cast a faint radiance over the house's front, but when she came to the corner, deep shadows lay everywhere. She glanced back at the driveway and for the first time realized she had not seen Michael's car anywhere. It might be parked on the other side, of course, but it would be reassuring to see it.

Walking along the side of the house was eerie. The house was on her left, and there was a narrow, uneven path. Nell could just about see her way, but trees and shrubs grew thickly along the side of the path, and overhead boughs dipped low, turning the path into what was almost a tunnel. Once she stumbled over a broken flagstone or a tree root, and only just managed to save herself from falling. She was starting to dislike the isolation of Fosse House very much, and she was wondering how Luisa Gilmore had managed to live here by herself for all those years.

She had been hoping to see lights at the back of the house, but it was in darkness and she could not make out any doors. The gardens were almost entirely in shadow, but beyond a sweep of slightly overgrown lawns was what looked like an inner walled garden. Hugbert had mentioned that; it felt strange to be actually seeing it.

Nell began to wish she had taken the number of the taxi driver who had collected her from the station. Still, it would be easy enough to call one of the enquiry numbers and find it – or if not, there would be a local firm who would come out. But if Michael was in the house . . . Yes, but his car was not here.

She stepped back into the tree tunnel, intending to return to the front of the house, but she had only gone a few steps when a dark figure appeared at the other end. Nell gasped, then drew a shaky breath of relief, because it must be Michael – he must have been out here all along. She was about to call out and go towards him when an alarm bell sounded in her mind. If this was Michael he would have called out. Her heart skittered unevenly, and she backed away, going towards the rear of the house again, desperately trying not to stumble on the uneven path, but reaching the corner safely. She risked looking back. The figure was still there, a black silhouette, featureless, almost two-dimensional, as if it had been cut out of the darkness and pasted on to the night. He was coming towards her.

Nell sent a despairing look at the dark house, then felt for her phone. But she would not be able to key in a number in this dimness, and she dared not stay here for long enough to make the call anyway – he was coming down the pathway towards her – she could hear his soft, light footsteps. If she could hide somewhere, she could use the phone, though. How quickly would the police get out here? And where could she hide that would be safe? Would there be an unlocked door into the house? But it would be almost impossible to locate a door in this darkness.

The walled garden was barely twenty yards away – she could see the glint of the black wrought-iron gates. If she could get in there she might be able to hide, or even climb over a wall. Nell thought she was so pumped with adrenalin she could probably scale the north face of the Eiger at the moment. She took a deep breath and, trying to keep to the shadows, ran towards the gate.

He came after her at once, as if he had known all along what she would do, and she heard him call out. But his voice was indistinct, and Nell could not tell what he said. It was not Michael's voice, though; Nell would have known Michael's voice if all the tempests of hell had raged and the skies had been rent asunder.

The wrought-iron gate was closed, but the latch clicked up easily. The door swung open with a squeak of sound; as Nell stepped inside, the walled garden seemed to envelop her with a scent of wet grass and the tang of box. She went towards the concealment of the tangled vines growing against the old wall and crouched down. But as she reached for her phone, he was framed in the gateway, turning his head this way and that, looking for her. Nell's hand had closed over the phone, but she hesitated. He could not fail to hear her make the call, and he would be on her long before help could get here. She pressed back into a thick mat of ivy, willing him to decide she was not here, praying he would go away.

She thought he called out again, and for the first time a tiny doubt brushed her mind, because his voice was hesitant, almost whispering. Or was that a ruse? For the first time she spared a thought to wonder who the man was – was he simply a chance intruder? Whoever he was, Nell was not going to risk letting him know where she was. She remained motionless, hardly daring to breathe.

The man seemed to hesitate, then stepped forward. If he closes the gate we'll be shut in together, thought Nell in horror. But he left the gate open and began to move around the edges of the garden. Nell, keeping her eyes fixed on him, edged away. If she could keep to the wall, she might manage to work her way back to the open gate and get out.

It was like a macabre game of hide-and-seek. Several times she thought the man whispered something, but she could not hear what he said.

She was about halfway round; the man was a good fifteen yards behind her, and she was trying to decide if she dare risk a quick sprint across the grass to the gate, when the gate itself swung closed. The man shot round to stare at it, but Nell thought it had only been the wind that had closed it.

Or had it? Because there were other sounds in the garden now; stealthy movements. Footsteps – not as light as the lone man's had been, but still the footsteps of someone who did not want to attract attention. Nell had no idea if she could trust this new arrival sufficiently to shout for help. Or supposing it was Michael? Hope surged up, because perhaps Michael had realized the arrangements to meet at the pub had gone wrong, and so he had come out here. But wouldn't she have heard his car or seen its lights?

Now there were more than one set of footsteps, and the garden seemed to be filling up with shadows – shadows that were not quite solid but not entirely transparent. Nell shrank back, a kind of disbelieving comprehension starting to unfold in her mind.

Stephen Gilmore had fled to this house all those years ago, and on a night in 1917 – a night about which a young German soldier had never afterwards spoken – four men had followed him to execute him. Had they cornered him in this very garden? Was this a weird, incredible replay of that long-ago event? It was the wildest idea in the world, and once Nell would have rejected it out of hand. But tonight, in the shadowy old garden, she believed it completely. It was Stephen who had followed her through the grounds of his old family home, whispering to her as they went – whispering and treading furtively because he had not wanted Hugbert and the soldiers to know where he was. Had he been trying to warn her? Or ask for her help?

The shadows – yes, there were four of them – were forming a circle around the single figure. This could not be happening, this was her disordered imagination, it was a trick of the light – several tricks. But the shadows were closing in on Stephen, and somewhere inside the sighing wind were faint cries, as if for help, spun on the air with such fragility that it was difficult to be sure that they, too, were not illusions.

Nell began to move, with infinite stealth and extreme slowness, towards the gate. She reached it without mishap and eased the latch up, praying that it would not squeak. It did not, and the gate opened smoothly, but she turned to look back. Were the shadows moving in on their prey? They were like smoke, so that it was impossible to be sure of anything. Oh, Stephen, she said silently, I wish I could help you, but there's nothing I can do. Whatever happened here happened almost a hundred years ago, and I can only hope you managed to get away, or that Hugbert – dear, nice Hugbert – found a way of saving you.

She made a rather shaky way to the front of the house, taking deep, grateful breaths of the cold night air. She was reaching for her phone again, to find a taxi or to try Michael again, but before she could do either, headlights swept the night and his car came around the drive. He parked untidily, leapt out and ran towards the house.

Nell called out, 'Michael. Over here.'

Michael stopped in mid-stride, saw Nell, and came straight to her.

'Thank God you're here,' he said, grabbing her and pulling her to him. 'I thought— I don't know what I thought. Are you all right? What on earth are you doing out here?'

'I'm perfectly all right. But the walled garden—' She broke off and looked back at the narrow side path. 'Michael, before I explain, could you bear to walk round to the back of the house to the walled garden.'

'Now? Tonight?'

'Yes.'

'Certainly I will, if it's what you want, but—'

He glanced uneasily at the house, and Nell said, 'I'm not suggesting we go inside.'

'Thank goodness for that.'

'I don't think there's any danger,' she said. 'I don't think there ever was. Well, not in the walled garden anyway.'

'What exactly happened?'

'I'm not sure. Are you honestly all right to do this?'

'No,' said Michael promptly. 'But we'll go along to see what beck'ning ghost along the moonlight shade invites our steps.'

'You do know how to add to an atmosphere. Where did you find that one?'

'I think it's Alexander Pope, isn't it?'

'One of the many endearing things about you is that you always assume other people are as knowledgeable as you are,' said Nell as they made a cautious way along the dark path.

The gate to the walled garden was wreathed in shadows, and there was a faint vapour on the air as if something had darted past it and left a barely-visible imprint.

Nell stopped. 'The gate's closed and latched.'

'Did you close it?'

'No. I left it wide open.'

They walked forward and peered through the iron scrollwork.

'We're like two children in a Victorian sketch,' murmured Nell. 'Staring in awe through the gates of the big house.'

Michael put his arm round her. 'Whatever you saw – and I think I could make a fair guess at what that was – I don't think there's anything in there now, Nell.'

'But don't you have the feeling that we've missed something by only a few seconds? That something's just happened and we were too late – or too early – or we didn't know the right thing to say?'

'I'm supposed to be the one who thinks like that. Talk about gamekeeper turned poacher.' He smiled at her. 'You appear to be level with me on research, or even ahead of me.' He looked back into the shadowy garden, then shivered slightly and turned away. 'Let's leave the ghosts to their lawful – or unlawful – occasions, and go to the Bell and compare notes over a meal.'

'Now you mention it, I'm starving,' said Nell. 'Wait a minute, I'll get my bag – I left it on the doorstep while I was chasing the ghosts. Or the ghosts were chasing me, I'm still not sure which it was.'

'I'll fetch your bag. You get into the car.'

They rounded the corner of the house together. The wind was still stirring the trees, causing the branches to cast goblin-fingered shadows across the old stonework. Most of Fosse House was in darkness, the windows black and blind. But at one window a

soft, flickering light showed, casting the silhouette of someone
who was seated at a desk or a table, writing.

'It's still there,' said Nell, stopping. 'That's the light I saw
earlier. I thought it was you – that's why I was trying to get into
the house. But that light – it's gas light, isn't it? Or even an oil
lamp. Because—'

'Because the house didn't have electricity in Stephen's time,'
said Michael softly.

'Do you know what that room is?' Nell's eyes were still fixed
on the glimmering light and the outline behind the curtain.

'I think it's the main drawing room. I glanced in there earlier
today. It had the air of hardly being used, but I do remember
seeing a writing table by the window.'

'I suppose there's no possibility of that being a – a real person?'

'Who, for instance?'

'The solicitor you spoke to?'

'He couldn't have got in without these keys.'

'Luisa's cleaner? She might have a key.'

'Writing at a desk by gaslight?'

'Well, no. What do we do?'

Michael looked down at Nell. Her eyes were dark smudges in
her face, and she looked pale, although whether with fear or
tiredness, he could not tell. He said with decision, 'What we do
is to drive away from this place like bats out of hell, and for the
next few hours we pretend there's nothing and no one in there.'

'We do?'

'Yes. But,' he said, smiling at her, 'we come back here
tomorrow morning, to see what daylight shows up.'

After the eerie shadows of Fosse House, it felt vaguely unreal
to be seated in the tiny dining-room, eating the Bell's very
substantial chicken pot pie.

Between mouthfuls of chicken, Michael gave Nell the gist of
Luisa's story. Nell listened with the absorbed interest that he
always found endearing, then said, 'Yes, I think I see. How sad.
Was she mentally unbalanced, do you think?'

'I think,' said Michael, and heard a slightly defensive note in
his voice, 'that she was affected by having spent her whole life
in that house. She hardly ever saw anyone or went anywhere. I

think most people might become a bit odd in those circumstances. And her father sounds very odd indeed.'

'I do feel rather sorry for her.'

'I think there was more in her life than it might sound. She was certainly regarded as something of an expert on the Palestrina Choir, and quite a number of very learned people used to contact her. I think there might have been a fair amount of interest – even purpose – in her life.' He laid down his knife and fork. 'Can I see Hugbert's letters, now? If you're having pudding, I could skim-read them.'

'I won't have pudding, but I'll share some cheese with you, please. You can skim while I eat.'

Michael read the letters, forgetting about the cheese, but occasionally reaching for his wine glass.

'Hugbert fills in a lot of the gaps,' he said eventually.

'Yes. And it sounds as if Luisa's journal fills in a lot more. There's still an awful lot we don't know, though.'

'I wonder if we ever will,' said Michael, closing Hugbert thoughtfully. 'The largest blank is what happened to Stephen, isn't it? Booth tried to find that out, but he doesn't seem to have done so. And his search was much nearer to it than we are now.'

'But in the end it led him to an asylum,' said Nell.

'I'd like to think he didn't die in there, but I'm afraid he probably did.'

'I'd like to know about Leonora,' said Nell. 'It sounds as if Iskander stowed her away with those people in Holland and collected her when they escaped from Holzminden – did you pick up that bit in Hugbert's letters?'

'I did.'

'Do you think she came back to Fosse House with Stephen?'

'Yes, I do. I know I've given you a potted version of Luisa's journal,' said Michael thoughtfully, 'but I don't think I've really conveyed the strangeness of it. There are passages where she almost sounds as if she thinks she actually is Leonora. Leonora had some kind of disability, according to Iskander – it sounds like club foot or something of that kind. Luisa seems to have developed a similar lameness.'

'So you're following all the traditions of classic hauntings which would argue that for Luisa to be – um – shadowed so strongly, Leonora must have lived at Fosse House at some stage?'

'Don't mock me, you heartless wench.'

'I'm not,' said Nell, smiling. She snapped off a piece of celery, then said, 'How about Stephen and the Holzminden affair? Do we think he really did shoot Niemeyer's brother?'

'You're remembering the sentence, aren't you?' said Michael, seeing her shiver slightly. 'Bayoneting.'

'It's horribly brutal, isn't it? Did the brother eventually die, I wonder? Hugbert doesn't say. I suppose it might be possible to find out, although I'm not sure where you'd start.'

'I can just about believe that someone else fired that shot at the brother,' said Michael thoughtfully. 'But it's stretching credulity to snapping point.'

'I could believe it. Those two were greatly disliked, and Karl – the Kommandant – sounds as if he was a vicious brute. Hugbert said the shots from Stephen's rifle went into the ceiling and the walls of the gatehouse, remember. And Stephen protested his innocence all the way through.'

'I think he'd do that anyway.'

'You don't believe he got away, do you?' said Nell.

'No, I don't. I think that's why he's still there.' He glanced at her. 'A violent death being one of the top ten favourite motives for a ghost to haunt.'

He said it with deliberate lightness, but Nell replied, quite seriously, 'Hugbert thought Stephen was still there. What was it he said?' She reached for the book. '"I think he's still at Fosse House . . . And it's a bad feeling to think of him in that lonely, dark old house."'

'Luisa thought Stephen was still around, as well. So did her father, although I suppose some of his evidence can be discounted, poor chap. But I'll swear I saw Stephen myself, on two occasions at least. Only – it's all so ethereal. What we're seeing are little more than shadows. Silhouettes at lighted windows. What was it you said in the garden tonight? That we're just too late or just too early to see the reality. By the time we get there, only the shadows are left.' He grinned a bit wryly. 'I do know how bizarre it all sounds.'

'You seem to attract the bizarre,' said Nell. 'But I'm getting used to it.'

'Are you?' said Michael, looking up. 'Enough to face a future filled with bizarre stuff?'

There was a pause, and he thought: damn, I've gone too far. I'm not even sure what I meant. But Nell said slowly, 'That might be rather a tempting prospect. Hadn't we better sort out the spooks first, though?'

'We'll go hand in hand into the spook-ridden sunset,' said Michael gravely.

'You know, I've almost sometimes wondered if you and I together are some kind of catalyst for ghosts,' said Nell. 'Like two chemical elements. You mix them or blend them and you get — I don't know – something explosive. Hydrogen or nitro-glycerine, or something.'

'You and I together are an explosive combination anyway, even without the spooks,' said Michael, putting his hand over hers for a moment.

'I know. We're very lucky, aren't we?'

'I do think,' said Michael as Nell withdrew her hand in quest of another sliver of cheese, 'that Luisa would like me to find out what happened to Stephen. I almost feel as if she was handing me the ghosts, that last night. That sounds really way-out, doesn't it? Do you think I might have had too much wine tonight?'

'For you, it isn't all that way-out. But you have drunk most of the bottle,' agreed Nell, looking round for the waitress to request black coffee.

'So I have. I don't think I'm actually drunk, although I might be slightly light-headed with relief at being away from that house. You may have to carry me up to bed.'

'How times change. Once it was the other way round,' she said, deadpan.

'Have you seen the stairs here?' demanded Michael. 'They're the steepest and the narrowest I've ever seen, and the bedrooms are on the second floor.'

'The sooner we set off, the sooner we'd get there.'

'That's true. Let's not bother with coffee after all.'

TWENTY-THREE

Thin morning sunlight fell across the old timbers of Fosse House's hall, but in the corners were thin spiked shadows, like severed spider legs.

Nell stood in the hall, looking about her. 'I see what you mean about it being eerie,' she said. 'Is that the library through there?'

'Yes. And that's the main drawing-room where we saw – whatever or whoever we saw last night,' said Michael.

'Let's save that for later. Can I see the Holzminden sketch? I've brought my camera,' said Nell. 'If the solicitor agrees, I could send one or two photos out for some tentative opinions.'

Michael would not have been very surprised to find the sketch had vanished from the half-landing overnight along with the rest of Fosse House's chimeras, but it had not, of course.

Nell stood in front of it for a long time. 'It's remarkable,' she said at last. 'At first you think it's just a charcoal sketch – quite a good one, I think – but nothing more. Only, the longer you go on looking at it, the more you see in it. I could wish Hugbert's wife hadn't destroyed the other one.'

'I find it unsettling,' said Michael, studying the sketch. 'And that's throwing roses at it.'

'It's very unsettling,' she said. 'I don't think I'd want to be in a room with it for too long.' She reached out a tentative hand to trace the outlines of the figure seated on the bed. 'So that's Stephen.'

'Is it how you imagined him?'

'Not entirely, but almost. He's younger than I thought. It's heartbreaking, isn't it? War's heartbreaking anyway, but that one took—'

'The flower of England? "They went with songs to the battle, they were young; straight of limb, true of eyes, steady and aglow . . ." I can't recall any more of it,' said Michael.

'Just as well. If you say anything about remembering them at the going down of the sun I shall dissolve in floods of tears. Is this the photograph from Word War Two?'

'Yes.'

Nell studied it intently. 'Yes, I see,' she said. 'You wouldn't see anything strange unless you looked at the sketch at the same time. He's just a man in the background. But there's the impression that he isn't quite in the photograph – that he's not entirely one of the group.'

'I wonder if any of those men saw him,' said Michael. 'Although it looks as if he's in uniform, so they might have accepted him as another patient.'

Nell repeated the gesture of tracing the shadowy figure in the photo, then stepped back. With an air of closing one subject and preparing for the next, she said, 'What now? There's a good hour before the solicitor will get here. The underground room?'

'Yes, but I don't think you'd better come with me. Will you stay up here?'

'No,' said Nell firmly. 'I'm coming with you. I want to know what happened to Stephen as much as you. And since we're quoting anything that comes to hand on this trip, isn't there a line about, "Follow thee my lord throughout the world"?'

'There is, but I'm a bit old for Romeo.'

'I don't care if you're the ghost of Hamlet's father, I'm not staying up here while you chase shadows in the cellars.'

'I'll leave the main door open, I think,' said Michael. 'Because if Pargeter turns up early, we mightn't hear his knock while we're down there.' He propped the door open with a small chair, then produced the key Luisa had given him.

Even seen halfway through the morning, the underground room was daunting. Nell shivered and thrust her hands into the pockets of her jacket as Michael shone the torch around the walls.

'It's like a shrine,' she said in a low voice. 'But a shrine for who?'

'Stephen, I should think. Luisa certainly seems to have had a bit of a romantic feeling for him.' The torchlight came to rest on the oak chest, and Nell gave a sharp gasp.

'So that's it.'

'Yes.'

'It's much bigger than I was imagining,' she said. 'And much deeper. It's almost waist-high, isn't it? It looks like a dower chest. Young ladies often brought them to their new homes when

they were married – they were intended to hold bedlinen,
mostly. They can be quite valuable. Can I have the torch a
moment? Thanks.' She knelt down, shining the torch directly
on to the chest. 'It's oak,' she said, 'and it's probably English.
Oh, and there's ebony inlay – can you see? Here and here. Some
of it's chipped, which is a pity. Those dreadful chains probably
did that. But the carving is lovely, isn't it? I should think it's
early eighteenth-century, which would make it very sellable.
It's a pity about the scratches and the chipped ebony, though,
because that will devalue it, and—'

'What is it?' said Michael as Nell broke off abruptly.

She was sitting back on her knees, staring at the chest. 'Listen,'
she said, very quietly.

'I can't hear anything. If it's footsteps, it's probably Mr Pargeter
arriving early—' Michael stopped, his eyes on the chest.

'Can you hear it?' said Nell in a half-whisper.

'Yes. It's something scratching. It might be mice,' said Michael,
looking about him. 'They might be at the back of the chest, or—'

Nell said, 'It's not coming from the back of the chest.' She
turned to look at him, her face pale. 'It's coming from inside it.'

They stared at one another. 'It can't be,' said Michael at last.
'It simply can't. Nothing could have got in there. Or if something
did – if something gnawed its way through the wood, it would
be able to get out the same way. At worst, it's mice.'

'How strong do you think that padlock is?' said Nell. 'It's
very rusty. I should think it would snap off pretty easily.'

Michael stared at her. 'You want to open it?'

'It's the last thing I want to do. But there's something in there,
Michael. And whatever it is, it's alive. Can you really walk away
and pretend you didn't hear it?'

'It probably is a mouse.' Michael was looking round the stone
room. In a very quiet voice, he said, 'Nell, I think we have to
walk away anyway.'

'Why?'

'Because there's someone in here with us.'

Nell stood up slowly, automatically brushing the dust from
her skirt. She looked about her, and her eyes came to rest on the
corner behind Luisa Gilmore's writing table.

In a very gentle voice, she said, 'Stephen?'

The shadows moved slightly, like smoke uncoiling. Nell reached for Michael's hand. Neither of them moved.

There was a sound like a faint sobbing – the faraway, long-ago resonance of something sad and somehow pleading, and then he was there, indistinct and blurred, like a photograph or an early ciné film not quite in focus. But recognizable. The young man with the leaf-blown scar and the nightmare-filled eyes.

Half to himself, Michael said, 'Of course he'd come in. We left the main door open.'

'I'll never believe you didn't leave it open deliberately,' said Nell, her eyes on the figure. 'Does he see us, do you think?'

'I don't know.' Michael had forgotten about beating a retreat. He said, 'Stephen – it's all alright. We're friends. We'll try to help you.'

There was no way of knowing if Stephen Gilmore heard or understood or knew they were there. His eyes were on the chest, and as he moved towards it, Michael was aware of Nell stepping back. But she's not frightened, he thought, and was grateful for her understanding.

The spoiled hands were reaching for the thick old chains around the chest.

'He's guarding it,' said Nell in a whisper. 'He thinks we're going to open it, and he's trying to prevent us.'

Michael had not taken his eyes off Stephen. He said, 'No, it isn't that at all. I think it's the other way round. He's trying to get it open. He's trying to get at what's in there.'

'Are you sure? Because if so, let's help him,' said Nell at once. 'Let's get the thing open. We both heard something in there – I don't care if it's dead or alive or something between the two – let's smash that padlock and break this bloody haunting wide open.'

But Michael was already halfway to the stairs. 'Hammer,' he said. 'In the kitchen. Come with me.'

He grabbed her hand, and together they half ran up the stairs. It was Nell who found a sturdy-looking hammer and a wooden mallet.

'This should do,' she said. 'If it won't, we'll have to call in a safe-breaker.'

They ran back through the hall and down into the cellar again.

'Is he still here?' said Nell, hesitating at the foot of the steps.

'I don't know. Let's just do this anyway.'

'Yes.' Nell went purposefully across to the chest. 'Hold the padlock away from the wood, will you? I don't care if the entire spirit population stands around gibbering at us, I'm not causing any more damage to this beautiful oak if I can help it.'

'Like this?' asked Michael.

'No, see if the chain's long enough to lay the padlock flat on the floor. Then I can bash it against the stone.'

The chain was just about long enough. Nell said, 'Good enough. Here goes. But be careful – stand clear of it in case it shatters.'

The padlock did not shatter, but the sound of the impact as she brought the hammer smashing down tore through the enclosed room and reverberated round the walls. Dust, dry and pale, clouded up from the stones.

'The lock's still holding,' said Michael, peering through the debris. 'Damn. Let me try.'

'No, you'll end up bashing your thumb or your foot or hitting the mains water supply.'

'I do love you,' said Michael, with sudden irrelevance, and she sent him a startled look.

'Well, good. But stand clear this time.'

This time, as the hammer impacted, the padlock cracked and the lock flew open.

'Got it,' said Nell with satisfaction. 'Now for the chain.'

Between them, they unravelled the chains from around the chest. It was necessary to tilt it slightly forward at one stage to drag the chains from beneath. It was heavy, but not as heavy as Michael had expected. But as the chest moved, there was the sensation of movement from inside, as if something had slithered from one end of the chest to the other. Nell shivered, but shone the torch on the lid, and Michael understood she was focusing on practicalities in order to ignore anything that might be watching from the shadows.

'I can't see a lock anywhere,' said Nell. 'I think we should be able to just lever it up. I can't hear the scratching now, can you?'

'No. But something shifted when we tilted the chest,' said Michael.

'I know. Let's try lifting the lid.'

She placed the torch on the floor so that its light shone directly on to the chest, then she and Michael each took a corner of the domed lid.

'It's stuck. Or even locked, after all,' said Michael after a moment. He glanced uneasily at the shadows in the corners, but nothing moved.

'I think it's just stuck down with dirt,' said Nell. 'We need something to scrape it out— Something that won't damage the wood. A nail file would probably do it – pass my bag, would you, I think there's one in there.'

By dint of scraping at the seam, the accreted dirt of the years came free in minuscule flakes and filaments. Nell worked her way round the rim of the lid with infinite patience, and Michael watched, feeling vaguely useless.

'I think that'll do it,' said Nell, straightening up at last. 'Let's try again.'

This time when they pushed at the lid, it moved, and at the third attempt a faint line of blackness showed under the lid.

'Be careful,' said Nell. 'The hinges could be rusted almost to nothing, and we don't want to send the lid smashing against the floor.'

The seams of the old oak creaked loudly as the lid came up, and the hinges shrieked like a soul in torment. As the air within was released there was a sighing sound, and something dry and infinitely sad seemed to breathe outwards.

The faint whispering came from the shadows, and they both paused.

'Stephen?' said Nell softly, scanning the darkness.

'I don't know. I expected – I don't know what I expected,' said Michael. 'But I thought that opening this would trigger something.'

He thought they had both been trying not to think about what might be inside the chest, but at first sight it looked as if there was nothing more than a yawning blackness, with a length of cloth folded at the bottom.

Then Nell reached down into the deepness of the chest and moved the cloth. There was the pale blur of bone, the impression of a human outline lying quietly beneath the cloth, and the glint of something bright. Nell recoiled, dropping the cloth over the bones, and straightened up.

'Stephen,' she said. 'It's his body. Oh, Michael—'

But Michael had reached down and, careful not to touch or disturb what lay partially covered by the cloth, drew out a small crucifix on a thin gold chain.

'I don't think it is Stephen,' he said. 'You'd know better than I do, but this looks like a very feminine thing.'

'Yes.' Nell took the small crucifix and looked at it. 'Yes, it's the kind of thing a lady would wear.'

'A lady who had spent her formative years inside a convent?'

They look at one another. 'Leonora?' said Nell.

'I think it might be.' Michael looked back at the dark well of the oak chest. 'Let's not move anything,' he said. 'We'll have to report what we've found, but for now let's quietly close the lid and leave it to the professionals to lift her out.'

'The annoying thing,' he said as they sat in the library, waiting for John Pargeter to arrive, 'is that we still don't know what happened. We're still only seeing shadows; we still haven't got down to the reality. "Shadows inside the rain," Stephen said somewhere in Luisa's journal – or Luisa thought he said. And that's what we're getting.'

'We probably won't ever see or know what the reality is,' said Nell, sadly.

But they did.

Pargeter and Associates
Solicitors and Notaries Public
Walsham

November 201—

Dear Dr Flint,

    RE: ESTATE OF LUISA GILMORE (dec'd)

    It was very pleasant to meet you at Fosse House recently, although the circumstances, of course, were sad. However, my colleagues and I are very grateful for all your help over this somewhat complex matter.

    We are also very grateful to Mrs West for her excellent advice and assistance over the selling of some of the more valuable furniture, china and glassware, and we are delighted that we have now been able to confirm the arrangements for her to handle the sale of the items discussed. (A separate letter regarding this has been sent to Mrs West at her Quire Court shop.) The sketch referred to as the Holzminden sketch is, I understand, already attracting some interest, and we will probably accept the suggestion that it is sold at auction by a specialist firm.

I am extremely sorry, however, that you and Mrs West had the distressing experience of finding human remains in the house. As you know, the police had to be notified of the discovery – any dead body has to be reported, no matter how long it might have been dead – and a post mortem was conducted. I do not yet have the results, but hope to let you know when I do. I can tell you, though, that the small crucifix you found in the oak chest is thought to be around a hundred years old, and possibly French in origin.

However, knowing your research into the Gilmore family history, I think you will find this next information of interest. Found beneath the body, at the very bottom of the oak chest, was a small sheaf of papers. They are handwritten and in English – very good, even colloquial English, although the writer appears not to have actually been English. I have taken photocopies and am enclosing them with this letter. They raise a number of interesting possibilities, and certainly suggest the identity of the body.

The funeral for Miss Gilmore is to be next Thursday, at the local church. Do please let me know if you, or anyone from Oriel College, would care to attend.

Kind regards,
John Pargeter

Michael read John Pargeter's letter twice. Then he read the opening lines of the enclosure. After this he reached for the phone to ring Nell.

TWENTY-FOUR

'We ought to read it together, I think,' said Michael, having provided Nell with a drink and seated her on the small sofa, where the light of the desk lamp fell across her hair. Wilberforce, who liked Nell, but would not admit it sufficiently far to actually sit on her knee, had positioned himself on the sofa arm.

'This is like old times,' said Nell, curling her feet under her and accepting the drink. 'Are these papers going to provide any answers, though?'

'I don't know. I only read the first sentence, then I tripped over Wilberforce to reach the phone to tell you,' said Michael. 'I don't know if this will give any more answers. But I think it's our last shot.'

'You didn't say who wrote it when you phoned,' said Nell. 'But I'm assuming it's Leonora.'

'I expected it to be Leonora,' said Michael. 'But it isn't. It's Iskander.'

He flattened out the papers, put one arm round Nell, and they began to read.

It's a tradition for writers from my country to pour out their souls in an orgy of confession and a raging tempest of dark angst and *weltschmerz*, not to mention the beating of breasts and rending of garments. I am perfectly happy to immerse myself in *weltschmerz*, but I am not inclined to be penitent, and if anyone's garments are to be rent they will not be mine.

It may be vain to believe someone, somewhere, at some time, will want to read what I have written, but although I do not admit to many faults, I do admit to some, and vanity is probably one of them, so I will believe it.

I have decided to write this in English. I learned a good deal of the language while in Holzminden and also on my travels, and I'm rather proud of my skills. And since this deals with events in this English house it seems appropriate.

It was the very young owner of this house who caused me to come here. Stephen Gilmore. A gentle soul, Stephen. He believed entering the conflict between his country and Germany to be noble and inspirational. Like thousands of other eager, idealistic young men, he went off to war, to the sound of cheering crowds, with flags waving and military bands playing, seeing only victory and glory. No one had warned them about the horrors and the despairs and the nightmares lying in wait.

I saw the nightmares, but I saw them from a distance, reporting for my newspapers. Like those stylish and disdainful reporters at the Crimean War, I sat on a safe hillside or in a field, partaking of smoked salmon and Chablis, exchanging languid observations with other newspaper men and writing about the theatres of war – theatres as bloody as anything ever dredged up from the pit of the Grand Guignol.

But bodies were shattered, eyes and limbs were splintered. And minds cracked.

When I met Stephen Gilmore in the prison camp at Holzminden where I had been ignominiously taken after being captured at Verdun, at first I thought him weak. Later I came to understand he was far from weak: he had fought his nightmares and his demons and he still fought them. A weak man would have given in to them. Stephen had not.

My reasons for escaping from Holzminden were not entirely altruistic. I genuinely wanted to get Stephen out of the camp, but I wanted to escape for myself, as well. I wanted to rejoin Leonora.

Leonora. She was like no lady I have ever met before or since. She was seventeen, convent-bred, small-boned and fragile with one leg slightly askew so that she limped when walking. She had a rather sallow skin, dark hair and eyes, and no one would ever have called her a beauty. But the moment I saw her I knew that even though I might live a dozen lives, and even though worlds might burn and mad

Prussian emperors storm across continents, I would never feel the same about anyone ever again.

Astonishingly, the convent years had not quenched Leonora's natural *joie de vivre*. Despite her sheltered life and the nuns' teaching, she took to the life of burgling as smoothly as silk. She took to love-making with the same delight as well. In my defence, I did try to fight that temptation, but one night, somewhere on the borders of Holland, Leonora metamorphosed from obedient waif into beckoning sprite. Like the fantasy play *Love in a Dutch Garden*, which I saw at the beginning of the war, a harlequin moon lay against midnight skies, and violet twilight enveloped the old rose gardens of a wayside inn. Nightingales even sang outside our windows. And no man is an angel all the time, and certainly not in such a setting. On that night, like Scaramel in the play, I was tempted and I yielded.

Afterwards, with the Kaiser's crazed stranglehold tightening on Europe, I left Leonora in Holland, in a comfortable, safe guest house with comfortable, safe people, and made my way back into Germany to gather more material for war articles.

If only I had not done so.

I have to be honest and say the first escape attempt from Holzminden was never intended to include Stephen Gilmore. I thought his mind was too fragile for him to cope and for me to trust him. But somehow he became involved, and it was as easy to abstract two German officers' uniforms for the attempt as one. And he was Leonora's cousin . . . So I took the risk.

On my own I might have succeeded. I might have talked my way through the guards – my German was very good by then – but Stephen, fearful and damaged, drew attention to our ploy, and found himself surrounded by armed guards. In desperate panic, he snatched a gun from them, although God alone knows how he managed that, and retreated into the gatehouse.

It was certain he would have been shot – all the camps had orders to fire on escaping prisoners – and the guards were already taking aim. From where I stood, held by two of them (but not very firmly), the only thing I could think of was to create a diversion. No one seemed to have realized that I, too, had a gun – a Luger pistol which had been with the stolen German uniform, and which was more or less hidden in the belt. There are times in life when you have to take risks, and I took one then. I fired the pistol, not particularly aiming at anyone. The fact that it hit one of the senior officers – actually the camp commandant's repulsive brother – was unintentional and disastrous. Everyone assumed that Stephen, cornered and panic-stricken, still in possession of the gun, had fired the shot. No one noticed when I kicked the Luger into a corner of the courtyard, because everyone was running around shouting orders. The commandant flew into a rage, I was hauled off to the cells, Stephen was dragged out of the gatehouse, and we were both sentenced to death – I for the escape attempt and impersonating a German officer, and Stephen for the same crime, along with the attempted murder of Heinrich Niemeyer.

To have confessed I had fired that shot at Heinrich would not have made matters any better. We would still have been executed. That was when I knew I had to get Stephen out of Holzminden and back to England.

Somehow I did it. I drugged some of the guards and bribed the others (there are times when having been a successful burglar is very useful), and we got out. I am not providing any more details, because I intend to write my memoirs, and I am not giving away the facts here. Suffice it to say we escaped, and I got both of us into Holland, to where Leonora was living.

I do not feel it to be any part of this statement to describe my reunion with Leonora; I shall say only it was a night to make the gods sing and the poets weep with joy.

The next day, by fair means and foul, by hedge and by stile, and despite the vagaries of the ferry system, the three of us reached England and this house.

We should have been safe here. How could I know that Karl Niemeyer – as mean and brutal a man as ever walked God's earth – would send his men to hunt us down all the way to Norfolk and Fosse House?

Michael leaned back for a moment, then turned to look at Nell.

'I think we're about to find out what happened,' he said. 'Are you sure you want to know?'

'Yes. I met Iskander while I was chasing Hugbert,' she said. 'And I rather like him. He was a rogue, wasn't he, but he had quite a lot of – well, of what he'd probably call honourable feelings. Let's go on.'

'Onwards and upwards,' said Michael, turning to the next page.

We had almost a week of relative peace at Fosse House. Stephen prowled around the rooms, occasionally venturing into the gardens, I made a start on my memoirs, using the library as my study, and between times Leonora and I—

Well, there is a walled garden here, and it is like a secret garden from a children's fairy story. Each afternoon Leonora and I went into that garden, and there was only the scent of the apples from the old trees overhead, and the feel of the soft moss beneath. No one disturbed us. No one knew we were there. We did not care that it was a cold English autumn – we hardly noticed.

When I met Stephen in the camp in Germany, he talked about wanting to see again the lamps burning in the windows of his home. It was an image he clung to. Tonight, in the drawing room at the front of Fosse House, I have lit those lamps for Leonora.

Earlier this afternoon I took a long walk. Stephen thought I was exploring the area, but of course I was reconnoitring the terrain. There aren't many large houses hereabouts, but there are some, and the coffers needed replenishing if Leonora and I were to make any kind of living—

I returned to Fosse House two hours ago. Twilight was falling – it's an odd kind of light, the English twilight. Smoky and strange. Walking up the drive, I had the feeling that something was near to me – something friendly and inquisitive, and that if I knew how or where to look, I should see it. Writing this, I've had the same feeling – as if there's something (someone?) wanting to see into the room, curious about what I'm writing.

As I came along the drive I liked thinking how Leonora would be waiting for me – and Stephen too, of course – and how we would make a meal for ourselves in the big old kitchen, and then eat it in the dining room with the windows overlooking the gardens. I am perfectly prepared to eat in a kitchen, in fact I have had some extremely pleasant encounters in kitchens, but if there is a comfortable dining room, with a polished table and silver cutlery, I will choose that every time. Even if it means helping with the washing up afterwards.

Approaching the house, I became aware of something wrong. At first it was only a feeling, but then it was more definite. Sounds. Movements. They were confused at first, but gradually they coalesced into stealthy footsteps and low murmuring voices. Then, clearly and sharply, a voice called Leonora's name, and the desperation and anguish in the voice cut through the dusk like a sword. I stopped, listening intently, and when the cry came a second time I knew it was from the gardens behind the house. I ran forward, making for the narrow path at the house's side. It's almost enclosed by trees and shrubs, and rather dark and narrow.

The shouts came again, and I recognized the voice as Stephen's, although I could no longer tell what he was saying. He had gone along the tunnel path, and he was at the back of the house, staring across the dark gardens. I followed his line of vision and saw the blurred figure of a female running towards the walled garden. There was a faint screech of sound as the gate was opened, and she ran through it. And then— I can't exactly say she vanished, which would be absurd, but she seemed to somehow melt into the darkness.

Stephen went after her at once, going through the iron gate, calling out as he did so.

'*Leonora* . . .' The name lay on the air, as fragile and insubstantial as silver filigree.

That was when the shadows in the walled garden reared up and were suddenly and frighteningly no longer shadows but men. Even from where I stood I could see who they were. Niemeyer's men.

It was instantly obvious what had happened. Karl Niemeyer had sent his men after us – in his vindictive, selfish determination to be revenged for his brother's shooting he had ignored the war and had sent soldiers to England, purely to recapture one man. Heaven knows how long they had been out there, but they had trapped Stephen in the walled garden. I edged closer, considering and discarding half a dozen plans. If there had only been two soldiers I might have risked a surprise attack and hoped to get Stephen away, but there were four, all armed. I tiptoed closer to get a clearer view and recognized two of the soldiers from Holzminden. The fat and essentially stupid Hauptfeldwebel Barth, and a younger man called Hugbert Edreich. Seeing Edreich gave me a glimmer of hope, because he had been a kindly and unexpectedly sensitive gaoler in the camp, always trying to help, certainly sympathetic to the likes of Stephen.

The two soldiers whom I did not know had taken Stephen's arms, and they were dragging him against an ivy-covered wall. He was struggling, shouting to them to let him go, calling for Leonora again.

'Leonora,' he cried. 'Please – oh, please . . .'

Edreich was looking about him, almost as if he might be seeking some way of preventing what was about to happen, but the other three soldiers were already raising their rifles. Then – and this is the part that grips at my vitals like steel fingers – they fixed the bayonets to the rifles' muzzles. It seemed Hauptfeldwebel Barth intended to carry out Niemeyer's orders to the last tortuous letter. Bayoneting. That had been the brutal sentence on Stephen, and I could not believe they would do it. But they were already tying him to a tree trunk, binding him tightly with a length of rope. He was sobbing and struggling, and I tensed my muscles, ready to bound forward. But it was already too late. The soldiers lined up, the bayonets tilted, and the order was rapped out. The men ran at the imprisoned figure. I heard the clash of bayonets, and I heard someone shouting. Then a single gunshot rang out.

The shocking thing – the thing that will remain with me all my life – was that the soldiers seemed not have heard the gunshot, and they continued with their grisly work. But Stephen was already dead. He had sagged against the tree, and something that was black in the moonlight ran down his face from his forehead.

From where I stood, I saw Hugbert Edreich very quietly and stealthily put a pistol back into the holder at his belt.

And now I am writing this in the long drawing-room of Fosse House, and my mind is scalded with the pity of it, and with pain and remorse. But within the anguish that I did not save Stephen is one tiny shred of comfort. He did not have to suffer the agony of being bayoneted. That single gunshot fired by Hugbert Edreich was done as an act of mercy – I *know* it was, I know it as surely as if Edreich had told me so. At the end, unable to save him, he gave Stephen a quick, clean death.

But even now I can spare only a small part of my mind for Stephen, for Leonora is filling my thoughts. I have no idea where she is. What I do know, though, is that the indistinct figure I saw running into the walled garden – the figure Stephen called to and followed – was not Leonora. It could not have been. Leonora could not run so swiftly and smoothly. She had a club foot, and she could not run at all . . .

Nell pushed away the remaining pages and went, almost blindly, to stand at the window, not looking at Michael, not looking at anything. When Michael went to her she turned away from him – the first time she had ever done so. She was not crying, but there was a dreadful blankness in her eyes, and Michael waited, not wanting to intrude, understanding that she was struggling with a deep, confused emotion.

At last, Nell looked at him. In a tight, desperate voice, she said, 'The figure they saw— The figure Stephen followed into the walled garden— Iskander was right to say it wasn't Leonora. What was it Booth Gilmore said about time bleeding backwards?'

'That's just a mad theory,' said Michael uneasily.

'But it's not, is it? Because I was the figure they saw. Stephen followed me into the walled garden – he thought I was Leonora. If he hadn't done that, he wouldn't have been caught. He wouldn't have died. I led him there – I led him straight into the hands of those murderers.'

Michael said, very forcefully, 'Yes, he would have died – that was inevitable. The soldiers wouldn't have waited very long, you know. When night fell, they would have broken into the house and dragged him out. It's what they tried to do the first time, only they saw—' He stopped, the words of Hugbert Edreich's letter in his mind.

I saw him open the curtains in a downstairs room and look out, Hugbert had written. *There was a lamp shining in the room, and we all saw him . . .* But who had they seen? thought Michael. I was the one who opened the curtains to look out of that window . . . There was a lamp shining from the desk behind me . . .

He thought he might tell Nell about this later, but for the moment, he said, 'My dear love, you don't believe that stuff about time bleeding backwards any more than I do. Stephen was never going to get away from those men – it was nothing to do with what you did or didn't do. And it might sound weird, but I'm inclined to be glad that Hugbert Edreich had the – the guts and the humanity to do what he did.'

This time when he put out his hand, Nell came into his arms, and clung to him. She was still not crying, but her eyes were dark and blurred with emotion. Michael felt something twist at his heart. 'I can't bear seeing you like this,' he said.

'Drama queen,' she said, managing a smile. 'Sorry. I think I'm glad Hugbert did it, too. I suppose he saw it was impossible to fight the other three soldiers – they were armed. But he wanted to save Stephen from the bayoneting.' She thought for a moment then, in a voice much more like her normal one, said, 'It even gives some logic to what Hugbert's wife said. She said he never spoke of what happened that night— But he had those nightmares, when he dreamed he was walking towards the house. When he thought Stephen came out to meet him. That was his guilt, wasn't it?'

'I think,' said Michael, 'that Hugbert came to reasonable terms with his guilt. He had done what he genuinely believed was the right thing. Let's think he had a fairly happy life – or as happy as any of us can expect.'

'You're getting awfully philosophical, aren't you? Shall we finish Iskander's statement?'

'Can you cope with it?'

'I can't cope with not knowing how it ends. Yes, of course we'll finish it.'

'In that case I'll make us some coffee,' said Michael, heading for the kitchen. 'I don't know if Iskander's got any more revelations, but I think I'll keep a clear head, just in case.'

The coffee brought a note of normality to the unreality and the horror of Iskander's account. Michael set the cups down on a low table and turned up the heating. Wilberforce, with the air of one who had been waiting patiently for this, padded across to the electric fire and lay down in front of it.

Michael sat down next to Nell again, and reached for the closing pages of Iskander's notes.

It's one o'clock. The smallest of the small hours. I have searched the house for Leonora, and once I was sure Niemeyer's men had left, I searched the grounds as well – difficult to do at this hour of the night, but not impossible, and I certainly could not leave it until daybreak. I wrapped Stephen's army greatcoat around him – he is lying against an old tree, and tomorrow I shall do something about making a grave for him.

But I had to find Leonora – I still have to find her. I walked along several of the lanes – the unknown church was chiming midnight as I did so. But I can find no trace of her, and no clue to where she might be, and so I returned here. The few belongings we managed to bring with us are all still in a bedroom cupboard, so clearly when she left this house she had no time to take anything with her. Did she flee for safety when Edreich and the soldiers arrived? Is she cowering in some dark, lonely hideaway, frightened to return? That thought is almost more than I can bear.

For the first time in my life I don't know what to do. Sleep is unthinkable . . .

. . . but after all it seems I must have succumbed to sleep, for I see that the time has ticked around to three o'clock. The fire has burned lower, and the room is colder.

I have the strongest feeling that something woke me. Something insistent, demanding, pulled me out of that dreary, exhausted sleep. I have no idea what it was though, for the room looks exactly the same.

It is half past three, and I know what woke me. A few
minutes ago I heard sounds, unmistakable and insistent.
Somewhere inside Fosse House, something is tapping on
a wall.

It might be a bird, or a trapped animal. It might be an open
window, or a door caught in a current of wind. It might even
be Niemeyer's men, returning for me. If so, they shall have
a good run for their money. But I don't think it is the soldiers.

I have lit a second candle and armed myself with a heavy
brass paperweight and a silver-handled letter opener –
absurd, makeshift weapons, but better than none at all. I
am about to embark on another search of the house to trace
the source of the tapping.

Four o'clock. I've been all over the house again, and I can
find no explanation for the sounds. Everywhere is locked
and secure, windows are fastened, doors are closed. But I
can still hear the sounds – they are a little fainter now, as
if whatever is making them is growing weaker. I think they
are loudest in the main hall, but there is nowhere in the hall
for anything to be trapped—

Or is there? Old English houses have panelling, and Fosse
House has some very fine panelling in its hall. Supposing
there's a concealed cupboard? If I take Fosse House apart,
I have to find out what the sounds are. Because Leonora
must be somewhere.

Later
Dawn is breaking through the windows, and I am writing
this from out of the most astonishing mixture of emotions
I ever expected to feel. But it is second nature for me to
record everything, and this, too, is part of Stephen's story,
so I am setting it down.

As the clock chimed the half hour after four, a faint dawn
was filtering into the house. Even so, I fitted a fresh candle
into the holder and set off to examine the panelled walls of
the hall. It was still shrouded in darkness, and the light from
my candle flickered wildly as if invisible creatures were
trying to snuff it. At first I thought the sounds had stopped,

but when I began to tap the panelling – hoping to find a cupboard – they started again.

My unknown reader may imagine my feelings. Somewhere in this brooding old house, with young Gilmore's body still lying in its grotesque huddle outside, someone was trapped. That someone might be my beloved Leonora. As I moved round the hall, my mind was tumbling with one particular thread that weaves its grim tale through the macabre literature of so many cultures. The doomed young girl, the virgin bride, accidentally walled up or entombed, mistakenly buried alive in a cell or a cupboard during a game . . . Not to be found until years later, as a poor, dried corpse . . . How much truth had there ever been in that story? Was it about to become a truth tonight? If she was here, trapped, would I find her in time?

Halfway round the hall's panelling, there was a different sound – a faint hollowness. My heart leapt, and holding the candle closer I saw the outline of a small door. There was a tiny keyhole, but when I pushed the door it moved, and when I applied more pressure, it swung inwards. Holding the candle aloft, I went down a flight of stone steps.

Halfway down I called out, 'Leonora? Are you here?'

My voice echoed in the enclosed darkness, then died away, and there was only the thick silence, pressing in on me. My skin was crawling with fear and with the horror of what I might be about to find, but, stepping carefully, I went all the way down the steps.

The tapping had ceased, and there was only the sound of my own slightly too-fast breathing, driven by the thudding of my heart.

I lifted the candle. A stone room – a cellar of some kind – with a few discarded items of household junk, and—

And a massive carved chest crouching in the corner. Carved and domed-lidded, and bound with thick chains and a padlock. In the candlelight it took on a dreadful sinister significance. The oaken chest, half eaten by the worm, where the ill-starred heroine found a grave . . . The living tomb . . .

As I stood there, a faint scratching came from within the chest. It was so faint it might have been made by goblin nails against a frost-rimed window-pane. It was so fragile it might be the last fading signal of a dying girl . . .

I set down the candle and knelt before the chest, dragging uselessly at the chains, cursing in Russian, calling her name, and pleading with any gods that might be listening to help me – I probably called on a few denizens of the darker side of heaven, as well. I did not care. If Leonora was in there, I would trade my immortal soul to rescue her and have her alive and living.

I could see no key to the padlock, and such a tiny key could have been anywhere. It might take hours of fruitless search. I could probably find an axe somewhere, and break open the chest – but to do that might wound or even kill what was inside. If, indeed, it was not already dead.

But I had not effected discreet entry into all those houses without understanding how to open a lock without the key. With the aid of a small thin implement without which I have never travelled, I had the padlock free in five minutes. I dragged the chain away and reached for the lid. Light years sped by, worlds died, universes crumbled to dust in those moments that I struggled with the heavy lid. If Leonora was lost to me, there would be nothing in the world for me anywhere ever again, no hope, no light, no joy . . .

The lid came up with a wail of old oak and disused hinges. She was there. Her hair was tumbled, and there was a smudge of dirt across one cheekbone. But she was pale and her eyes were closed—

Then she opened her eyes, saw me, and in a hoarse, dry voice, said, 'I thought you'd never find me—'

'I'll always find you,' I said, and I lifted her out and held her against me. She was crying, and so was I.

She cried again when I told her about Stephen, and it wasn't until later in the morning that she was able to tell me what had happened, and even then it came out in fragments. My poor Leonora – she blamed herself.

It seems that while I was prowling the lanes, she and Stephen saw Niemeyer's men skulking in the gardens. Leonora was all for running out of the house – perhaps

making for the church and asking for sanctuary. But Stephen
would not leave. He insisted that this was the only place
where he could be safe. They would barricade themselves
in, he said. And to be entirely safe, Leonora must hide.

'In the oak chest,' I said.

'Yes. Alex, I argued against him, but he was adamant.
And there wasn't much time anyway, so I gave in. He said
even if the soldiers found the stone room – which was very
unlikely – they wouldn't bother with an ancient chest. He
said to make sure, he would lock it.'

I am not sure about the next part, because I think Leonora
was frightened and confused, and I don't think her recollection
is entirely to be relied on. Nor, I should say, does she.

But she thinks Stephen came running down to the cellar
and called to her that the soldiers had gone, and that they
were safe. Then he tried to get her out. It's somehow typical
of Stephen – poor, well-meaning Stephen – that he had not
used a key for the padlock, he had simply snapped an open
padlock into place around the chain with no thought of
unlocking it afterwards. And so he was unable to open it again.

Leonora thinks he shouted to her that he would get her out
somehow – she thinks he tore at the chains and the lid, trying
to force it open. She could hear his hands beating uselessly
at the wood, tearing at the chains for a very long time.

Then, quite suddenly, he stopped. She thinks he said in
a low voice that the soldiers were coming back, and he
would hide in the grounds. But he would come back for
her, he said. She must trust him in that. He would come
back. Then she heard, very faintly, his steps going away,
and the door in the panelling closing. And then there was
nothing, only the silent darkness within the chest.

Michael said, 'I think we have the explanation. Stephen ran into
the gardens to hide, saw a figure and thought it was Leonora
and that she had managed to get out by herself. Or perhaps he thought
Iskander had come back and got her out.'

He looked down at Nell, who was leaning against his shoulder,
her eyes on the pages. She said, 'It's all right, I'm not going into
high drama all over again. I'll cope with having been a ghost in

a garden.' She thought for a moment, then said, 'That all seems to fit. And it would explain why Stephen was trying to get back into the house, wouldn't it? He must have realized right at the end that it couldn't have been Leonora he saw, and—'

'And he died believing he had to get back into the house to get her out of the oak chest. Everyone who encountered him,' said Michael thoughtfully, 'assumed he was running to the house to get away from Hugbert and the others, but he wasn't.'

'He was running to get to Leonora.'

'Yes.'

'Did we resolve it for him?' asked Nell. 'When we opened the chest? Did we – what's the expression? – send him to rest?'

'We'll probably never know for sure. But I'm going to think so.'

'So am I. There's another couple of paragraphs,' said Nell, turning the last page. 'Let's read them.'

The final entry was quite short.

> Later today, I shall bring Stephen's body into the house, and we will seal it up in the oak chest. Leonora wants to do this – she wants Stephen to be in the house, where he felt safe, rather than to be in the garden where he was executed. So I shall do what she wants, and then I shall put these pages with his body. Leonora will put her gold crucifix in as well. Then we'll lock up the house and leave. I have no idea yet where we will go, but wherever it is, it will be good. I will make it so.
>
> One last thing . . .
>
> I can't forget that shadowy figure who darted across the darkness just before Stephen was killed. I know this is absurd, but I wish there was some way of letting her know that I saw her and that whoever she is or was – or will be – that brief memory will stay with me.
>
> In the meantime, here, for anyone who finds it, is Stephen Gilmore's story.
>
> Alexei Iskander.
>
> Fosse House. 1917.

TWENTY-FIVE

Memo from: Director of Music, Oriel College, Oxford
To: Dr Michael Flint, English Literature/Language
                Faculty

                                          November 201—

Michael,

Thank you again for all you did over that rather unfortunate Fosse House business. I really am immensely grateful.

I feel our *opus* on Music and the Great War Poets is shaping up very well. Dr Bracegirdle has provided some excellent material and has even managed to inject a thread of humour into his gleanings. Considering the focus of our book, this is a remarkable feat, even for him.

I believe you and Nell West will be attending Luisa Gilmore's funeral – which will also be the funeral of the poor man whose remains you found in the house. I will be present as well, of course. After the extraordinary bequest to the music faculty I certainly wish to pay the respects of myself and of College, so I hope to see you there.

In view of the absence of any family I don't suppose there will be any kind of funeral bak'd meats, so perhaps you and Nell would care to have lunch with me after the service? I recall you spoke well of the Bell, where you stayed.

Kind regards,

J.B.

The little church was filled with music – beautiful, intricate music sung by a small choir. It ebbed and flowed and wove its enchantment, as its creator, Giovanni Palestrina, had intended.

'Specially requested,' murmured Michael to Nell.

'By you?'

'By J.B.' Michael hesitated then said quietly, 'But the next reading is my request.'

It was taken from the Edward Melbourne poem, *Before Action*.

> 'I, that on my familiar hill,
> Saw with uncomprehending eyes
> A hundred of thy sunsets spill,
> Their fresh and sanguine sacrifice,
> Ere the sun swings his noonday sword,
> Must say goodbye to all of this.
> By the delights that I shall miss,
> Help me to die, O Lord.'

There was a brief, but very deep silence when the vicar's voice ceased. Then the congregation rose for the final hymn and blessing, and under cover of the small flurry, Nell said huskily, 'That was almost unbearably right for Stephen. I can't think of anything better.'

'I thought he would have liked it,' said Michael. 'Call me a romantic old fool, if you want.'

'You're a romantic old fool. And I love you,' she said.

As the small congregation walked away from the graveside, Michael and Nell fell into step with a lady who appeared to be on her own. She looked as if she was in her mid thirties, and she had dark hair and eyes, and slanting cheekbones.

'Are you one of the family?' asked Michael, conventionally.

'Very distantly.' She had a slight accent, which might have been French. 'It's three, or even four generations back,' she said. 'My great-grandfather – maybe one more "great" – married a Gilmore. He was Russian – a bit of a disreputable old boy if any of the legends can be believed, but I always rather liked the sound of him. And his disreputable ways, whatever they were, seem to have paid off, because he's supposed to have ended up quite rich.'

Michael felt Nell's reaction, but she only said, 'Do you live locally?'

'Not at all. I've been working in France – I'm half French – but I've always wanted to come to this part of England where my family lived. I'm director of a small music academy just outside Paris. We've been thinking of having a base in England for some time, and we hope Fosse House might be that base.'

'Really?' said Michael, hardly daring to believe this.

'It's exactly the right size, and between the academy's funds and an Arts Council grant, as well as the dosh my great-great-grandfather left, it's looking as if it can be done. Our idea is to have residential weekends and conventions for researchers and youth orchestras. Also summer schools, perhaps.'

'I think Miss Gilmore would have liked that very much,' said Michael warmly. He pushed open the lychgate, and the stranger and Nell went through. As they walked across to the parked cars, he said, 'By the way, I'm Michael Flint, and this is Nell West.'

'I'm Léonie,' she said. 'And I'm so pleased to be coming to Fosse House.'